D0045977

Red Beans
and
Vice

Also by Lou Jane Temple

The Cornbread Killer
Bread on Arrival
A Stiff Risotto
Death by Rhubarb
Revenge of the Barbecue Queens

Red Beans and Vice

Vice

LOU JANE TEMPLE

ST. MARTIN'S MINOTAUR ✹ NEW YORK

www.minotaurbooks.com

Library of Congress Cataloging-in-Publication Data
Temple, Lou Jane.
  Red beans and vice / Lou Jane Temple—1st ed.
    p. cm.
  ISBN 0-312-28013-0
  1. Lee, Heaven (Fictitious character)—Fiction.   2. Women detectives—
Louisiana—New Orleans—Fiction.   3. New Orleans (La.)—Fiction.
4. Women cooks—Fiction.   5. Cookery—Fiction.   6. Nuns—Fiction.
I. Title.

PS3570.E535 R43 2001
813'.54—dc21
                                                              2001019676

First Edition: August 2001

10 9 8 7 6 5 4 3 2 1

To Ron Megee,
friend and creative inspiration

Acknowledgments

Writing a book about New Orleans is a great undertaking. The city has a history like no other. My thanks to the forefathers who kept such good records. The three museums in the French Quarter run by the Louisiana State Museum system, the Cabildo, the Presbytere, and the Old U.S. Mint, are all great. So is the Historic New Orleans Collection at 533 Royal.

Thanks to Susan Spicer at Bayona and Anne Kearny at Peristyle for inspiring me to have a women's chef dinner in the book, and to Jo Anne Clevenger at Upperline and Anthony and Gail at Uglesich's for feeding me so well while I did research, among others of course. The Napoleon House, my favorite bar in America, gave me loads of creative moments. I'm grateful to my daughter, Reagan Walker, and my daughter-in-law, Kelly Walker, for helping me with research.

I appreciate the Ursuline nuns for sending me their book, *A Century of Pioneering: A History of the Ursuline Nuns in New Orleans, 1727–1827*, by Sister Jane Francis

Heaney. Many other good reference books about New Orleans helped me, but the best was written in 1895. If you ever see a copy of *New Orleans: The Place and The People*, by Grace King, get it.

Thanks to Margaret Silva for providing a safe haven where I can get some work done.

Red Beans
and
Vice

Jambalaya

1 whole head garlic, roasted
3 stalks celery, sliced thin
1 large onion, peeled and diced
1 green pepper, seeded, quartered and diced
1 red or yellow pepper, or both, seeded and diced
1 large can Italian tomatoes, smashed up
1 can artichoke hearts, drained and halved
1 qt. chicken stock
1 qt. shrimp stock
1 small can tomato sauce
12–15 cherry tomatoes, halved
¼ cup oregano leaves, chopped
2 sprigs thyme
1 lb. large shrimp
1 lb. Polish sausage or andouille
½ lb. crabmeat
1 lb. white long grained rice
1 T. Louisiana hot sauce
olive oil
kosher salt
black pepper
white pepper
1 T. Worcestershire sauce
1 tsp. cayenne
1 T. green Tabasco sauce

This is a great party dish that has suffered too much exposure of late. Remember to put the shrimp in last so they don't turn to rubber. My version gets great flavor from the roasted garlic and the two stocks.

To roast the garlic: In a baking dish, put a tablespoon of good olive oil and a sprinkling of kosher salt. Split the head of garlic and place in the pan face down. Bake in a 350 degree oven for 20 minutes or so, until the garlic is soft and browned on the bottom.

To make the shrimp stock: Peel the shrimp and place the shells in a large saucepan. Add the tops and bottom of the celery bunch, some parsley stems, green onion tops, half an onion with the skin on, and a carrot that has been washed but not peeled. If there is any open white wine in the refrigerator, throw some in. Cover this with 2 qts. of cold water and bring to a boil. Reduce the heat and simmer, occasionally skimming the top of the stock, until you have reduced the liquid by about half. Strain and cool.

In a large, heavy Dutch oven or something like it, heat 4 T. olive oil. Add the trinity: diced onion, celery, and peppers. When they have softened and the onion is translucent, add the rice and toss. Then add the tomatoes and the tomato sauce. Squeeze out the roasted garlic cloves into the pot. Bring up to a simmer for a couple of minutes, then add the chicken stock and herbs. Simmer 20 minutes. Add the cherry tomatoes, artichoke hearts, and sausage. As the liquid cooks away, add the shrimp stock and the seasonings. Taste every once in a while to test the rice. When the rice is just tender, throw in the shrimp and crabmeat. If you need more liquid, add water, chicken stock, or shrimp stock, whatever you have to keep it moist. Cook just long enough for the shrimp to turn pink, adjust seasonings and serve.

One

So, first they sent women from Paris to be brides of the French settlers, then they sent these nuns to help birth the babies and start schools and stuff." Heaven Lee was pacing around Sal's barbershop, waving a hardcover book. Sal was getting ready for his day, setting out his clippers and combs and scissors in a neat, orderly row. Murray Steinblatz, the maitre d' at Cafe Heaven, had brought Lamar's doughnuts to the barbershop and Heaven had brought coffee from the restaurant across the street. She would only drink Sal's coffee under crisis circumstances. The other member of this impromptu coffee klatch was Mona Kirk, the owner of the cat gift store right next to Cafe Heaven. She was the only one who seemed interested in Heaven's history lesson.

"And that was how long ago?"

"Really early, as far as American history goes. Seventeen twenty-seven. My friend sent me this history of New Orleans and it tells all about them, the sisters," she said, waving the book again. "Can you imagine a bunch of

nuns coming across the ocean to God knows where."
Heaven was glad to have an audience. "New Orleans was
just a swamp with a few houses then."

Sal turned his head to face the crowd rather than talk
through the mirrors that lined the room as he did when
he had a customer. "So what's different from right now?
That city is still under sea level and still filled with alli-
gators and other slimy two-legged critters, from what I
read in the newspaper."

The word newspaper pulled Murray away from the
one he was reading, the *Kansas City Star*. Murray was
really a journalist who had dropped out for a while and
was working at Cafe Heaven. He used to write for the
New York Times and was sending them a column once
again entitled "Letters From the Interior." "That's right,
Sal," Murray said. "That city is full of corruption. Once
I flew down there for a story when the vice squad had
to be disbanded because it was just too corrupt. What a
comedy. The bar owners on Bourbon Street complained
because the cops would come in and help themselves
to the bills in the cash register, just scoop out money
and walk away."

It did seem comical but also exciting, and they all
chuckled wistfully. Kansas City rarely had scandal anymore, and when it did, it was a more boring, stolid Midwestern variety.

"Remind me, Heaven," Sal said. "What do these nuns
have to do with you going down to ol' NOLA?"

"Nola?" Mona Kirk asked peevishly. She was the only
one who had been attentively listening and she didn't
remember a Nola being a part of the tale. "Who's Nola?"

Heaven patted Mona's leg and knocked some glazed
doughnut leavings off her slacks. "NOLA is just a nick-
name for New Orleans, Louisiana. N and O for New

Orleans, and LA is the state abbreviation for Louisiana," she said in a slightly condescending manner.

"I knew that," Mona said crossly.

"The nuns?" Sal asked again. Once Sal started tracking on something, he wanted to get it straight.

Heaven looked around the room like an old maid schoolteacher, pursing her lips slightly. "Now everybody, pay attention. The history stuff was just to show that I'm not leaving you all for some unimportant, trivial pursuit in another city. The nuns, the Sisters of the Holy Trinity, are a very important part of New Orleans history, and my national women's chef group is helping Susan Spicer and Anne Kearney, who are restaurant owners and chefs in New Orleans, we're helping them put on a benefit for the sisters because the sisters' thing is education and that happens to be important to the women's chef group too." She could see by the way Murray's eyes were glazing over that she was losing them again. "And a woman I knew when I was a lawyer, a woman who used to live here but married someone and moved to New Orleans, just happens to be on the committee for this benefit. She called personally and asked me to be one of the chefs and so I couldn't say no to a good cause and an old friend, now could I?"

Murray gamely tried to act interested. "Old friend? I've never heard you talk about an old friend in New Orleans."

"Well," Heaven said defensively, "she was a law school friend. I always liked her; we just didn't keep up after she moved out of town. I've seen her a couple of times when I've been in NOLA."

Sal turned back to his brushes with a roll of his eyes. "You know, it's not a crime to just take a vacation. You could say, 'Bye everybody, I'm off to New Orleans for a few days.' No, you have to go and get involved with some big production number. That New Orleans society is different, Heaven. I had an uncle who lived down there. Lots of Italians came through there after the famine of—"

"What are you saying, Sal, that you think Heaven can't breeze through a little Southern society event?" Mona broke in. "Heaven single handedly kept the Eighteenth and Vine dedication from going to hell in a handbasket, with a little help from me, of course. New Orleans will be a piece of cake for Heaven."

"That reminds me, what are you cooking?" Murray asked, trying to change the subject. Sal and Mona could bicker about almost anything.

"We don't have that figured out yet. That's one of the reasons I'm going down there tomorrow, so we can assign the courses and decide where everyone will do prep and take a look at the convent. But Pauline and I have been working on some kind of an outrageous pie with praline bits and strawberries and other decadent things. We're calling it Nola Pie."

Murray stood up and shook the doughnut icing off his trousers. "Well, let me know when you need a taste tester. I'm leaving. I've got errands to run. See you later."

"You're working tonight, aren't you?" Heaven asked.

"I'm working for the next four days, while you're gone, remember? I'll expect you to give me my instructions tonight, before the open mike."

"It's time for me to open the shop," Mona said as she folded up the newspaper Murray had left in a tangle on his chair. They all knew Sal hated a messy newspaper in the shop. Why couldn't Murray just fold it up himself when he was done with it?

Sal noticed what Mona was doing and gave her a reluctant grunt. "Thanks, there, Mona."

"Bye, Sal," Heaven said and blew a kiss in his direction.

"You might need a trim before you go down to New Orleans," Sal barked, trying to act like he didn't really notice Heaven's hair.

Heaven stopped at the door. "Good idea," she said as she checked her red locks in the mirrors. "Let me go see what's up in the kitchen and I'll come back over later. Are you busy all day?"

"Eleven," Sal said without turning around as the two women banged the door shut.

Heaven and Mona crossed 39th Street to their businesses, stopping for a quick hug on the sidewalk between the two places. "Later," Heaven said vaguely in Mona's direction as she watched the mailman stuffing envelopes in the mail slot of her cafe. She said hello to him as they passed on the street, then unlocked the front door with the key she'd slipped in her shirt pocket when she went to Sal's for coffee. Heaven didn't like to leave the front door open early in the morning. People could wander in off the street and the kitchen crew wouldn't know they were in the dining room. Once, a couple of years ago, Heaven had found a derelict sleeping across a big table hours after the kitchen crew had been working in the back. In the morning, deliveries needed to come to the kitchen door anyway.

The minute Heaven set foot in the restaurant, she felt like a ball in a pinball machine, moving from one problem or task to the next without having a big plan for the day, propelled forward by who needed her the most. The produce guy was on the phone, and Heaven and he talked about what spring lettuces and vegetables were available this week. The accountant called and asked a bunch of questions concerning a few pieces of new equipment he was trying to amortize. Pauline, the baker, and Brian, the lunch chef, had a squabble that Heaven had to referee. The night dishwasher called with the news he had broken his wrist on Sunday playing baseball with his kids. He was waiting at the medical center for a special waterproof cast to be put on and he might be late for work. Because she was thinking of New Orleans, she decided to make Jambalaya for a special, so she started the prep for that.

The next thing Heaven knew, it was time to go get her hair cut. As she headed into the dining room she spotted a stack of mail piled on the bar where a waiter had thrown it so Heaven could look through it. She grabbed it and headed across the street to Sal's.

"Don't let me forget the coffeepot," Heaven said as she walked in the door of the barbershop, shuffling through the mail as she talked. Sal was brushing off the neck of a uniformed policeman. Heaven sat down and started opening envelopes, ripping a few of them almost in two to indicate they were junk mail, putting the rest on the bottom of the pile.

The cop shook hands with Sal, paid, and left. Heaven sat down in Sal's battered leather barber chair. She held up a plain white envelope with a handwritten address and tossed the rest of the mail on Sal's countertop. "Look at this, Sal. It sticks out like a sore thumb among the rest of the day's mail. Guess why?"

Sal moved the unlit cigar he kept in his mouth most of the day from one side of his face to the other. "Easy," he grumbled. "Handwritten, not computer type. No return address, either."

Heaven smiled. "Sal, what a mind. I hadn't noticed

the lack of a return address. I hope it's a party invitation." As Sal put a clean smock around her shoulders, she ripped open the envelope. Silence followed. Sal didn't notice for a minute because he had to find his best pair of snipping shears to work on Heaven. By the time he turned back to the chair, Heaven was holding out the letter, her hand shaking.

"What?" Sal asked.

"Look," she said with a small voice Sal hadn't heard before. He took the single sheet of paper and read. The text was in some generic typeface:

CAFE HEAVEN IS FULL OF AIDS INFESTED FAGS.
THE COOKS PICK THEIR NOSE IN YOUR FOOD.
EAT THERE AT YOUR OWN EXPENSE.

Sal folded the letter carefully by the edges. "I hope none of the guys is that way," he said gruffly. "I think a lot of Chris and Joe."

Heaven started crying. "See. That's what happens when someone writes down that kind of filth. Even you, you who know us all, you tend to believe something that's written down. Not that having AIDS is something that makes a person bad, but the intentions of this letter certainly are."

"Hell, I guess lots of waiters are gay. It would make sense some of them might be sick . . ." Sal trailed off, red-faced.

Heaven stood up, tears streaming down her face. "Yes, but as it happens, none of my waiters, who are also my friends, are sick. And having someone slander them that way, about something life and death . . ." She sank back down in the chair. "What a monster." She wiped her nose with her arm like a kid. "What if they sent this to someone else? What should I do, Sal? Why would any-one . . ."

"Honey, there are lots of deranged people out there. Your restaurant is popular and that makes some people want to destroy, to tear it down."

"But what should I do? Should I tell the guys?" Heaven whimpered, her usual competency shattered.

Sal patted her shoulder and handed her a wad of tissues. "I tell you what we're gonna do. We're gonna cut your hair real pretty for New Orleans. Then you're gonna go back to the cafe and keep your mouth shut. That's the plan. I'm gonna call Murray and show him this thing and he's the only one we're gonna tell. Not even Mona, you understand?"

"Can't I tell Hank?" she asked, like a petulant child.

"Not now," Sal said gruffly. "Just buck up and shut up, like a big girl."

Heaven saw the glitter of tears in Sal's eyes. Embarrassed at being caught under the sway of his emotions, he spun her around, away from the mirrors.

Monday nights were busy at Cafe Heaven because it was open mike night. The actors and poets and musicians of Kansas City came in and performed free because they knew it would be a full house and a tough crowd. If they could make it there, chances were their act would fly anywhere else in town.

The open mike had been over for about an hour. It was after midnight and Tony, the bartender, was counting his drawer. Most of the waiters had checked out with Murray and a couple were helping the busboys set up the tables for tomorrow's lunch. Heaven was at the bar nursing a glass of Veuve Clicquot. She'd left the kitchen cleanup to the rest of the line. Murray came and sat down, ordering a Diet Coke with lime. "You usually don't drink that bubbly stuff this late at night," he remarked to Heaven.

"It's good for all times of the day and night," Heaven said dully.

"You expecting someone?" Murray asked.

"No. I thought I'd drink the whole bottle tonight, all by myself."

"Now, Heaven, calm down. I know you're upset about the letter. I think this is just a crank who wrote that thing. Chances are by the time you get home at the end of the week, nothing will have come of it."

"That's a sick person, Murray. If that's someone's idea of a joke, he's insane and should be put away. If someone is starting a campaign to ruin my business, well . . . those seem to be the two choices we have. Insane or vicious. Fun, huh?" Heaven threw back her champagne. Tony looked up and tried to make eye contact with Murray, like he was asking, "What's up with the boss?" Murray kept his head down. Heaven reached over and poured herself another glass of champagne out of an ice bucket on the bar. She must have told Tony to keep the bottle handy. She gave Murray a don't-fuck-with-me look.

"I'm afraid I have another piece of bad news concerning this hate-mail thing." Murray couldn't put it off any more. "Sal and I decided that I shouldn't call any of my contacts at the newspaper. Why get people thinking about something they may not have any reason to think about, right?"

Heaven sighed. "And?"

"But one of my contacts called me. A reporter, someone with a city hall beat. His letter said the same thing yours did. He read it to me."

"Great. Why the city hall beat? Why not the food editor?" she asked.

"Oh, maybe going for the food safety angle. That's what we guessed. Now, don't worry. My reporter talked it over with his editor and they would never print something like that, unsigned and unsubstantiated. But it does get folks thinking."

"Thinking about what? What folks?" Heaven asked heavily. She shot back another gulp of champagne.

"Well, it made the editor think about doing a story about people in food service that are HIV positive."

Heaven moaned. "So even if it doesn't affect us, some poor waiters somewhere could be outed as being HIV positive?"

"You know, does the public have the right to know who touches their food, that kind of thing. It could be good, remind people that you can't get AIDS that way," Murray said quietly, wishing he wasn't having this conversation.

"Next it will be produce pickers with TB, cooks with hepatitis. This could win someone a Pulitzer," Heaven said. "In the meantime, do you think anyone else got that letter? If they sent it to one reporter, they could have sent it lots of places."

Murray patted Heaven's hand. "Just go on your trip and leave this at home. There's nothing you can do about it anyway. I called my friend at the FBI—"

Heaven broke in sarcastically. "Oh boy, I thought we weren't going to tell anyone."

"I didn't. I asked him some general questions about paper documents. Said I was doing a piece about hate mail, which I may do. My friend said it's hard to trace if the perp wishes to remain anonymous and had used gloves and generic paper, but that sometimes the person wants to let their victim know who they are."

Heaven moaned again. "Something to look forward to. The maniac reveals him or herself. Oh goody."

Suddenly a familiar voice came from the vicinity of the front door. "What does a doctor have to do to get a nightcap around this place?" It was Hank, Heaven's boyfriend, who worked in the emergency room of the medical center a few blocks away from the restaurant.

Heaven turned toward Murray with fire in her eyes.

He quickly put up his hands in defense. "I did not call because you decided to drink an entire bottle of Veuve by yourself and then drive home. I called because Sal and I were worried about you. This letter is creepy stuff, Heaven. I didn't want you driving all the way downtown by yourself tonight. Just in case this nut has something else in mind. So I called Hank and I told him about the letter. Sal said you'd wanted to tell him anyway."

Hank had moved to stand between the two, listening to Murray try to explain his way out of a tongue-lashing. Now he kissed Heaven on the cheek. "Got a beer for a poor ER dog?"

Heaven smiled in spite of herself and threw her arm around Hank's shoulder, pulling him onto the bar stool on her other side. "People are so screwed up, you know that, honey? Tony, get this man what he wants, please."

"Just a Boulevard, Tony. The wheat ale if you've got it," Hank said, requesting a popular local brew. He smiled at Heaven and tapped her champagne glass with his beer bottle as soon as it arrived. "Don't tell me about screwed-up humans tonight. I've had a good dose of them today, including my last patients, two sisters who stabbed each other. They're both still alive and mad the other one survived, I'm happy to report."

"And it's only Monday," Murray observed. "I thought you saved the good stuff for the weekends in ER."

"Take me home, baby," Heaven said to Hank as she got up and finished the last bit of champagne, tipping the bottle up to her mouth grandly, then tossing it over her shoulder for effect. It landed with a thud on the carpet behind her, not breaking, and rolled toward the bar. "I'll leave the van here in case the kitchen needs it for something. I can hardly wait to get to New Orleans where everyone knows folks act crazy."

Murray got up and shook Hank's hand, then gave Heaven a little hug. "Don't worry about us. We'll be just fine here." He sure hoped he was right.

Profiteroles Filled with Brie and Artichokes

For the Profiteroles:

¾ stick butter, cut into pieces
1 cup water
1 T. sugar
dash salt
¾ cup all-purpose flour
4 large eggs

Preheat oven to 400 degrees. Bring butter, water, sugar, and a dash of salt to a boil in a heavy 3-qt. saucepan, stirring until butter is melted. Over medium heat, add the flour all at once. Beat with a wooden spoon and cook until the mixture pulls from the sides of the pan and forms a ball, about 1–2 minutes. Transfer to a bowl and beat in eggs one at a time with an electric mixer or by hand. Transfer the mixture into a pastry bag with a medium-large tip. Pipe the mixture onto a baking sheet in 1–2 inch diameter mounds. Bake for 10 minutes. Reduce oven temperature to 300 degrees and continue to bake until the puffs are crisp and golden. Cool and halve horizontally with a serrated knife.

For the filling:

a kilo of Brie (2.2 lbs.)
1 can artichoke hearts, drained, and chopped fine

2 T. cream
white pepper
paprika
cayenne

Create a *bain marie* with a stock pot half full of boiling water and a stainless steel mixing bowl that fits over the top of the pot. Cut the Brie into chunks and remove the rind. Melt the Brie in the mixing bowl along with the cream. When the cheese is melted, add the seasonings and the artichoke hearts. Keep over the heat until the mixture is thoroughly mixed. Cool and fill the profiteroles with this mixture.

Two

The room was filling up fast now and the babble of feminine voices grew louder. Heaven had finally figured out what made this different from the dozens of other committee meetings she'd attended over the years. It was the perfume. Heaven would have laid odds that every woman in the house, with the exception of herself and the ordained sister present to represent the nuns, had applied a different brand of perfume with abandon. Heaven felt slightly nauseated from the assault on her nose. She hardly ever wore the stuff herself because it interfered with her ability to judge the aromas of food and wine. She would have to have a no-perfume zone if she ever opened a restaurant in the South, she thought.

"Who is this gorgeous creature with the red hair?" a voice cooed.

Heaven turned to see who was flattering her and at the same time spotted her old friend from Kansas City hurrying in the door.

Mary Whitten had informed Heaven on the phone that she was still practicing law with an international trade firm. She wore a tailored brown dress and the look of a harried attorney who was running late. Other than the harried look, Mary appeared very much the way she had when she and Heaven went to law school together twenty years ago. She was tall, thin, with short dark hair and a classic American profile, including a cute, small nose and good cheekbones. Her dark hair had one shock of white streaking through it that hadn't been there twenty years ago but Heaven thought it made Mary's appearance more striking.

As Heaven waited for her friend to make her way across the room, she returned her attention to a gray-haired grande dame type in an expensive navy blue suit, the stranger who had addressed her. "I'll answer to 'gorgeous creature' any time," she said to the older woman, and smiled. "I'm Heaven Lee. I own a restaurant in Kansas City."

"Oh, dear Lord. A Northerner," the grande dame said with chuckle. "I used to hire some of your musicians. That Count Basie was a hoot."

"I wish I'd met him," Heaven said, catching herself before she mentioned how long the Count had been pushing up the tulips. She herself couldn't stand it when people marveled at the fact she actually saw the Grateful Dead play concerts live. "Did or do you own a restaurant or jazz club here in New Orleans?" Heaven asked politely.

"Oh, mercy me, no," the dowager replied. "I used to own a whorehouse, and a damned good one it was, too. We could afford to have the likes of Count Basie play for the amusement of our clients, darlin'."

Heaven was not going to let this old gal get the best

of her. "If you could afford that kind of entertainment in the parlor, I can only imagine the treats waiting in the bedrooms."

A big laugh came out of the little old woman. "Nancy Blair, Heaven. Nice to have you on board."

Mary Whitten hurried over to the women, giving air kisses to both Nancy and Heaven. "I'm so sorry I couldn't get you at the airport. Did you find this place all right?" she said breathlessly.

"The taxi driver gave me a history of the sisters when I told him where I wanted to go. His version was much more colorful than that book you sent me," Heaven said. "You didn't tell me the nuns were all going to go back to France in a huff when the United States bought this territory."

"But Thomas Jefferson sent them a handwritten letter and begged them to stay. Said he couldn't do it without them." Mary gave a little wave to Nancy, who was already embroiled in another conversation, and then pulled Heaven to two empty chairs at the conference table. She sat down and fanned herself with one hand as though she were exhausted.

Heaven sat down beside her and leaned in. "I want to hear little Miss Nancy's story later, like how does a madam get to be on the committee for the nuns' party?"

"Like everything else in this town, Heaven, it's a long saga but a good one. Maybe we'll get around to Nancy tonight. I'm glad you're staying with us. I haven't seen you in years. Where's your luggage?"

"In the gatehouse. I thought we could get it when we leave and I wouldn't have to lug it in here. I didn't realize this wasn't the actual convent anymore. I was trying to respect the nuns and not act like it was a hotel."

"This is actually the site of convent number one and number two. Then they moved downriver, in 1824, I think. Even then, the Quarter must have gotten too racy for the sisters." The two women laughed just as Susan Spicer called the meeting to order.

For the next hour, everything went along just fine. Tea and coffee appeared along with profiteroles filled with some kind of Brie-and-artichoke deliciousness. The two chefs from New Orleans, Susan Spicer and Anne Kearney, plus Heaven from Kansas City and Rozanne Gold from New York, who was on a cookbook tour and in town, figured out who should cook what course, deciding for the chefs not present, like Lidia Bastianich and Edna Lewis and Joyce Goldstein.

The other committees gave their reports and Heaven could see a lot of work had been done already. Sometimes preparing the food was the easy part. Filling the tables with paying guests was usually the hard part and that was going well. A month before the event and it was ninety-five percent sold out.

They talked about sticking a few more tables out in the inner courtyard and to that end they all got up to go take a look; Susan showing where the tent kitchen would be placed and Mary and her committee figuring out that they could get four more round tables for ten in by the herb garden without killing the herbs. When they arrived back inside at the conference room, someone was waiting for them.

"Uh-oh. It's Amelia Hart," Mary whispered.

"Who's she?" Heaven asked, noticing that this woman had already changed the dynamics of the group without saying a word. The easy talk had died down and everyone was eying the newcomer.

"A local television reporter and a real troublemaker," Mary replied.

Amelia Hart was one of those burnished African-American women that, had they chosen a life outside of New Orleans, could have passed easily as a white person from a Mediterranean country. She was extraordinarily beautiful, tall and haughty-looking, her hair up in an elaborate but professional French twist, her bronze-colored outfit expensive enough to give Nancy Blair a run for her money as the best dressed in the room. It was in fact Nancy who spoke to Amelia's presence first, before she herself gave them any indication why she was there.

"Amelia, darlin'. So nice of you to come but we'd rather save the publicity until a little closer to the night of the dinner. We don't want the sisters to be criticized for working on a fund-raising project during Lent, now, do we?" Nancy said firmly as the committee members silently took their places around the long oval table.

Amelia had taken the best seat for herself, at the head of the table where Susan Spicer had been sitting. Susan found a side chair and quietly pulled it to the table downstream from Amelia, who now stood up dramatically. "Thanks, Nancy, but I'm not here professionally. Truth is, I could give a rat's ass if the lovely Sisters of the Holy Trinity here were the laughingstock of New Orleans for hustling during Lent. They were slave owners themselves, you know."

Nancy Blair had remained standing until now, the better to face down her opponent. "Well, then what in the hell are you doing here, Ms. Hart? And I'm sure you're gonna tell us." Her voice held about equal parts ice and humor as she took her seat. Heaven noticed she had changed the way she addressed the other woman from Amelia to Ms. Hart. When you want something, she's Amelia. When they want something, she's Ms. Hart.

"Boy, no one worries about cursing in a religious institution, do they," Heaven whispered to her friend.

Mary, intent on what was going to happen next, shushed her with a finger over her lips.

Amelia was ready to let loose now. "What I want to know is, if you Uptown ladies, and you too, Nancy, have so much time on your hands and need to help someone, why the sisters? There's another religious order that is just as much a part of our history and they always get passed over for the blessed sisters. The Sisters of the Holy Trinity may be dying out but they get more attention than they worth, that's fo' sure," she said, losing a little of her anchorwoman pronunciation.

Nancy Blair, ignoring the cut that Amelia had slipped in to make sure everyone remembered Nancy was no Uptown lady, seemed to be enjoying her role as spokesperson for the group. "I'm not going to argue our choice with you, Ms. Hart. And you know as well as I do that the sisters have educated thousands of underprivileged children over the years, black and white. But go on. Who's more deserving, in your opinion?"

Amelia had her own script and timing worked out in her mind. Heaven wondered if she'd been lurking outside waiting for the group to take a break so she could make her stand. Now she smiled for the first time, a dazzling smile. "When I decided to have a career in television, I legally changed my name to Amelia Hart, in honor of my great-great-great-grandmother of the same name. Does that ring a bell to any of you who are so interested in preserving history?" She made a brief sweep of the table with her eyes. "Amelia Hart was the daughter of the sister of Henriette Delille, the founder of the Sisters of the Holy Family, the free woman of color who dedicated her life to the education of the children of slaves and other people of color. She is who you should be honoring, not a group who were brought to this country to continue the exploitation of others."

Heaven couldn't believe it. Nowhere in Kansas City could you get a bunch of folks to argue about the past like it was just yesterday. This woman was talking about stuff that happened in the eighteenth century with a passion most midwesterners couldn't muster for a crisis that happened last week. But enough was enough. Amelia Hart could create a serious problem for the event they were trying to plan. Heaven tried the old outsider ploy. She stood up and the room became all atwitter.

"Amelia, I'm Heaven Lee, a chef from Kansas City. I know very little about those you speak of, yet as an outsider it sounds to me that both groups have done good for the children of New Orleans and especially for their education, yes?"

Amelia narrowed her eyes at Heaven, trying to figure out where she was going with this. But around the table there were enough yeses for Heaven to continue without waiting for Amelia to counterattack.

"As a member of the Women's Chefs and Restaurateurs, and also of Chef's Collaborative 2000, I'm dedicated to the education of children and women. That's why I'm here. And I'd be glad to come back next year and do the same thing we're doing now for your aunt's order. We could make it an annual event, one year for one group, the next year for the other."

Well, if the feminine racket before the meeting had been loud, now it was deafening. Everyone had an opinion and they wanted it heard by everyone else. Heaven had blown Amelia totally out of the saddle and Amelia knew it. Even the Uptown ladies, who never would have come up with such a compromise on their own, were having trouble finding fault with it. From the look on Amelia's face, so was she.

"Nice work, girlfriend," Mary hissed through her teeth with a little pat on Heaven's hand and a laugh.

The meeting would have been hard to call back to order after Amelia and Heaven's exchange, but then something happened to ruin that possibility forever. The janitor burst into the room with a wild look on his face. "Sister, you better come," he gasped, indicating the nun at the table. "You better all come. Streetside courtyard. I'm calling the police," he said, and turned around and hurried out.

Not only did the former convent have a spacious inner courtyard, where the dinner was to be held, but it had a second courtyard between the high brick fence on Ursulines Street and the building proper. Boxwood shrubs formed elegant patterns. As the group poured out into this space, elegance wasn't what they saw. The walls of the courtyard were splashed with red paint, ugly words scrawled all around: Parasites, Bloodsuckers, Witches. But as upsetting as that seemed to Heaven, most of the women were aghast at something else, or the lack of it.

"Oh my God," Mary Whitten said. "They've stolen the cross that the sisters brought from France on that first trip in 1727. It's the sisters' most prized possession."

The Carousel Bar at the Hotel Monteleone had a real merry-go-round in the middle of the room. A round, garish confection that rotated slowly, the bar supplies and bartender were located in the middle of this affair. The room was filling up fast with a combination of local businessmen and tourists too shy to start out their drinking at Pat O'Brien's over on Bourbon Street. Mary and Heaven rushed in. They were meeting Mary's husband and they were late.

The crisis at the convent had taken time, what with the police and the archdiocesan people, who had offices at the convent, all hovering and asking the committee members questions they couldn't answer, like what time had they gone outside to the inner courtyard, had they heard any strange noises, and stuff like that. For every question there had been multiple answers from the ladies:

"We were outside for at least thirty minutes."

"It wasn't more than fifteen minutes we were in the garden."

"I thought I heard something."

"You couldn't hear yourself think what with all the expert opinions in that room."

"Well, you know, Amelia Hart did show up uninvited to the meeting with trouble on her mind. Maybe she . . ."

Heaven herself tried not to jump in the middle of a police investigation as she would if she were in Kansas City. She felt Amelia certainly wouldn't feel bad about defacing the convent property on moral grounds. But why would she come in and let them know she was gunning for them if she'd just tossed paint around on the other side of the entry hall? And where was the cross? Certainly not with her in that meeting. She could have hired an accomplice to do the dirty work, but Heaven thought she was smarter than that. And not quite so twisted.

A man Heaven vaguely remembered as Truely Whitten stood up as they crossed the dimly lit barroom. He had been sitting with two men, one of whom was red-faced with anger. As Truely stood up and buttoned his jacket, he offered his hand to the angry man, who jumped out of his chair, ignored the hand, and went out of the bar into the hotel, away from Mary and Heaven.

They arrived at the table just in time to hear the second man saying, "This isn't a joke, old man," as he also walked away. Truely opened his mouth to say something to the retreating figure, then started when he finally noticed the two women standing next to him. Heaven had imagined he'd noticed them and had stood up in greeting, but judging by his look of surprise that turned on a dime to a fabulous grin, that was not the case. It was the grin of a Southern male, an aren't-I-something-and-I-know-I-am-cause-my-momma-told-me-so grin. It was also a good acting job.

"Dear lord, Mary Beth, you scared the bejesus out of me. Where in the hell have you been, sugar?" Along with this playful rebuke Mary (Beth?) received a kiss on her cheek. Then he turned to Heaven. "I guess it's been almost ten years since I've seen you, Heaven. You were married to that uniform manufacturer. Welcome to New Orleans, darlin'. Sit down right here."

As they took the two seats warmed up by the departed men, Mary asked about them. "Wasn't that Leon Davis?"

"Yes, sugar."

"Who was that with him?"

"His plant manager. They spotted me sitting here all by my lonesome and made a beeline over to give me grief."

"Who's Leon Davis?" Heaven asked, realizing it sounded nosy.

Mary sniffed. "He owns the other coffee company. He's always trying to get Truely to sell him ours."

"Now, Mary Beth, you know I don't pay him a bit of attention. He's like an old jaybird, fussin' around."

Heaven blanched. He must call her Mary Beth all the time.

Truely just grinned that grin and signaled to the waitress. "Martinis all right?"

Heaven nodded. "Remind me I can only have one, even if I'm not driving. I get into trouble if I have more than one. Bombay up with an olive and a twist, please."

Truely tapped his empty martini glass to indicate more of the same and Mary ordered hers, "Absolut Citron up, please, with a twist. Oh, make it a Cosmopolitan, what the hell," and shook her finger at her husband. "Wait till we tell you what happened over at the convent. You won't believe it. But first, just tell me why Leon's man was saying it wasn't a joke and Leon himself looked like he was about to blow a gasket?"

"Mary Beth, you know how it is. He thinks if he throws enough zeros behind his offer, I'll say yes. My daddy would roll over in his grave. His litt'l ol' manager thought he could lean on me. It was nothing. Now what could have happened over at the convent to get you two so wound up? You both are hummin' close to warp speed. By the way, the excitement sure makes your eyes pretty, Heaven. Green, aren't they?"

Heaven had to smile. It was a classic and expert example of flattery and bald-faced lying combined into charming Southern cocktail conversation. Truely had blonde hair flecked with gray and a lick of it fell over his forehead. What a charming scoundrel.

Mary thought about calling him on such obvious bullshit, but she let it slide, cocking her head at him as if to say, "We'll talk about this later." She wondered what he and Leon had really been talking about. It could be something totally unimportant. Truely sometimes just lied to stay in practice. She knew that about him. But now she wanted to tell him about the missing cross.

Pear Honey

8 cups pears suitable for cooking, (or as my son
    recommends, any pears off an old pear tree)
6 cups sugar
1 ½ cups crushed pineapple (optional)

Cook pears with sugar on low heat until the mixture looks
clear and begins to thicken, about 1 ½ hours. Add the
pineapple and cook 10–15 minutes longer. Seal in hot,
sterilized jars, and process in boiling water bath. If you
don't want to put up in jars, use within the week.

Three

Heaven found the kitchen. "Damn, Mary, I almost had to call 911 to get help finding the coffeepot. This house is big."

Mary Whitten smiled. "But isn't that a great ol' suite up there?" she said as she poured Heaven a cup of coffee. "And it's only the third floor."

"Where are we? I didn't pay attention last night."

"Audubon Place. It's hot shit, as far as an Uptown address goes." Mary patted a chair for Heaven next to her at a big wooden table positioned in a bay window in Mary's gigantic kitchen. A black woman in a uniform was working over at the sink. At least two more staff members came and went while Heaven and Mary ate breakfast.

"What's in here?" Heaven opened a linen napkin folded in a basket.

"Biscuits, of course. And there's some sausage that our butler makes himself. It's spicy."

Heaven put a biscuit on her plate and pulled it open.

Then she reached for the preserves. "Pear honey?" she asked.

"You got it," Mary answered as she bit off a corner of her own biscuit.

Heaven finished building a biscuit sandwich by slathering the pear honey on one half of the biscuit and plopping a round of sausage on the other. She closed it up and bit in, a little moan escaping her full mouth. "Delicious. So, how much time do we have?"

"What do you mean?"

Heaven looked up at a beautiful antique railroad clock on the wall. "How much time before you have to go to work?"

"I've got a deposition this afternoon, so I want to go in by nine, nine thirty. Why?"

"Good. That gives me an hour to grill you. Where's Truely?"

"Already gone. He said to tell you he made reservations for us at Bayona tonight. Had to use your name to get us in. He was very impressed. New Orleanians choose their friends by who has more pull at Galatoire's."

Heaven started at the top of her list of things to quiz Mary about. "So, what's with the Mary Beth thing?"

"Well, it is my middle name. Truely at first just called me that as a tease. Then I noticed he would introduce me as Mary Beth, said it would help me fit in better. My mother-in-law, God rest her selfish soul, never said my first name until we added the Beth. Mary was too Presbyterian for her, I guess."

"So, in court, do they call you Mary Beth?"

"No, Miz Mary Beth, or Mary Beth, honey," she said with a straight face. Then giggling at Heaven's consternation, she added, "I'm pulling your leg. It helps me in court to go by both names. Every one of the good old boys goes by three names, usually all three suitable for last names."

"What's Truely's?"

"Truely, with an E for some reason, Fortier Whitten. His mother was from a real Creole family, the Fortiers. His daddy was a carpetbagger, which any Uptown lady will tell you about Truely if she gets a chance."

"Sounds like a senator. So, do I call you Mary Beth from now on?"

Mary shrugged her shoulders. "If it seems too weird, don't sweat it. I'll know who you're talking to."

"Let's try it. So, Mary Beth, how's the coffee business?"

"New Orleans is now the biggest coffee-importing city in this country. Twenty-seven point eight percent of all the beans that come in come in here. And Truely does most of that importing."

"Well, something must be going right, because this is a great house full of beautiful antiques. Do you like living in New Orleans?"

"I've been here eighteen years so I guess if I didn't I would have left by now. It grows on you, that's for sure."

"That's not the most enthusiastic endorsement for a marriage I've heard. Is there a problem?"

Mary smiled and got up. "Oh, God, no. I fell for that goofball twenty years ago and I haven't fallen out. But these Southern families are so complicated. And the town is too. I spent ten years feeling like an outsider and I became terrified when the day came I didn't feel like an outsider anymore. It's a club I'm not sure I want to belong to."

"The Groucho Marx Syndrome," Heaven said with a grin. "I've been there myself."

The phone rang and Mary grabbed it. She waved it at Heaven and put it down. "It's for you. I'm going up to put my lawyer face on."

Heaven wondered who was calling her. She hoped something terrible hadn't happened at home. "This is Heaven."

"Heaven, this is Nancy Blair. I wonder if you're free for lunch today, or does Mary have you all booked up?"

"I'm free, Nancy. Wasn't that an ordeal yesterday?"

"Welcome to New Orleans, Heaven. How about Antoine's at one?"

"It's a date," she said and hung up.

She poured another cup of coffee and walked around the first floor, touching the lovely finish of a table or admiring a porcelain figure or a bronze bust. It really was quite a collection. Heaven thought about the full-time uniformed staff around to keep all this stuff clean. She herself had house cleaners, a team of jovial lesbians. Was it the fact that all of Mary's employees were African-American that made Heaven uncomfortable? Was it their uniforms? Mary came down the stairs and found Heaven in the living room.

"This place is full of good shit."

"I'll take that as a compliment. Who was on the phone?"

"Nancy Blair wanting to have lunch."

"Oh, dear, how fun. I'm sorry I've got this deposition or I'd butt in."

"Give me the twenty-five words or less on Nancy Blair, will you?" Heaven asked.

"She made tons of money selling sex to those who could afford it, invested her money well, bought herself a seat on a couple of boards, and then got religion. She gave lots of money to the sisters for their school because in the old days they would let her girls' children go to the academy on the cheap. They parade her out like their own little Mary Magdalene."

"Whoa. Do I sense some cynicism?"

Mary picked up her briefcase by the front door. "Everybody, I'm leaving. Take care of Heaven," she yelled to the air. She turned to her friend and patted her arm. "Cynicism is as Southern as pecan pie, Heaven. I'll see you later."

Heaven was following the meeter/greeter/seater from the front desk through the labyrinth that was Antoine's. Since its birth in 1840, Antoine's has kept the secrets of the powerful of New Orleans. Private dining room waiters hurried through the hall, one with a Baked Alaska ready to be set on fire at the last possible moment. As hokey as it was, Heaven loved every minute, wondering what the kitchens were like, how many walk-in coolers they had, how many people on the payroll. When they arrived at Nancy Blair's table, Heaven smiled. "I see you chose the spot with your back to the wall, not the door. Hello, Nancy."

Nancy Blair was wearing a red suit today, as fine in its detail as the navy one had been the day before. She had on dark glasses and white kid gloves. "Pardon me for not getting up, Heaven. I'm creaky. Oh, yes, you always want to be able to keep an eye on the door, and know where the back door is too."

Heaven laughed and sat down on Nancy's right side. "Where do you get all these fabulous suits?"

"Paris," Nancy answered. "Thank God Karl Lagerfield took over Chanel, not one of those knuckleheads from England that can't sew a seam. Tailored suits have been my trademark for years, Heaven. They always made a good impression in court."

"Did you have to go often?"

"Depending on the mayor or the police chief at the time. I think thirty-three arrests in a year was my record. But many of my colleagues were arrested hundreds of times in a year. I spent my bribe money wisely. Are you shocked?"

Heaven blushed. She had been thinking about her own brush with the law. "No. I was a lawyer, but I did something stupid years ago and lost my ability to practice. I'm no saint. And you know what? Life does go on."

"And the bills still have to be paid, don't they? I ordered us a nice bottle of white Burgundy, a Puligny-Montrachet, if that's all right with you. They have a good French wine list here."

For the next hour, Heaven and Nancy enjoyed good food and wine and each other's company. Heaven was fascinated with the matter-of-fact way that Nancy told racy tales of her life as a landlady, as she called it.

"You know, Nancy, I realize that there must have been some great landladies in Kansas City. It was a wide-open town for a few years in the twenties and thirties. Yet, I've never heard any of the stories."

"They dead now, child," Nancy said with the first tinge of nostalgia Heaven had detected. "I'm just lucky I lived in a town that couldn't survive without the likes of me. I have a professor from New Orleans U. who's writing a book of my life. She comes over four times a week and I talk into a tape recorder. Says it will make a movie, for sure."

"But you didn't ask me to lunch to rehash old war stories did you, Nancy? You don't seem the type that lives in the past."

Nancy went right to the point. "Heaven, I'm fond of the Sisters of the Holy Trinity. I don't like what happened yesterday, not one bit. Of course, it's easy to pin it on that little bitch, Amelia Hart. But really, she's no fool. Why would she come in and make a stink if she'd set up the snatch of the cross and all the other?"

"I'm sure the police will—"

"Bull," Nancy broke in. "The police may come up with a couple of black kids they say did it, but it won't lead us to the cross, or the slick behind all this."

Heaven wondered if she had a sign on her back that read "Meddling Redhead for Hire. Works Free." "You know, Nancy, I'm going home tomorrow and I won't be back for a month. I don't know how much help I can be."

Nancy Blair's eyes narrowed and she signaled for the check. "You're an outsider, Heaven, and that gives you an advantage. Just keep your eyes and ears open. You never know where that cross might pop up. And I've got a bad feeling that this wasn't an isolated incident."

Heaven's wheels were turning. "I guess it wouldn't kill me to go over to the convent and see a photo of the cross. I didn't really pay attention to it yesterday when I arrived."

Nancy Blair didn't even have to present a credit card. She just signed the check and started gathering up her things to leave. The white kid gloves went back on. She was thinking out loud. "No matter what I said earlier, I wouldn't rule out Amelia Hart. She carries a heavy chip on her shoulder, Heaven. Chips make you stupid."

Heaven stood and gave the older woman a hug. "Thanks for sharing your history and for lunch. That fish in the parchment paper was just as good as the press on it said it would be."

Nancy slipped her arm around Heaven's waist for a moment suddenly very sexy for a little old lady, then released the younger woman. She must have been a pistol in her day, Heaven thought. "I'm sneaking out the side door, where all the sinners come and go." She handed Heaven a calling card with just her name and a phone number; heavy ivory paper, deep engraving. "Here's my card if you need to get in touch with me. I'll see you next month." She turned and, out of nowhere, two managers appeared and swept her away. Heaven hadn't noticed them hovering or anything. Pretty attentive service.

Heaven walked down Bourbon to Ursulines and then over to Chartres, where the convent was located. She let the French Quarter take over her senses for a few minutes, loving the sights and sounds. It was almost three and leisurely lunches were running into afternoon cocktails. The bars along the Bourbon strip weren't full but they sure weren't empty either. Farther down Bourbon, the gay bars were opening the wooden French doors that allowed the late-night crowd to spill out on the street. The sidewalks had been hosed down and hadn't received their nightly dose of regurgitated Hurricane cocktails yet. Azaleas were blooming everywhere on second-story balconies. The place was maddening, with all the hidden courtyards, the indication of lives being lived behind closed doors in these ancient buildings that looked like a good wind would blow them all over. Heaven loved it.

Suddenly, a garage door flush to the street opened and a silver Porsche almost ran over Heaven, sticking its sleek nose out on the sidewalk. She jerked to attention abruptly brought back to earth from her flights of fancy. She shot an angry look at the driver, a very distinguished man with silver hair. He gave her a bemused glance and turned his car out onto Ursulines. While the automatic door slowly came down, Heaven caught glimpses of banana trees and flowering bushes in pots, and a wrought-iron table and chairs set on a brick terrace.

Neither the man nor the car were the kind Heaven was usually attracted to: Well-polished middle-aged men with expensive cars were such a cliche. Still, at that moment, Heaven was intoxicated with the promise of the situation. She wanted to be kissed on that terrace, with the scent of magnolia in the air. By that man. Reminding herself he was probably gay, she crossed the street and entered the small office and gift store in the gatehouse of the former convent.

Originally, Heaven had intended to go to the diocesan offices and ask for a photocopy of a picture of the cross. She even had a good reason. She was going to say that she intended to make a duplicate out of chocolate or spun sugar or some damn thing. But when she got to the convent, a tour was starting and she paid her money and got in line with a group of Catholics from Minnesota. It couldn't hurt to learn more about the place and the sisters.

First stop was a video history of the convent that Heaven had trouble concentrating on because it had very poor production values, and bad lighting and narration. It did show the cross, a filigreed iron affair that reminded her of all those movies of the evil white explorers claiming some choice piece of real estate from a group of aborigines. Maybe the Indians were behind the attack on the convent. Heaven racked her brain. What Indians had lived here, the Choctaws? Maybe a few Choctaws had decided to get revenge. She realized the video was over and their guide, a crusty old guy with an accent that sounded to Heaven like Brooklyn, was loudly trying to get them to move out in the hall.

"The staircase from the original convent, which was right over there where the parking lot is now," he yelled, gesturing to his left, "was moved to this building when it was occupied in 1750. Now let's go see that staircase, original in the first convent building and finished in 1734."

The crowd, about thirty of them, shuffled down the hall, Heaven bringing up the rear. Before she got around the corner she heard a choked gasp coming from their guide, then, "Oh, dear Jesus, what the hell?"

Screams popped out of a few Minnesota throats. Heaven pushed into the entry hall of the convent where the staircase led to the second floor, a graceful curve of thick cypress boards. But no one would want to walk up those stairs at this moment because they were covered with insects; wriggling ones, flying ones, thousands of them, millions of them. Heaven felt her stomach heave. She turned away.

"Termites!" the tour guide yelled.

Heaven was doodling on her napkin when Mary walked into the Bombay Club. "Did you get my message?" she asked.

"I'm here, aren't I?" Heaven said with less than her usual good humor. Her stomach refused to calm down. She hated bugs. "Did you get mine?"

"Yes, and I can hardly wait to hear. You just said there was another problem at the convent. What are you drawing?" Mary sat down and waved for a waiter. "What are you drinking?"

"First question: I'm drawing the stolen cross from seeing it on a video. I'm thinking of re-creating it in choc-olate. I went to the convent to get a photo of it but that became impossible. Second question: I'm drinking a Bombay martini. Since we're in the world-famous Bom-bay Club, what else? And what happened at the convent was really disgusting."

"I'll have a Cosmopolitan," Mary said to the waiter. "Heaven, why in the world would you use the word *disgusting*? Horrifying, mysterious; but disgusting?"

Heaven stuck her re-creation of the cross in her purse and leaned in toward Mary.

"Bugs. Millions of them. Termites actually. And they were eating the ancient cypress staircase that's the only surviving part of the oldest building in the Mississippi Valley at a rapid clip."

"Termites?" Mary said as her drink appeared and she held it up in salute to her friend. "Well, that's terrible, but I thought someone had vandalized the place again. Although I am surprised the diocese didn't take better care of that staircase."

"They swear they have it checked for bugs twice a year. They live in mortal fear of a termite. They're sure it was sabotage."

"You're kidding!"

"No, and what's more, they had just given a tour at one o'clock and the stairway was fine. I guess the people at the diocese archives office don't use the streetside door. Actually, I learned that the convent was built to face the river, so the entrance on Chartres is actually the back door. But the office workers come in and out a side door near where they park their cars. Someone brought millions of termites in and planted them on the staircase between two and three in the afternoon and didn't get caught."

"Ugh. What did the diocese people do?"

"Called an exterminator, and the police," Heaven said with a little shiver. She could still see the masses of silver wings.

"Well, if there's one thing we are experts at down here in the swamp, its killing bugs and vermin 'cause we got plenty of 'em," Mary said.

"Who's killing vermin?" Truely Whitten asked as he bent down and gave his wife a kiss on the cheek.

Heaven looked up and couldn't believe her eyes. Standing right beside Truely was the man, the silver-haired, Porsche-driving man that Heaven had fantasized about not two hours before. She felt her face turning pink. He pulled two chairs from an empty table next to them. The man must be with Truely.

"Heaven, this is my best friend in the whole world, Tompkins Wilson Tibbetts."

Heaven couldn't help herself. She giggled. "Tompkins Tibbetts, huh?"

He sat down next to Heaven with the comfortable slouch of a person who was at home at the Bombay Club. He grabbed a handful of goldfish crackers out of a bowl on the table and gave Heaven that bemused glance again, then actually winked. "That's why my friends call me Will. Sorry I almost ran over you today," he said with a great deal of humor and not a hint of apology in his voice.

A waiter approached their table again. Heaven couldn't remember the last time someone had winked at her. It was so corny. "Maybe, just this once, I could have a second martini," she said.

*   *   *

"That's what New Orleans does," Mary said as she handed Heaven the aspirin bottle along with her coffee the next morning. "It makes people break their own rules. You, the girl with the one-martini limit."

Heaven was clutching a glass of ice water, a huge glass of ice water. She pressed it against her face and then moved it to her lips and downed three aspirin. Next she took a big gulp of coffee. "At least I stopped at two and switched to that Far Niente cab. What a great dinner. I loved the thing with the duck and the jalapeno jelly and the caramelized onions."

"You and Will were having a ball," Mary said with a sly smile.

"Oh, stop it. It was just a harmless dinner flirtation. I forget. Is he married and did I take any clothes off?"

"Divorced and not a one. Well, I think your shoes. I seem to remember your foot working up his leg. Do you remember you promised Truely you'd come to the coffee warehouse today?"

"That I remember. I'm looking forward to it. I'm into coffee. We use a single estate bean and grind them at the restaurant to ensure freshness."

"Well, la-de-da," Mary said with a laugh. "I must admit, I had a ball last night myself. I haven't laughed that much in months. Your rendition of the termite story got funnier as the night went on."

"Speaking of the crises at the convent, I need to go upstairs and pack my stuff. My plane leaves at three and I want to do a little investigating before I leave, and also visit Truely. Where's his office?"

"In the warehouse at the beginning of Magazine Street, you can't miss it. Don't forget your lunch," Mary said.

"My lunch?"

"You're having lunch with Will at K-Paul's at 12:30. Aren't you glad I hadn't been traumatized by termites so I could keep track of you?"

Heaven got up and kissed her friend on the top of her head. "Yes, I am. I would have remembered. The coffee is kicking in. Thank you so much for your hospitality."

"I wish you'd change your mind and stay here when you come back next month."

Heaven shook her head. "I want to stay in the Quarter so I can be close to the venue for the dinner and to Peristyle, the kitchen I'm prepping in. I got a small suite at the Hotel Provincial. It's not even a half block from the convent. I'll be more productive there."

"Heaven," Mary said seriously, "about this investigating. I know you're famous for catching the bad guy at home, but New Orleans isn't Kansas City."

"Which means?"

"Nothing is ever the way that it seems here. Everything is more dangerous than it seems."

"That seems like the Surgeon General's warning for life in general, not just New Orleans. Now go to work. International law needs you."

Mary shrugged. "Be careful. I mean it."

Heaven waved confidently from the kitchen door.

The television station that Amelia Hart worked for was right in the Quarter. Heaven hadn't called ahead and had no idea if Amelia would be there or even remember who she was, and if she did, would want to talk to her. She pressed the buzzer on the street and when the receptionist answered she bluffed with, "Heaven Lee from

Kansas City to see Ms. Hart." That got her in the door. The next fifteen minutes were spent cooling her heels in the waiting room, but then the woman behind the desk said that Ms. Hart would be out shortly.

And she was, walking toward Heaven with her hand outstretched. "This is a surprise."

Heaven got up and shook the hand. "I'm leaving to go back to Kansas City this afternoon and there were a couple of things I wanted to talk to you about before I left."

"Come in then," Amelia said in a businesslike voice. She used a code to get them through a door to the warren of equipment, cables and props that constituted a television studio. "I have something that resembles an office," she said as she turned the corner into a tiny room crammed with a desk, a computer and printer, hundreds of clippings and books and files, and photos of Amelia with various celebrities push-pinned to the cork walls. Amelia sat down in front of her computer screen and removed a big pile of magazines from the only other chair in the room. Heaven sat.

"It looks like you read a lot. I promise I won't tell on you and ruin your reputation as just a talking head."

Amelia smiled involuntarily but didn't warm up. "You said you wanted to talk about a couple of things. I'm sure one of them is the trouble at the convent."

"Did you hear what happened yesterday?"

"I'm in the news business, remember?"

"Did the police question you because of your, eh, concerns about the benefit dinner for the sisters?"

"Now, why is that any of your business?"

Heaven tried a sweet smile. "Look, it's nothing personal. I just met you. You came into a meeting I was attending and raised hell with a bunch of women that weren't used to having someone talk to them like that. That's why I thought the police would make you Suspect Number One."

"And what about you? Is that how you see it?"

"Doesn't play that way to me. While you're saying your piece, the courtyard is trashed and an antique cross is stolen. You don't seem dumb. Why would you call attention to yourself if you'd already done physical damage to the place?"

"So, what? Are you going to defend me to the cops? Since you've got this all figured out, you want to take me down to the precinct and straighten them out?"

"No, I wondered if you had any ideas about who might have done it. I can't imagine this is high priority to the cops, even if everyone does love the sisters."

Amelia smiled. "Obviously, not everyone loves the sisters. I've already told you I'm not a fan. But carrying a million termites into the convent is not my kind of revenge. I can't stand the sight of one cockroach."

"And you would have needed an accomplice for the other job since you didn't come in the meeting holding the cross high above your head like Don Quixote."

"My, my, you have been thinking this through," Amelia Hart said as she leaned back in her chair, looking Heaven over like she was noticing her for the first time.

"So, if we both believe you didn't do it, who did?"

"It is intriguing. I'll grant you that. For all the crime in New Orleans, folks leave the churches pretty much alone. We don't have to lock 'em up like you do up North."

Heaven handed Amelia her card. "Will you call me if anything happens while I'm gone? I'm concerned that whoever is doing this is just getting started: that the benefit dinner could be a real disaster. You're in the business of knowing what's happening in town. You hear and see more."

Amelia noncommittally took the card and put in in a desk drawer. "What was the second thing?"

Heaven fished around in her purse and pulled out a slim booklet. "I went back to the convent yesterday. By a stroke of bad luck, I was there when the termites swarmed. But that's not the second thing. I bought this little book about your ancestor in the bookstore. *Henriette Delille: Servant of Slaves.* Imagine my surprise when I read that she herself had a slave. And you all upset about the Sisters of the Holy Trinity."

Amelia Hart flared, of course. "We're all victims of our times, Heaven. By the time Henriette was a grown woman, in 1850 say, it was very hard to free a slave. You white folks had made sure of that. She would have had to put up a big bond, plus the slave had to leave the state. Maybe her . . ." the word was hard for her to get out, "slave didn't want to leave New Orleans."

Heaven stood up. "I didn't know a thing about any of this until just two days ago. I'm just trying to understand. It does seem strange that any of these religious women, whether black or white, would not see that to own another human being like you own a dress is wrong."

"Easy for you to say, standing here now."

"I also noticed in the booklet that Henriette received her slave from her sister. Was that your great-great-great-grandmother?"

"Fuck you, Heaven. Are you saying I've got the same blood on my hands your white ancestors have? Not in a million years. Now get out of here."

Heaven paused at the open door. "I meant what I said about coming back next year and cooking for your aunt's order," she said as a parting peace offering. She didn't wait for a response, just found her way to the reception area and to the street. "Well," she said out loud as she walked down Chartres, "that certainly went bad fast."

The Pan-American Coffee Company warehouses were what you'd expect; right on the wharf, an outdoor concrete dock with a tin roof and filled with wooden pallets, some empty and stacked high on top of each other, others loaded with fifty-pound burlap bags of coffee beans from all over Central and South America. It was basically the same story inside some ancient-looking warehouses, bags of beans everywhere.

Heaven was following Truely around, trying to act interested. He noticed she was distracted.

"What's the matter, Heaven girl, still hungover from last night?"

Heaven shook her head. "No, I'm over that. I went to see Amelia Hart this morning."

"Doing some of your famous sleuthing? Watch out for that one, Heaven, she's hell on wheels."

"And I made her so relaxed and comfortable by reminding her that her free-woman-of-color religious great-great-great-aunt, or whatever it is, owned at least one slave."

Truely laughed. His lanky frame held a suit beautifully. "Now what ever possessed you to do that?"

"Well, I got this book over at the convent about her aunt. I just couldn't get over the fact she pitched such a fit, and her family owned slaves, too. I'm new at this Civil War stuff. It's still so vivid to folks here. Of course, we had our own problems out in the Midwest, but they don't seem to come up in conversation very often. Right where I live, in Kansas City, the Kansas folks were on one side of the Civil War and the Missouri folks were on the other. But I guess, because it was new territory out there in the 1860s, we don't have the same long history with slavery as you all do down here. New Orleans is older than the United States, for God's sake."

"A fact we like to bring up as often as possible," Truely said as they headed back through the warehouse to his office.

"I guess my point is, I'm not claiming any moral superiority because my great-great-grandparents didn't keep slaves. The prairie settlers were way too poor for that. But because it isn't part of my family history, it seems like it would be kind of creepy."

Truely stopped and pointed around at the vast room they were standing in. "I'm the ninth generation of my mother's family to import coffee. I've got forklifts and conveyer belts and electronic tracking systems up the ass. We run this whole warehouse operation with just forty employees. Of course, we've got lots more people out at the roasting and shipping facility. But I know as well as I know my name that this room, or one on this very spot, was filled with slaves in, say, 1850, doing what those forklifts and conveyers belts do now. It's eerie," he said softly and took Heaven's arm.

They stopped at a state-of-the-art coffeemaker. "Want a cup?" Truely asked as he poured himself some. Truely's coffee cup seemed permanently attached to his hand. He gestured with it gracefully.

"What is it?" Heaven asked, embarrassed to be such a snob.

"This is from a Jamaican estate right across the valley from Blue Mountain. Good enough?"

She nodded and accepted the cup, slurping as they walked. "Delicious. Is it as expensive as Blue Mountain?"

"About half the price. So, Heaven, who do you think is fooling with the convent?"

"I think it will take much more New Orleans knowledge than I have to even identify all the suspects," Heaven said.

When Heaven and Truely rounded the corner into Truely's office they were surprised by a man sitting in Truely's chair. He was a big man, no, a mountain of a man, like a former professional football player at age forty. The guy wasn't fat but he wasn't all muscle either. Tall, too. He startled both of them, Truely more than Heaven. "Where you been?" the big man demanded.

"Showing my friend from out of town around," Truely said cautiously, not introducing Heaven and the unexpected visitor.

"I thought we had an appointment yesterday?" the big man said, ignoring Heaven completely.

"Yes, I guess we did," Truely admitted.

"I guess we'll have it right now," the big man said, looking at Heaven dismissively.

Heaven got the hint. There was no way to pretend the guy wasn't emasculating Truely. He was sitting in Truely's chair behind Truely's desk and he didn't bother to get up when Truely came in. That was fairly insulting. "I've got to go anyway. I'm meeting your best friend at K-Paul's."

Truely's eyes looked sad that Heaven had been exposed to this big lug, but he still smiled politely and gave Heaven a hug. "Watch that boy. He's a pistol. We'll see you next month." With that he almost pushed Heaven out in the hall and closed the door. Heaven walked slowly away from the office, hoping to catch a piece of conversation, but no yelling erupted that she could hear. Maybe it was just rudeness on the part of the other man, nothing more.

But here in New Orleans, where superficial manners were an art form, rudeness jarred Heaven. This guy wasn't one of the rival coffee people who had confronted Truely at the hotel bar. He was someone else who wasn't happy. Heaven shivered. Something was wrong.

"I don't remember it being so upscale," Heaven said as she and Will were seated.

"Just another way the world is going to hell in a handbasket. K-Paul's has gone and cleaned up," Will said as he rubbed his hands together gleefully. "The food is still good, though."

"I sure had fun last night," Heaven said before she thought. "The four of us, I mean," she quickly added.

"Me, too. How come I haven't met you before? You're sure the best one of Mary Beth's Northerner friends."

Heaven couldn't resist. The scene at Truely's was just too fresh in her mind. She switched the conversation. "Speaking of friends, yours says for me to watch out for you, says you're a pistol."

Will looked like he had just been called a captain of industry. But before he could reply an older man in a linen suit stopped by the table. "Tom Tibbetts, don't get up. Just call my office this afternoon. We may be able to do something with that Chef Mentuer property." He walked on.

Heaven looked quizzically across the table.

"I told you only my friends called me Will. I can't be the only one at this table with several names. You can't tell me your momma named you Heaven."

"Katherine O'Malley," she said, wanting to turn the conversation back to Truely. "Will, can I ask you something that isn't any of my business?"

"I've been married twice, well, three times if you count that month in my senior year of high school."

"I've got you beat by two, if you count that month in your senior year of high school. But that's not what I want to ask you. Is Truely's business all right?"

The waiter arrived and they ordered; gumbo and a miniature eggplant version of a pirogue, the flat-bottomed boats of the bayou, filled with spicy crayfish for Heaven, and some oysters and blackened snapper for Will.

"And we'll have a bottle of that good Sancerre, the Pascal Jolivet," Will said as he handed in their menus. "Why do you ask about Truely's business?" He didn't say she was barking up the wrong tree, she noticed. Answering a question with a question was old but it still worked.

"Well, today I went over to the warehouse, to see how a coffee operation functions, and when we went back into Truely's office, there was a great big man sitting in Truely's chair behind his desk, which I found to be the highest form of insult."

Will started the spin control for his friend. "If someone sat in Truely's chair and he didn't give them hell, they must be a good friend. How old?"

"Forty, maybe. He looked like someone who had played for the Saints about ten years ago."

"Heaven, you've been living in Kansas City too long,

where those Italians were into everything in the food world and were always dropping by to get their cut."

"Duh, New Orleans can keep up in the organized crime department," Heaven said haughtily, thinking of her Italian/American/Vietnamese neighborhood back home.

"Truely Whitten is not mobbed up, Heaven, no way. Is that what you're trying to say? Did this guy look Italian?"

"No, he looked like a big bohunk from the University of Nebraska, twenty years removed."

"What happened?"

"The guy said Truely had missed an appointment and then they kicked me out. Truely didn't even introduce me and, for such a Southern gentleman, that spoke volumes."

"Oh, it did, huh? Heaven, I think this trouble at the convent has got your imagination going on overtime."

Heaven refused to be waylaid. "And there's more. The other day we met Truely at the Monteleone and these two guys were with him and one of them left looking real mad and the other one said, 'It's not a joke,' and they were from the rival coffee importer."

Will gave her that grin. "Boy, you are Nancy Drew, aren't you? Sounds like Leon Davis to me. He's full of bull. I doubt he could buy Truely out if Pan-Am were for sale, which it isn't. Heaven, honey. Relax."

Their first courses arrived and Heaven bit her tongue for a minute, then slipped in one more try. "So, everything's fine with Truely?"

"Let's talk about us, instead. Are you involved with anyone in Kansas City?"

"Yes," Heaven said hurriedly, with a follow-up smile

that she knew was flirtatious. Sometimes she couldn't help herself. She felt guilty about that. She loved Hank. "And you?"

Will shrugged. "This and that. When you're as handsome as me, you have to fight 'em off with a stick."

Heaven got ready to give him a stinging reply, and he winked. "Just kidding. I know you have a sense of humor, 'cause I saw it last night. I've only been divorced this last time for a year. I'm not ready to get hooked up again, just yet. So, what about us having a mad affair when you come back next month?"

"Said with about as much passion as you had when you were talking about your real estate business last night. I get the feeling you don't take much seriously, Will."

"You didn't answer my question."

"Any affair planned a month in advance like a dentist's appointment wouldn't be worth having," Heaven said.

"Touché. Then let me show you my place after lunch. It's right over on Governor Nicholls. It's on the historical register. That bad boy Clay Shaw lived there once."

Heaven thought back. She was sure Will and his Porsche had been coming out of a courtyard on Ursulines, not Governor Nicholls. But before she made a fool of herself about French Quarter geography, she'd check it out when she returned next month. Will must know where he lived, after all. And he could have been visiting a friend. "How about splitting a piece of sweet potato pecan pie instead?" she said sweetly.

Fish in Parchment

For six servings:

6 6-oz. fillets of sole or pompano or other flat-bodied
   fish. (Have the butcher save the bones and heads if
   possible.)
Parchment paper is cut in large rounds or a heart
   shape, one for each serving.
1 onion, peeled and diced
1 shallot, peeled and diced
2 cloves garlic, diced
6 T. butter
1 cup white wine
1 cup fish stock or chicken stock
1 T. thyme
1 T. tarragon
1 T. white vinegar
red or yellow baby tomatoes, three for each serving
1 cup crabmeat
1 cup diced cooked shrimp
2 shelled oysters per serving (optional)
kosher salt
white pepper

If possible make some fish stock with your fish bones, a
stalk of celery, an onion quartered, a carrot, and some
parsley in a large sauté pan or wide mouth saucepan.

Cover the bones with cold water, bring to a boil and simmer, skimming the top of the pan. Add ½ cup white wine and reduce to a quart.

The fish:

Melt 3 T. of the butter in a large, heavy sauté pan. Add the onion, shallot, garlic and sauté to soften. Add the liquids, the herbs, and reduce 10 minutes. Add the vinegar, tomatoes, and seafood (except the fish and seasonings). Reduce again 5 minutes. With a fork, beat in the remaining butter. Remove from heat and cool.

Oil the inside of the parchment paper. Place a fish fillet in the middle of each piece and sprinkle with kosher salt and white pepper. Place a scoop of the vegetable and seafood mixture on the top of each fillet. Close and crimp the paper to seal.

Roast at 450 degrees for 15 minutes. Rip into the paper, take a big sniff of the wonderful aroma and dig in. This is a much lighter version of the classic New Orleans dish, which has a thickened sauce. You can add some cayenne if you want a little heat, or sometimes I sprinkle a touch of ground cinnamon in the package.

Four

And that's why I'm so glad to be home," Heaven said with a big sigh at the end of a sparkling recitation of all the problems that had occurred in New Orleans.

Sal and Murray and Mona were speechless for a minute. "You left Tuesday morning and got back Thursday night and that much happened?" Murray asked, in awe. "You could write a whole novel just from those three days."

"It's really more like two days. You have to take time off for flying there and back," Heaven said smugly.

"Heaven, what in the world will happen when there's food involved?" Mona asked. "Troublemakers love it when there's food involved."

"That worries me too. But no one even mentioned canceling the event. Ninety-nine percent of the people of New Orleans seem to really love the sisters and what they mean to the city."

"What happened to the cross?" Sal said, leaving the

obvious comment that it only takes one percent to screw everything up left unsaid.

"I thought about that on the way home. It has great historical value, of course, but I don't know what someone in another city would pay for an eighteenth-century iron cross from France and I don't think anyone in New Orleans could display it in their home if they bought it on the black market. So I don't think it was stolen for that. It could have been thrown in the river by someone who just wanted to destroy the outward trappings of the sisterhood."

"Like that Amelia Hart," Mona threw in.

"Of course, they could use it to commit a crime. That would irritate the sisters. I don't know if it's heavy enough to break the window of a bank or anything. And I don't know if the point on top is sharp enough to impale anyone," Heaven said, speculating.

"Heaven, stop," Mona ordered like an old maid schoolteacher.

"Well, whoever stole the cross isn't likely to have it polished and return it, you know," she said defensively.

"People are just no damn good," Sal said as two high school students entered the shop for trims of their military-style haircuts, so popular with the kids at the moment. He looked at Heaven as if to say, no more crime stories.

"I better get to work. How are the reservations for tonight, Murray?"

Murray looked at Heaven intensely. "Busy. Let's go over and look at the reservation book. There are a couple of problem areas, like right around seven o'clock."

"Seven is always a problem on Friday night," Heaven said. "Bye, Sal."

Sal's unlit cigar moved from one side of his mouth to the other, a gesture they all took for good-bye.

Heaven and Mona and Murray got up and walked out the door. "I'll talk to you two later," Mona said as they walked across 39th Street.

"You better tell Mona about the letters pretty soon," Murray said in a low voice. "She'll be pissed. . . ."

"You mean if she finds out some other way, like in the newspaper?" Heaven hissed under her breath as they walked into the cafe. "Has something else happened?"

Murray looked down and nodded. "Sal's connection at city hall says the health department got the same letter you did sometime this week. Just like the newspaper, they don't follow up on unsigned accusations because they've been used for some personal vendettas. I guess an ex-wife pissed off at her ex-husband, who owned a little cafe out on Wornall, made a big stink last year, saying he had rats, roaches. She sent the letters unsigned but got antsy they weren't closing him down fast enough and called up. Health department has caller ID. They went out and interviewed her and saw she was trying to cause trouble for her ex."

"I get the picture, Murray. The health department doesn't like to be used in personal vendettas. But the idea gets planted."

"Just like the newspaper. It gets them thinking that maybe they should have a policy about people working in the food industry with HIV. I guess all the honchos are meeting with the docs, trying to see what's what."

"They already have rules about what you're supposed to do if anyone has hepatitis. Everyone takes a gamma globulin shot," Heaven said, knowing that had nothing to do with the current problem. "Damn."

"I'm going, I'll see you tonight. Heaven, I don't like the sound of things in New Orleans. Whoever is doing this is working up to the big benefit dinner. You know that."

"But what can I do? We've got some nut up here trying to destroy my business. The sisters are on their own for a while." Heaven stalked into the kitchen with a heavy heart.

"Heaven, get out of here. You must be exhausted, after the trip to New Orleans and all." Sara Baxter, the lead line cook—she refused to be called the sous-chef—was trying to spare the kitchen the grief of having Heaven around while they cleaned up. It took twice as long to clean when Heaven was there because she was always finding nooks and crannies that she wanted them to pull everything out of and wipe down with bleach water. Not that it wasn't a good idea, just not tonight. They'd gotten their butts whipped tonight.

Heaven wouldn't hear of it. "I wonder how many orders of those fish in parchment we did? I should have thought when I decided to do it as a special it would come from my station. What a night. I do ache, I must admit. But I'll stay and help," she said cheerfully. Heaven wanted more physical labor. Sometimes, when you can't figure out a problem, getting slammed on the saute station on a busy Friday night and then organizing the walk-in cooler was the next best thing. But before she could protest further, Murray stuck his head into the kitchen via the pass-through window. He had a big grin on his face, which pissed her off. He shouldn't be smiling after the night they'd just experienced. "Guess who just walked in the door?"

"Don't fuck with me, Murray," Heaven said shortly.

"Trust me. This will make you happy. Just come out here," Murray said, insisting.

Sara took the dirty kitchen rag from Heaven's hand and untied her apron. "Bye," Sara said firmly.

Heaven went over to the tiny kitchen bathroom and did her sixty-second beauty routine. She took off her chef's jacket. She splashed water on her face to get any large chunks of food loosened and rinsed off, then applied bright pink lipstick. She mussed her red hair with wet fingers, giving it a little life. Then she stepped back out into the kitchen and slipped on a 1950s men's sharkskin sports jacket that she always had hanging there, to give her tee shirt and tights a little boost. She didn't bother to change from her kitchen clogs to high heels. "Thanks for working so hard. Lucky us. We get to do it again tomorrow night," she said to the kitchen crew and stepped out in the dark of the dining room.

Every time Heaven entered the dining room it gave her a buzz. If the kitchen was backstage, the dining room was front and center. Hitting that swinging door, having your eyes adjust to the dim light, your skin be caressed with the coolness, your ears with the sound of Ella Fitzgerald and snippets of conversation from guests having a good time, it was a real high for Heaven. In those first few seconds of being in the dining room, the chaos of the kitchen, the sales tax due in a few days, the broken bar sink that would have to be fixed tomorrow, Saturday, at overtime rates, even the anonymous hate mail seemed like a small price to pay for standing there in the dining room in a world you'd created.

Heaven looked over at the bar and saw why Murray had insisted she come out. Jack was back.

Jumpin' Jack, as he liked to be called, was a neighborhood fixture. For years, he wore only army camo gear and insisted he had served in Vietnam. Actually, he was raised a rich kid in Mission Hills, had never been in the armed services, and was ten years too young to have gone to Vietnam even if he'd been well enough to be in the military. His family didn't want to deal with him and his neuroses. They gave him money to stay away. Jack had helped Heaven out of some jams and in those cases his military delusions had come in handy, as he could could pick a lock and do surveillance with aplomb. But Jack had become confused and agitated more than a year before, and Heaven had insisted that his parents help him. Menninger's was just sixty miles away in Topeka, Kansas, and couldn't be beat for an expensive shrinking. This was the first time Jack had been seen since he went there to be fixed.

"Hey, stranger, long time, no see," Heaven said and gave Jack a big kiss on the cheek. The camo gear was gone, replaced by jeans, a black Gap tee shirt and a tweedy sports jacket. His old beard was also gone and, clean shaven, Jack looked almost like a college professor. Heaven thought he was puffy though, probably from his medication. A few months ago, Murray had found out they were having trouble finding the right combination of chemicals to soothe Jack's demons. Now, his eyes looked clear and friendly.

"Did ya miss me?" Jack said, like a regular person. Before he had spoken in military speak.

"We missed you terribly," Heaven said. "Murray and I tried to come visit you but they said it would interfere with your progress. Can you have a drink?"

"My doctor said one drink a day will be fine," Jack said.

"Tony, get this man what he wants, on the house. I notice you have a new wardrobe."

"Scotch and water, Tony. I had to give up on the Vietnam thing. Hell, people who did go there have to give up on the Vietnam thing, let alone me. But that doesn't mean I can't help you if you need me, Heaven."

"Tony, give me a glass of that new Adelsheim Pinot Noir, please. I'm gonna have a drink with my friend."

While Heaven and Jack sat there, the rest of the staff meandered over and gave Jack a hello. Joe and Chris insisted on bringing him three desserts, on them. Murray told him about how he was writing again on a part-time basis. Everyone was happy to have Jack back, safe and seemingly much more sound.

"I don't want to accuse you of ulterior motives, but you don't invite us to dinner at your restaurant on the house every day. Is something wrong?" Rabbi Michael Zedek and his wife were enjoying their dessert and coffee, having polished off a lamb shank and some hot, hacked chicken.

Heaven sat down at an empty chair at their table. "Patently transparent, eh? I love having you in the restaurant but, yes, I wanted to ask you something. I know that guy who got the genius grant and tracks the hate-crime people is your friend."

"Howard Yukon, yes."

"And I know that he keeps a very low profile because he gets death threats and all that stuff. I didn't even try to look him up in the phone book. I just assumed he wouldn't be listed."

"No, he even keeps his residence as much of a secret

as possible. It's a classic case of killing the messenger. These groups see him on some national television show explaining that there are *x* amount of white supremacists in Missouri and *y* amount in Idaho, and they think he's told the government their secret locations," Rabbi Zedek said.

"Do you think you could arrange it so I could talk to him? Even over the phone would be fine. He could call me. I wouldn't have to know his number. I could promise not to look at the caller ID. Or, we could meet in person. Whatever you think is best."

"Will you tell me why you want to speak to him? I assure you it won't leave this table," the rabbi said, and his wife nodded in agreement.

"Oh, I trust you. It's just, well, someone has written a vicious unsigned letter about Cafe Heaven and sent it around town. So far I've gotten one, and the health department and the *Kansas City Star* each got one too, all the same text."

"Any ideas who sent it?"

"Haven't a clue. That's why I thought if I spoke to the expert, maybe he could help me figure it out."

Rabbi Zedek shook his head. "I'm so sorry this has happened to you. The reputation of a restaurant is so delicate. Even for someone to claim they got food poisoning at a cafe can be damaging. I think Howard will want to talk to you. I'm not sure he can solve the mystery, however."

"Have you ever been through this yourself?"

"Many times. I get vicious E-mails and snail mail all the time. Because I'm on that radio show with Father Tom and Reverend Hill, I'm the Jew that killed Christ in many people's minds."

"Do you ever find out who writes them?"

"E-mails are rarely rerouted, so I know where they come from. The snail mail is too much trouble to trace. Occasionally someone will become so fixated, they want you to know who they are and they confront you physically or start signing their sick work. But you should talk to Howard. He and I have a conference call with someone in California tomorrow at two. Why don't I arrange for him to call you after that. Will you be here?"

"If Howard is calling, I'll be here. Just let me know if for some reason he can't. I'll be back here in the restaurant by two if I go out to run any errands." Heaven stood. "Have a good Passover and thanks for the help. Don't forget you're coming to my house on Easter."

"We'll be there, and thanks for dinner," the rabbi said as he turned his attention back to the dessert plates.

Heaven was in the office when Howard Yukon called, wrangling the invoices into some semblance of order for the part-time bookkeeper.

"Cafe Heaven."

"Heaven, this is Howard Yukon. I'm here in Michael's office and he said you've been the beneficiary of some unsigned mail."

"Oh, Mr. Yukon, thank you so much for taking the time. This really is very disturbing because a restaurant just can't have bad press."

"Pardon me," the voice on the other end said. "But didn't someone die in your restaurant and didn't a group of people have a bad experience with some contaminated flour as well?"

Heaven took a deep breath so she wouldn't snap the man's head off. "Notoriety seems to be okay. But this is much different."

"I know it's hard, but you must tell me exactly what the note said."

Heaven told him.

"How was it arranged on the paper?" he asked.

She closed her eyes and could see it as though it was lying in front of her. "Three lines, each centered on the page. Why?"

"Although I don't know their identities; some of these individuals have become familiar to me by the style in which they write these notes, and of course, the object of their hate."

"Do you think this hatred is directed toward gay waiters, or personally toward someone who works for me? I'm concerned for my employees, and I don't want a maniac to screw up my business with this bullshit," Heaven said, more emphatically than she'd meant to. The poor guy didn't need her to yell at him, just because he took the time to call and help.

"It could be one of those reasons, or another one," he said quietly. "You are a high-profile woman. Your name and photo have been in the paper quite a bit. Many times this creates fixations, like the Jodie Foster stalker."

"But this person doesn't want me, they want to destroy me. I know you understand better than I what's involved here. But I'm not a religion or a government that can survive this kind of opposition. If this letter was to get wide circulation, even if people didn't really believe it, the damage would be done. If you were trying to figure out where to go to dinner and the nose-picking cook came to mind, you might choose another cafe, even if the choice was subconscious."

"You're right. And places like the *Kansas City Star* and city hall aren't the most secure. I had a friend who was an educator. Someone wrote a hate letter saying he was abusing young children. The letter was sent to the board of education office in his district. They discussed it with him, told him that they didn't respond to unsigned accusations. But the letter got copied. Soon enough parents had seen it that they demanded the teacher's resignation. He moved far away and has never taught again."

Heaven felt sick. This was just what she feared. "What can I do? This is such a vulnerable position for me. I'm helpless," she said.

"Do not give in to despair. If you do, this individual will have accomplished at least one of the things he was trying to do, and that's to get the better of you. He didn't say the waiters in all the restaurants in Kansas City were AIDS infested. He said the waiters in your restaurant were. That makes it personal."

"But how can I fight this thing?" Heaven was in tears again. One trickled down her face.

"Tomorrow you are going to messenger the original letter out here to Michael's office at the synagogue. Keep a copy for yourself, but send me the original. Then you are going to call your contacts at the *Kansas City Star* and at city hall and you are going to tell them that you will be down to pick up their originals in person in an hour."

"What if they won't—"

Howard Yukon broke in quickly. "It won't guarantee that there aren't already copies made. But it will stop the casual stopping-by-the-file-cabinet-to-view-the-gory-details kind of thing. And I've seen those photos of you in the paper myself. Don't tell me a beautiful redhead can't get her way with those boys downtown."

Right now Heaven couldn't talk a blind man into new

eyes. "Thanks for the vote of confidence. What if I need to talk to you, what if something else happens?"

"Just call Michael," the voice said soothingly.

"Thank you. Can I ask one more question?"

"Of course."

"Why do you have to have the original letter?"

Howard Yukon paused. "Sometimes I can feel them. I'll know if it's any of my regulars." Then he hung up.

"Do you think this is the original?" Murray said as he held a piece of paper up to the light streaming in the front windows at Sal's.

Heaven shrugged. "I wouldn't have a clue. I'm sure the copy paper at the *Star* isn't the same paper as the original, but I'm not a paper expert."

"So what happened?" Sal asked as he finished off a trim of an elderly man.

"Well, thanks to Murray, who called his friend and absolutely insisted that he give me the letter, it was easy. I went to the front desk. Murray's friend came down with an envelope, gave it to me, and shook my hand. Said as far as he could tell it was a dead issue in the news department, except for a more general story that was still brewing."

"You sure they don't have copies all over the office already?"

"No, Sal. I could have made the man sign in blood but, if he didn't have physical control of the letter at all times, he wouldn't know whether someone else made a copy. I didn't make him lie to me."

"What about you, Sal?" Murray asked as the customer shuffled out. "What about city hall?"

"Heaven doesn't even have to go down there. My guy

is dropping it off on his way home tonight. Said he didn't know who had seen it, but he was willing to pull it out of the crank letter file, without a trace. Not that it hasn't been copied, but not by my guy," Sal said gruffly.

Heaven was slumped in one of Sal's chrome-and-Naugahyde chairs. "And after we collect these so-called originals, and if there are copies, they could be copied again and again. No one is going to bother to check and see if it's the real thing. It's filthy sleaze and if a person is copying it, they don't care about what's right."

"Don't think like that, Heaven," Sal said. "That hate-crime fellow, he gave you good advice about going around collecting the letters. It's just too bad we didn't think about it when we first heard other people had received that garbage."

Heaven went over to Murray and took the letter out of his hand, kissing the top of his balding head as she tore it up. "It wouldn't guarantee anything. It only takes two seconds to copy something. Thanks, guys, for your support during yet another Cafe Heaven crisis."

"Don't you think you should keep that, for evidence?" Murray asked.

"As I learned back in Criminal Law 101, because we have no chain of evidence, this is tainted and useless. We already have one copy in the office and that's more than enough. I hate even touching it, and I'm taking the copy home tonight. I don't want one of my employees to come across it by accident," Heaven said as she stuffed the paper shards in her jacket pocket, went out the front door and headed back across the street.

Sal and Murray watched as the late-afternoon sun hit Heaven's hair. It shimmered like fire.

*   *   *

Heaven looked around. The house didn't look too bad. She couldn't believe Easter had crept up so fast. The last few weeks had flown by. Now the Fifth Annual Spring Renewal, Resurrection and Rejuvenation Brunch, held on Easter Sunday, was officially over. It had been a big success. Even under duress, worrying about the hate mail and about New Orleans, Heaven could throw a party.

Now she was alone. Hank had to go to the hospital and he would be there all night, working the emergency room. The dishes were clean or at least the last batch was in the dishwasher. All the empty bottles had been deposited in the Dumpster outside by the waiters from Cafe Allegro Heaven had hired to work the party. She didn't want to ask any of her employees to work as they were all invited to be guests. There had been about a hundred people in and out of the house in the period from eleven to four. The last group left about five.

Heaven's home helped her entertain. A two-story building constructed in 1890, it was an Italian bread bakery before Heaven moved in. The coal-burning bread ovens were still installed in the brick walls, extending from the exterior of the building like an ear. The first floor was one big entertaining/kitchen/living room combination. Before the restaurant, Heaven had run a catering business out of the space. It still had rows of baker's shelves lined with platters and baskets and antique culinary treasures, such as Heaven's collection of two hundred plus drinking glasses. When she had a big party like this, she put out a huge tray filled with all different kinds of glasses, from 1940s juice glasses to etched wineglasses, and let people take their choice.

Now she busied herself for a few minutes carrying glasses back to the shelves.

The phone rang. "Oh, shit," Heaven mumbled and grabbed it.

"Mom, I'm tired and I want to go to bed. I thought you were gonna call after your party."

It was Iris, Heaven's daughter, who lived in England. "Honey, I'm so sorry. I started putting away glasses and I guess I spaced out. I've got a lot on my mind. Happy Easter, honey."

"That doesn't sound good. First, tell me about the party. What did you serve this year?"

Heaven always tried for a menu that skirted around the traditional Jewish Passover food and Christian Easter items. "I did a Zakuski table this year, very Russian."

"Zakuski?" Iris echoed.

"In the really old days in Russia, before it was just potatoes and cabbage, on their plantations or whatever they called them, people would have food out on their sideboard all the time because when travelers would get to your house they were usually from far away, and they'd been traveling a long time and they were hungry. The steppes you know. So it's the Russian version of Tapas, kinda."

"Like what?"

"Blini all piled up with mushrooms. Caviar, beet caviar, eggplant, pirogi dumpling things, and a Kilebiac, a salmon in puff pastry. Other stuff. These Armenian pastries filled with farmers' cheese. Yum."

"How exotic. Did you serve vodka?"

"Of course. I put the vodka bottles in milk cartons full of water in the freezer. And I put flowers in the water so the vodka looked very festive, in an iceberg of flowers."

"Sounds like Martha to me, Mom."

Heaven bristled. "People were putting their vodka in icebergs long before Martha Stewart."

"So, what's the problem? You said you had a lot on your mind."

How much did she want to tell her daughter? "Someone wrote this horrible unsigned letter about Cafe Heaven and also sent it to the newspaper and to the health department."

"Mom, what did it say?"

She decided to paraphrase. "That our waiters had AIDS and our cooks put nose boogers in the food."

"Mom, that's horrible!"

"Yes, it is. There's virtually no way you can stop people from doing something like that. And it can ruin your business."

"The newspaper isn't going to print that crap is it?"

"No, but who knows what this sicko will do next. And I have to leave town next week."

"Where to?"

"New Orleans. I'm cooking at a benefit for the oldest nuns in America."

"Poor old dears," Iris said sweetly.

"The order is old, not the actual nuns. But that's not going too well either."

"Tell me."

"I went down there a few weeks ago to a planning meeting and while we were there in the convent, someone wrote bad words in red paint on the convent walls and stole the eighteenth-century cross they brought from France and put termites on their historical staircase."

Iris giggled. "I'm sorry, Mom. I shouldn't laugh but

you just painted quite a picture. Did all that happen at once, the graffiti and the cross and the termites?"

"Not quite. But enough about me. You left a message and said you had a good new gig?" Iris had been writing since she finished up at Oxford. Her father was a well-known English rock star and she was writing about music for magazines.

"I go to Brazil next week for a magazine kind of like *Tattler*. I don't think they have it in America. I get to stay two whole weeks and write a what's-going-on-in-Brazilian-music piece. Won't that be fun?"

"Just be careful—tourists are always getting shot on the beach in Rio—and don't go to any late-night clubs by yourself."

"Mother! You've got a lot of nerve fussing at me about being safe. Some nut is writing hate mail to you and you're heading off to New Orleans where another nut is after the nuns. Nothing that could happen on the beach in Rio could compare. Besides, you-know-who will be with me most of the time." You-know-who was Iris's boyfriend, another member of her father's band and a man as old as her father. It infuriated Heaven.

"Then you'll have bodyguards and a driver and all that. Good," Heaven said shortly.

"Mom, let's not hang up mad. I'll be fine and I'll call you from there next week, if I know where you'll be."

"I'll put the phone number at my hotel in New Orleans on your machine in England. You can get it off that. Or call the cafe. They'll have my numbers."

"I'm worried about you, Mom. Have you told that detective friend of yours about this?"

"No, but that's a good idea, Iris. Bonnie couldn't come to the party today or maybe I would have thought of that when I saw her. Now go to bed, honey. Alone, I hope."

"As alone as one of your nuns, Mom. Be careful. I love you."

"Love you too, honey," she said as Iris hung up.

Heaven, dialing, could hardly wait to talk to her friend Sergeant Bonnie Weber, of the Kansas City Police Department. She couldn't believe she hadn't thought of it before.

Bonnie would know what to do.

"I don't know what to do," Bonnie said between bites. She and Heaven were having lunch at the Classic Cup, a bistro owned by one of Heaven's friends, Charlene Welling. Charlene had sent them lots of food: a Cobb salad; a bacon, lettuce, tomato and Brie sandwich; two bowls of two different soups and a piece of grilled salmon with a mango salsa on top. They had it all in the middle of the table and were grazing. "I'm a homicide cop. What do I know from poison-pen letters?"

"Don't play dumb with me. You're always going to those conferences and I know they aren't always about murder. Now that you're a big shot sergeant." Heaven couldn't resist teasing her friend a little bit. Bonnie had resisted taking the sergeants' exam for several years, saying it would take more time away from her family. But now that her kids were in high school, she'd moved up.

"Heaven, I don't blame you for being upset and scared. These creeps can bring a person down. And the extra added element is that you serve food. That makes it easy to start rumors and it makes you vulnerable to people's fears about their health. All of these food safety problems, the killer hamburgers and stuff. It's made the public gun-shy."

"Gun-shy. Good one," Heaven said wryly. "Can't you rummage around and find a profile on this type of weirdo?"

"Yes, I probably can. But you already talked to one of the top experts in the country and he gave you good advice, it sounds like, even if it was a little late. I'll go into the FBI web site and see what I can find. Heaven, it could be anyone."

She had to laugh. "You mean I'm universally hated?"

"Start in and move outward. Personally, it could be a spurned lover from years ago who harbors a grudge. Or it could be someone who has obsessed over you from seeing your picture in the papers and reading about your brushes with death. That can be sexually exciting to some people."

"What's the next circle out? My business?" Heaven picked a big slice of avocado out of the Cobb salad and popped it in her mouth.

"Yes, I would say that's next. Someone who didn't get a job and wanted one, or did get a job and couldn't keep it. Someone who got bad service or had to wait for a table or thinks he got sick from the food. Someone who doesn't like the open mike nights. Someone who personally doesn't like one of your employees." Bonnie waved for a waiter. "Could I have some coffee?" she asked when one hurried over. Heaven's table was always considered VIP at the Cup.

"And then?" Heaven asked glumly.

"People who don't like the groups mentioned in the letter. Someone who hates gays, or waiters, or cooks," Bonnie said calmly, not feeling Heaven's sense of doom and drama.

"What's the largest circle?" Heaven asked.

"The poison-pen version of random violence. Someone who could have chosen any restaurant to terrorize, and you just happened to get chosen."

Out of nowhere three desserts appeared, compliments of Charlene, who waved at them from behind the coffee counter. The two were quiet for a while as they tasted a baked apple with cinnamon ice cream, a dense dark-chocolate brownie, and a piece of key lime pie.

"Will you do one thing for me, Bonnie?"

"You know I will within my limitations."

Heaven polished off the last bite of the brownie. "Will you ask around the department? Maybe some other restaurant has been getting these too and we just don't know about it. Or maybe some other kinds of businesses that hire lots of gay people have been targeted. We might be able to eliminate one or two of these possibilities."

"Now that I can do," Bonnie Weber said.

Heaven rolled over on Hank again. She kissed his neck and the little hollow where his collarbone fit on his chest. She licked his shoulder, wanting to set the taste of him in her mind. "I'll miss you," she whispered.

Hank ran his hand through her hair. "You're only going to be gone for a few days. Why are you acting this way?"

"I'm afraid."

Hank pulled her down until her head was on his chest. He wrapped her up in his arms and let the beat of his heart calm her. After a few minutes he sensed that she was more relaxed. "I don't think I've ever heard you say that before, that you're afraid. What of?"

"The fact that there are people out in the world that I don't know that may want to do me harm scares me. Whoever wrote that letter about my restaurant scares me. The person who vandalized the convent in New Orleans scares me. The fact that some or all of these things could be just random really scares me."

Hank stroked her head. "If you know what you're up against, you can figure out how to fight it. I know you're a warrior, Heaven."

"I'm a tired warrior. I feel defeated."

"Then I'm going to take your mind to a completely different level for a minute. I have a favor to ask you."

"Anything, as long as it doesn't require warrioring," Heaven said, rolling over and propping her head up with one arm so she could look at Hank.

"I have a package of little gifts and a letter that I'd like for you to take to my cousins in New Orleans. They live in a Vietnamese enclave just out of town. Its called Versailles. I think it's very well known and shouldn't be hard to find."

"Of course, but why not send them UPS?"

"Because I want them to meet you, that's why. This way there will be no embarrassment, no one has to ask the other to dinner or something that might be strained. You can deliver the package and they will get to meet you. And you them, of course."

Heaven was touched. "Is this because your mom has told them what an evil white witch I am? You want to show them I don't have horns?"

"I want them to see the remarkable woman that I love. That's all."

"Aren't you afraid that when they see how old I am, plus being an Anglo, it will just make things worse?"

Hank laughed. "Two of my cousins are general practitioners and run a family practice together, and a third is a dentist. They should be able to handle any geriatric medical emergencies that might occur."

"I think I'm having one now." Heaven grabbed Hank's hand and put it on one of her breasts.

"A medical emergency?"

"Yes. Heart palpitations," she whispered in his ear, and pulled him to her.

Trinity Rice Cakes

3 cups cooked rice
1 onion, peeled and diced
3 stalks celery, diced
1 green pepper, diced
1 red pepper, diced
3 cloves garlic, diced
3 T. olive oil plus a little oil for frying
3 eggs, separated and the whites beaten stiff
2 T. flour
1 tsp. baking powder
½ cup grated Parmesan cheese
your choice ¼ cup fresh herbs: basil, rosemary, thyme,
    marjoram, parsley, oregano
kosher salt and black pepper

Heat the oil in a heavy sauté pan and add the onion, peppers, garlic, and celery. Sauté until soft. Add salt, pepper, and herbs, and sauté another couple of minutes. Remove from heat, cool a little and then pulverize in a food processor. Toss the rice with the flour and the baking powder. Add the vegetable and herb mixture and the beaten egg yolks to the rice and mix, then add cheese and beaten egg whites. Heat some oil in a crepe or sauté pan and drop in small dollops of the dough, flatten and fry on each side until the edges are crispy. Drain on a paper towel and serve with a curl of prosciutto or country ham for a starter. You can make a larger version as a side dish for an entree. You can also mix in some cooked wild rice or some barley.

Five

Heaven, if I didn't know better, I'd say you were the one who caused all the trouble at the convent. Not one bad thing has happened since you've been gone." Nancy Blair was teasing Heaven over lunch at Galatoire's.

"Do you think I should have stayed home?" Heaven asked as she tasted her Pompano Almondine. "This is great. I wonder where they get the pompano."

"Florida. But who knows what it really is? Any old flat-bodied fish, they call it pompano nowadays."

Heaven was surprised Nancy knew about the types of fish bodies. "Are you a cook, Nancy?"

"We had great food at my houses. We were known for it. Not that I wanted our clients hanging around eating food. No, I wanted them to do their business and get out. But there is another level of customer that demands food and drink along with their romantic interludes. At first I had Antoine's send over food and a waiter, but there is little markup in something that's already retail, so I started providing that service myself."

"You sound like a savvy businesswoman, Nancy. No wonder you're rich."

Nancy Blair ignored the compliment, lost for a moment in reverie. "Back then, on Sundays I'd cook for all the girls. They could have their children come to dinner, too. If I was in a good mood, I'd let them invite their pimps. I thought pimps were utterly useless, didn't understand why girls that worked in a respectable house like mine still felt the need to give their money to some man, money they'd worked hard for. By the time I took mine and the pimp took his, the working girl didn't have a chance."

The irony of what she had just said was lost on Nancy, Heaven could see. Her exploitation had been just, while the pimp's exploitation was unjust? "What would you cook?" Heaven asked.

"Pot food. The south has a great history of pot food, something made out of a cheap cut of meat and cooked for a long time to be tender. I made great ox tails, Jambalaya, gumbo. Sometimes I'd roast a turkey or some ducks. One of my husbands was a hunter, and we'd have venison stew."

"Now we're getting to the good stuff," Heaven said with a smile. "The husbands."

"I wish they'd been the good stuff," Nancy Blair chuckled.

"How many times were you married?"

"Counting my present husband, six."

Thank God she beat me, Heaven thought. "I didn't realize you were married now. You seem like a single woman and you didn't mention a husband when we had lunch before."

A look of genuine pain came over Nancy's face. Heaven wasn't sure if she was sad or having a physical attack. "Most people think we're divorced. Jimmy's been gone from New Orleans for two years now. He was considerably younger than I was."

"Where is he?"

"I wish I knew. I sent him money about three months after he left. He was in San Diego then. I haven't heard since. Don't know if he's dead or alive."

"I know this is nosy," Heaven said, "but was the amount of money you sent enough to tide him over for a year and a half? Maybe you'll hear from him when he needs more."

Nancy laughed. "I'm not that generous, Heaven. Even if he invested wisely, he's been out of money for a year. After all, I wanted him to come back at that time. I wouldn't give him enough rope to go and hang me with."

"And now? Do you still want him to come back?"

"I could say no and mean it right this minute, but if he was to come through that door, I don't have a clue what I'd do; fire my revolver at his pretty head or kiss him."

Now it was Heaven who laughed and decided it was time to change the subject. Digging around in an old woman's love life was a little too intimate. "Let's talk about the sisters for a minute. After our lunch at Antoine's, I went over to the convent again and that's when the termite incident happened. The next day I went to the television station and talked to Amelia Hart. Aside from making her mad by mentioning the fact that her aunt, the servant of slaves, owned one herself, I accomplished little. What about you?"

"I have considerable connections with the antique dealers around here. I'm one of their biggest customers. So I put out the word about the cross, not that the police hadn't done that, but I just thought I might have better luck." She paused, as if considering what to say next.

"Because you've been known to buy stolen goods?" Heaven asked, trying to keep any sense of judgment out of her voice.

"Buy 'em, sell 'em, hell, I've even done the stealing on occasion," Nancy said with good humor. She was relieved Heaven wasn't some Goody Two-shoes.

"Nancy, I've got a problem back in Kansas City and I want to talk to you about it." Heaven was surprised that she felt like bringing up the letters. Something about this older woman made her feel safe. Maybe it was because her own mother had been dead for so many years. Maybe she missed having an older woman to talk to. She shifted uncomfortably in her own skin. Her mother had been a farm woman in Kansas. She would not appreciate having her daughter choose a surrogate mother who was a former madam in New Orleans. "But first, give me your honest opinion, Nancy. Do you think we're out of the woods with this big dinner? Do you think whoever stole the cross and stuff is done?"

"I wouldn't think so, honey. Why would you shoot your wad on a committee meeting of old girls when you could have four or five hundred of the city's best Catholics in your grasp? There's more to come, I believe."

"That's what I think, too."

"Now tell me about your problem in Kansas City, Heaven," Nancy said as she signaled for the check.

As they finished their coffee, Heaven told her about the unsigned letter and how it had rocked her foundation, how she didn't know how to fight this.

She felt better. No matter if Mamma O'Malley would

shake her head and purse her lips up in heaven, she liked this old lady.

Heaven paid this time.

Nancy, who had been quiet while Heaven poured out her heart, asking a few questions but basically just letting the younger woman talk, took Heaven's arm for help getting up and then gave it a little squeeze as they left the table. "If we ever find out who wrote that, they better watch out. Your enemies are my enemies now, child," she said.

Sometimes unconditional support is better than logic.

Heaven called Mary at the office. "I know I said I wanted to stay here in the Quarter, but can I still see you?"

"Actually, I was going to call you. How about dinner? I told Truely I'd get a hold of you and the day just slipped away," Mary said.

"When will you be done? It's five now."

"I'm almost done. Truely said to meet him at Napoleon House at six."

"Why don't you meet me first and go with me up to the convent for a minute."

"Okay, but what for?"

"Well, I got a letter saying to please use the herbs from the convent herb garden, that it was important, historical. So I want to go see what's growing there. It won't take a minute."

"Are you sure it wasn't a scam? After what happened last month I'd be wary of anything suggesting you go to the convent," Mary said, her attorney's caution turned up on high.

"The letter didn't say wait on the corner in front of

the convent with a bag of cash. And it was from Susan Spicer, on Bayona stationery. Now come on. I'm at the Provincial. I'll be in the lobby."

In a few minutes Mary and Heaven were standing in the inner courtyard of the former convent. When they'd explained Heaven was one of the chefs for the benefit, the caretaker had let them in and then Mary and Heaven had given him a tongue-lashing. "When you insisted that he take our drivers licenses until we came out again to the gatehouse, he looked at you like you were crazy," Heaven said.

"No wonder the cross is gone and termites ate half the staircase," Mary said disapprovingly.

"Mary, what's the deal with the herb garden?" They walked toward the river side of the courtyard, where the retaining wall was embedded with bas reliefs of saints. The sky was a gorgeous shade of blue. The sound of ship horns blaring on the river carried throughout this side of the Quarter.

"Oh, honey, the herb garden is part of New Orleans history. Part of the contract between the Company of the Indies and the sisters was that they'd plant an herb garden. Sister Xavier Herbert was the first woman pharmacist in North America and it was her garden. Course then it was across the street. The sisters had a big piece of the Quarter at the time. They had livestock and a vegetable garden and all." Mary bent down to pull off a twig of rosemary and held it to her nose. "What will you use? What are you fixing, by the way?"

"Two appetizers and a dessert I named Nola Pie. I'm going to make seasoned rice cakes and put a thin slice of tasso ham on top, tiny cakes for passing. I'm calling them Trinity rice cakes, named after the sisters and the trinity that's the base of so many Cajun dishes: diced onion, celery, and green pepper, which I'll use with the rice. I can use an herb in the mixture so I thought we'd see what's here." Heaven started walking slowly down the brick path. The beds were full of green plants, with climbing roses planted behind them going up the back wall. "Lemon verbena, a bunch of different basils, thyme, lavender." Heaven read off the signs stuck in the ground next to the plants. She bent down and picked a mint leaf from a large bed of mint and stuck it in her mouth. Quickly she spit it back out. "Yuk, something's wrong." She picked another sprig of mint and held it to her nose. "Let me smell that," she said as she took the rosemary out of Mary's hand. There was an acrid smell about both herbs. "Does this smell funny to you?"

"It's not quite the way rosemary usually smells. Can something smell bitter or is that just a taste thing? Heaven, what's the matter?"

Heaven bent over and retraced her steps down the row of plants, peering intently at each herb. "Do you know anything about gardening?"

"I'm a Southern wife. Of course."

Heaven pointed at something on the ground near the lavender bush. "What's that?"

Mary looked down. There were small, light-colored granules on the ground. "Something that shouldn't be here. I think it's a combination weed killer and insecticide."

Heaven turned and walked rapidly over to the side of the convent where an old stable was used for maintenance. There were several large trash cans with lids. Heaven jerked off the first lid and started poking gingerly at the trash. "You'd think this outfit would have a Dumpster. Mary, start looking for the weed killer."

"You don't need a Dumpster in the French Quarter, Heaven. They pick up the trash twice a day."

"And people still complain about the smell." Heaven pulled out a round canister and looked at the label. "Would 'Bug Be Gone' be it?" she asked Mary.

Mary took the canister and read quickly. "Yes, but you would never use this product around things you were going to eat."

"And why is that?" Heaven asked.

"Because it's a systemic insecticide. You sprinkle it on the ground and it's absorbed into the root system of the plant when you water. Then the plant becomes poisonous and when the bugs eat it, they die."

"My point exactly," Heaven said grimly.

"Heaven, I remain convinced this is sheer incompetency, not another part of the vast plot against the Sisters of the Holy Trinity." Will Tibbetts was starting to piss Heaven off with his antiplot stance.

Truely, Mary, Will and Heaven had met at Napoleon House as planned, then gone around the corner to Emeril's French Quarter restaurant, NOLA, for dinner. They were drinking their second bottle of Burgundy and arguing over the herb garden situation.

"How can you say that?" Heaven retorted hotly. "The herbs are a crucial part in the story of the sisters. It would be a natural place to attack them. And now, none of the herbs can be used. In fact, the whole herb garden has to be dug up and the soil replaced before they can replant. And what if I hadn't gone over there? Every dish at that party would have contained contaminated herbs. Everyone would have gotten sick as a dog."

"You don't think any other hotshot chef would have

noticed the bug killer when they went to pick herbs?" Will shot back.

Mary shook her head. "The gardens have watering systems in the ground. The caretaker said that the riverside gardens are watered in the evening, the streetside courtyard in the morning. If we hadn't been there right then, the stuff would have dissolved and probably wouldn't have been detected. There was a funny smell, but it probably would have faded when the granules dissolved."

Truely held up his hand. "Normally I wouldn't do this, but I'm gonna have to side with the girls on this one, Will, ol' buddy."

The two women didn't even give him shit for calling them girls. They both gave Will a thumbs up and high-fived each other across the table. "If this were the first incident over at the convent I might be able to back you," Truely continued. "But having this convenient accident with the herbs just before the big dinner?"

"All right, I know when I'm outnumbered," Will said, holding up both hands in a defensive position. "Just for that, I'll pay for dinner." The other three diners clapped.

Heaven stood up. "I hate to break this up, but for the next two days, I actually have to work. They have volunteers to help us, but still. Four hundred people is quite a few to feed. I'm going back to my hotel and my legal pad and my lists. Will you check on me tomorrow at Peristyle?"

"Yes," Will said, even though Heaven was looking at Mary. "Are you sure, in these uncertain times, that you don't need an escort back to your hotel?" he offered slyly.

Heaven pinched his cheek. "No way. Mary, Truely, it's

been a joy. You too, big boy. It's my turn to pay next."
She hurried out onto St. Louis Street and turned onto
Chartres.

The sweet scent of magnolias filled the air, mixed with
the aroma of fried fish from Johnny's Po-Boy down St.
Louis. Music drifted out of bar doorways; laughing
troops of conventioneers passed Heaven on their way to
the next drink. When she reached Jackson Square, she
turned and headed toward the river. The square, scene
of artists and fortune-tellers, pick-up brass bands and
fire eaters during the day, was quiet at night, the gates
of the park itself closed, the streets sparsely littered with
bits and pieces of debris from the thousands of tourists
that passed by there daily. Heaven was surprised it didn't
look worse.

The prospect of going back to her hotel room actually didn't appeal to Heaven. She was upset and elated
at the same time due to the incident at the convent. She
was glad they had thwarted the herb garden scheme,
but worried about the next crisis.

Why wouldn't anyone consider the idea of canceling
the dinner? She had brought it up again tonight and
the other three, Truely, Mary and Will, looked at her
like she was crazy. New Orleanians have never let adver-
sity keep them from a good meal, they told her.

Heaven crossed over Dumaine, walking by Café Du
Monde, full as always with coffee drinkers and beignet
eaters. She went up the ramp to Artillery Park, then
down the steps on the other side, across the streetcar
tracks to the Moonwalk. She walked a short distance in
the direction of Canal Street and found an empty
bench.

Heaven was pleasantly surprised at how many people
were walking by the river. Many were couples, romanti-

cally entwined. She tried to forget about problems she couldn't do anything about and watched the Mississippi River flow by for a while. A giant freighter moved silently upstream in the night. Heaven caught a snatch of conversation coming from the darkened deck in a tongue she didn't understand or recognize. Someone turned a lantern on and off, the silhouette of a crew member appearing and disappearing. The hulk slid by. Heaven wondered if it was a Greek ship, or maybe Swedish. She was imagining a life cooking for sailors as her friend and employee, Sara Baxter, had done in her youth.

All of a sudden, she was jerked back to her body, adrenaline pumping. Someone was trying to strangle her. A piece of cloth, a pillowcase or a tee shirt, had been slipped over her head.

Heaven was borderline claustrophobic. She grabbed at her neck, trying to pull the piece of cloth loose. So far her attacker had done nothing but grunt. Heaven found a wrist and dug her nails into it, such as they were. Cooks had short nails. Now a male voice hissed near her ear. "Listen to me, bitch. Don't stick your nose in where it doesn't belong or you'll be sorry. Why don't you go back where you came from."

Two things happened next. Heaven started to scream and even through the cloth over her head she let out a pretty blood-curdling cry. Then two German tourists who were actually jogging down the Moonwalk at eleven at night must have seen what Heaven couldn't see because they started yelling in a mixture of English and German, "Get away from her" being the idea they were trying to get across. With the noise coming from all sides, Heaven's attacker let up the pressure on her neck for a second. Heaven threw off the makeshift hood, turned and ran for the streetcar tracks, all in one motion. She didn't take time to look back and see who had done this to her. The attacker's voice was still ringing in her ear and it wasn't familiar.

The riverfront streetcar ran back and forth from the French Quarter to the Riverwalk shopping mall. Heaven had never ridden it because she liked the walk, but a streetcar was coming from the lower Quarter and Heaven beat it across the tracks and hopped on, along with seven or eight other passengers. She had a small evening bag with her and fished out the $1.50 to ride. Only then did she look out the open sides of the car toward the river. The streetcar took off as a man came jogging toward it, following in Heaven's footsteps. Heaven knew he was the one. She couldn't see much, a white guy with dark hair.

Why she got on the streetcar instead of running over to Café Du Monde she had no idea. Her heart was pounding. She couldn't think straight. She wanted to put space between her and the attacker but maybe going to a public place and calling the police would have been a better bet. Was this the same person who had defaced the convent and all the rest? What else had Heaven stuck her nose in? The scene at the coffee warehouse popped into her head. But this wasn't the big man that she'd seen there and technically she hadn't really interfered in Truely's business. She'd only asked a couple of questions about Truely's business, inquiring innocently to Will, Truely's best friend. Heaven peered into the darkness behind the streetcar but her pursuer was nowhere to be seen. Maybe he'd given up on following and was taking a shortcut. A guy in reasonable condition could run down to the end of the line as fast as the car traveled, what with the stops. The car slowed down and they were at Riverwalk.

Heaven walked rapidly toward the doors of the shopping mall. They were locked tight, of course. "What an idiot," she said aloud to herself. She hadn't worn a watch to dinner and hadn't thought about how late it was. She hadn't taken her cell phone with her to dinner. "I'm totally unprepared for this," she muttered and looked around. She needed to get away from the front of the closed mall. It was fairly dark. But, she tried to tell herself, the chances of the guy having followed her were slim. After all, he had delivered his message. Also, even if someone wasn't chasing her, she shouldn't be standing around in the shadows of a locked shopping mall.

All of sudden, from the river side of the big building, Heaven saw him appear. He was jogging, not running, and he spotted her but didn't increase his speed. If the distance was straightened out, he was still more than a block away. Heaven turned away from the direction he was coming and started across the street. She spotted the big casino, Harrah's, on the other corner. "Perfect," she said, and ran into the sparkling gambling emporium as fast as she could.

Heaven went looking for the security office, then thought better of it. No one would make a scene in a casino. An assault here would be met with zero tolerance. Heaven spent a few minutes lurking around the front door waiting to see her attacker enter and then realized there were entrances on other streets. He could already be in the building, could have already spotted her, could be making his way toward her right now.

She looked around nervously and walked into the

ocean of slot machines, bought a roll of quarters and sat down in front of a Triple Wild Cherry slot to think.

The blinking, ringing, chinking, the soundtrack of the casino, was soothing to Heaven. She put quarters in the machine automatically and won a few back. Maybe, if she just stayed there a few more minutes and didn't see the bad guy, she'd get a taxi back to her hotel and the whole thing would be over. The cheery bell told Heaven she'd won again, and this time twenty or thirty dollars worth of quarters must have poured down in the trough. She put them in one of the plastic cups stacked by the side of the slot machine and walked over to another set of machines.

That's when she realized she should have kept moving from the very beginning. Her red hair made her easy to spot. She sat facing a different direction, her eyes scanning. Another five minutes went by and Heaven was beginning to breath normally. She would just get up and go to the Poydras Street entrance to the casino and get a cab. It would be easy. She shoveled as many quarters as she could in her small purse, leaving the rest next to a slot machine.

At that moment, her attacker appeared on the false horizon of slot machine tops. He was in another room coming her way, moving his head slowly from side to side, like a robotic surveillance camera in a convenience store. Heaven hadn't seen him except at a distance in the dark, but there was no question in her mind that it was him. He was shorter than he'd seemed up close, more compact.

She shrank down, hoping he wouldn't see her hair. Maybe he didn't even know she had red hair. It had been fairly dark by the river. But he must have followed her to the Moonwalk. He didn't just go up to the first park bench he passed and tell the woman sitting there to stop being nosy while strangling her. When had he started following her? When she left the convent? The restaurant?

Now, of course, Heaven wanted to kick herself for not going straight back to the hotel right after dinner. But if this guy wanted to spook her tonight, or was being paid to spook her tonight, he must have had a plan for the hotel, too. Heaven felt a trickle of sweat run down the back of her neck. She usually never broke a sweat, not even in the kitchen on a hot Saturday night.

She made a dash for the door, looking for a security guard. There was one standing by the cash-in booths and she made for him and turned to pinpoint her man.

Heaven grabbed the guard's hand. "Thank God you're here. My ex-husband," she pointed at the attacker, who still hadn't seen her, "is here looking for me. He said he'd kill me if I gambled again. He's a religious fanatic and I'm afraid of what he'll do if he sees me. I'm leaving, but please don't let him follow me."

"Where is he?" the guard asked gruffly.

Heaven pointed. "Right over there. The one with the gray windbreaker." As Heaven pointed, she knew she'd screwed up. Her excited energy flowing toward the man made him turn in their direction. He started toward them instinctively, then saw the guard. He paused and Heaven turned and ran toward the door.

"Help me," she shouted over her shoulder in the guard's direction.

Heaven stopped just once to look over her shoulder. She saw what she had feared. The guard was standing empty-handed in the middle of the room, hands on hips, looking around. Her man, as she now thought of him, was nowhere in sight.

She slipped off her high heels and took off running down Poydras toward St. Charles, past the new W hotel, past Mother's. She wasn't a runner and by the time she got to St. Charles she thought her lungs were going to burst. The St. Charles streetcar pulled up to its stop right across the street. Heaven grabbed some of her quarters and got on.

The trip out St. Charles was painstakingly slow. At every stop, Heaven debated getting off. At every stop, Heaven was sure her man would walk up the steps and in the door of the streetcar. She looked around. There were other people with her, it wasn't just her and the driver. Most of them looked like hotel and restaurant workers going home. She wasn't sure when the last run was but she thought it was around midnight, which must be soon.

She checked her money. With what she'd had before and the quarters, she had forty-seven dollars and a credit card. She thought about getting off at Tulane University, or by the gates to Audubon Place, where Mary and Truely lived. But then she would have to get to their house and it was way down on the other end of the street. Plus it was gated and what if they'd gone back to the Napoleon House for a nightcap and the guard called and the Whittens weren't home?

The streetcar lurched on and that option was behind her in the dark New Orleans night before Heaven realized that she could just ask the guard to call the police. She was mad at herself that, with all the times she'd seen them, she hadn't asked for the business cards of the two patrol officers who always showed up at the convent. She didn't have the name of a police officer who might be familiar with the trouble she seemed to be involved in.

Heaven changed seats several times, peeking out on each side of the avenue. Now she went to the back of the car, half expecting her tormentor to be running behind the streetcar. When it slowed to turn onto South Carrollton, she decided enough was enough. She put her high heels on, pulled the buzzer and got out. Just across the street was the famous Camellia Grill. She headed for it and was about halfway there when she heard a car door slam. In the strip mall parking lot a half block from the Camellia, standing there coolly lighting a cigarette and leaning against his car, was her man. She wanted to get a good look at him. She hadn't really seen him. But as usual he was just far enough away to escape a positive identification later. She was sure he wanted her to see him, though, and for her to know that he'd followed her all the way with no problem, that she was dead meat if he wanted her to be.

The door of the grill opened and three people came out. Heaven searched the double horseshoe counter for the places they'd vacated. It was a quiet time for the grill, after dinner and before the tipsy late-night crowd hit the doors needing a pecan waffle to sober them up. There were no waiting customers and Heaven slipped onto a stool and, even scared and confused about what just happened to her, was immediately drawn into the scene before her. African-American waiters in starched white jackets and black bowties spoke their own language with short-order grill men of amazing grace. One minute the grill was covered with a shimmering mass of raw eggs, the next minute that mass had been transformed into three beautiful omelettes, each with different ingredients nestled in the middle. Beside the grill, waffle irons spat pieces of batter onto the stainless-steel tables they were bolted to, great collars of built-up batter creating a crusty outline. With two grills and two waffle irons, the horseshoes of the counter created a mirrored universe: different dancers, same dance.

Heaven jumped when her name was suddenly called. "Heaven!"

She spun around, ready for the worst. It was Will Tibbetts, grinning his charming grin as if nothing had happened since he last saw her.

"Will, you scared me to death. What are you doing here?" she demanded crossly, stealing a look outside as she spun her stool around.

Will sat down beside her. "I'll answer that question but then you better be ready to do the same. I followed Truely and Mary home for a nightcap. When I left their house, I decided I needed a piece of grilled pecan pie. Now, what about you, the one who said she just had to get home to her list-makin'?"

Heaven felt a wave of apprehension. She didn't believe him for a minute. But she couldn't help but be relieved to see him. She got up and walked outside looking up the street. Her man was gone. He was just playing with her, showing her he could keep track of her. And what, if anything, did Will have to do with it? She went back inside. "He's gone."

"Who's gone?" Will asked.

"It all started when I was walking through Jackson Square."

The waiter came and gave them glasses of water, a look of expectancy on his face.

Will smiled. "Hello, Henry. I'll have a piece of that good pecan pie, grilled nice and warm, and a freeze. And what is it for my bride?"

Heaven smiled in spite of everything that had happened. Will was so corny with the winking and the "my bride" stuff. All of a sudden she was starved. "A hamburger with everything but onion, a piece of pecan pie, and what's a freeze?" If she was going to die, she'd be full.

Will pulled his fancy Porsche up to the locked gate at the hotel and honked. "Things sure are interesting with you around, Heaven. That was quite a story. I don't want to leave you here alone. I suggested either staying with you or taking you home with me. Those are two good offers still on the table."

Heaven shook her head. "I do still have to make prep lists for tomorrow. Now that I've survived another night here in New Orleans I'll be expected to produce some product tomorrow. Thank you for seeing me home. You still think I shouldn't call the police?"

"More trouble than it's worth, in my opinion. But talk to Mary about it in the morning." He reached over and kissed her on the lips.

She was too wrung out to give him any static and the next thing she knew she was kissing right back. She broke away finally. The concierge was standing at the open gate watching them. Without saying a word or letting Will say one, she quickly got out of the car and waved good-bye.

French Onion Soup Beignets

3 onions, sliced
2 T. olive oil
2 T. butter
1 T. kosher salt
1 T. sugar

8 oz. Gruyere cheese, cubed
1 cup milk
2 T. butter
2 tsp. dry yeast or 1 pkg. dry yeast
1 tsp. sugar
1 egg
3 ½ cups flour
grated Parmesan cheese

To caramelize onions: peel and slice three onions. Heat the 2T. each butter and oil in a large sauté pan, add onions and reduce the heat. When the onions have turned translucent, add the sugar and salt, and stir. Sauté over low heat, stirring occasionally, until the onions are a caramel color, about an hour. Cool and refrigerate. This can be done a night ahead of making the beignets.

For the beignets: Scald the milk with the butter and let cool to lukewarm. Add yeast and sugar and let stand about five minutes, until the mixture is bubbly. Add egg and flour and mix well. Let rise about an hour. Punch down and roll out the dough on the floured surface to about ¼ inch. With a 1 ½ inch round cutter or the top of a juice glass, cut rounds from the dough.

To assemble the beignets: Cover a cube of cheese with a spoonful of onions. Put in the middle of the dough round and seal with a little warm water. You can roll these so they are round or let them be irregular. Chill for at least an hour, then fry in about an inch of medium hot peanut or canola oil. Using tongs, turn the beignets until they are brown on all sides. Drop them in a plate of grated Parmesan and roll them around. Serve warm so the cheese in the middle will be soft.

Six

"Heaven, you have a delivery," a voice called from the front of Peristyle.

Heaven had been working at the restaurant for several hours, trying to get most of the work done on her two starters today so she could concentrate on her dessert tomorrow.

Heaven was no pastry chef and Pauline Kramer, the pastry chef and bread baker at Cafe Heaven, had sprained her wrist badly and couldn't come to New Orleans to do her thing as they'd planned originally. But with the help of the whole Kansas City kitchen staff Pauline had formed four hundred thirty—thirty extra for breakage—individual pie crusts made out of a very special shortbread dough in throwaway pie pans, baked them, frozen them, and sent them overnight UPS to Heaven packed in dry ice. Heaven was going to have to do the rest.

Heaven went up to retrieve her package. It had been relaxing to work in the kitchen, after the stress of the night before. Now, in the cold, clear light of day, she was embarrassed she hadn't just gone straight to a phone and called the police.

"And Susan said to remind you and Annie that there's a short meeting over a bottle of wine at Bayona around 5:30. The others chefs will all be here by then," the maitre d' reported. He was there confirming reservations for the evening.

Heaven took her package to the back and opened it, to check the condition of the pie shells. They looked good. Pauline had packed them well with bubble wrap and other materials plus plenty of dry ice. Heaven set them in the freezer. They would defrost tomorrow in the time it would take to assemble the rest of the dish.

Committee members and local chefs had rounded up a group of volunteers to help with the preparations and at the dinner. Two volunteers had been helping Heaven with the rice cakes. They were cutting small rounds out of sheet pans filled with the thick rice batter and placing the rounds on baking sheets covered with parchment paper. Tomorrow the cakes would be finished on the flat top grill that was part of the portable kitchen.

While they were cutting out the cakes, Heaven had worked on the other starter, assembling all the pieces so the volunteers could put them together.

"What's next?" one of them asked Heaven as they smooched the last rice into a biscuit cutter and tamped it down.

"Next is something I've named a French onion soup beignet. I've already rolled out the beignet dough. Now what you do is take one of these cubes of Gruyere cheese and wrap some of these caramelized onions around the cube. I cooked the onions earlier and cooled them down so they should be easy to work with."

Heaven looped some of the cold onions around the cheese. She'd brought a full set of biscuit cutters with her and now found a small one and cut a little round out of the dough. "Then you wrap the cheese and onion into a ball with the dough pulling the dough slightly and sealing it with a little water on your fingers and rolling it round again," she said as she did just that to show them how. She had two shallow bowls of water there for them to work with. "We'll put these in the walk-in and chill them good so they stay together. Then tomorrow night they get fried and tossed in Parmesan cheese."

"Now that's what I call a New Orleans-style appetizer," one of the volunteers said approvingly. "Fat and grease."

Heaven worked with them for a while, making sure they got the hang of it. She was lost in thought when once again a voice called to her from the front of the restaurant. "Heaven, a friend of yours wants to see you."

Heaven walked out, expecting Mary. They hadn't actually talked yet so Heaven could tell her about the attack. She'd left an urgent message but Mary was in court until this afternoon. To her surprise it was Amelia Hart, gorgeous in a peach-colored sleeveless shift.

"Amelia, what are you doing here? I mean, after last time, I didn't think you'd ever speak to me again if you didn't have to."

"I didn't think so either," Amelia said with a slight grin.

There was an awkward pause.

Amelia cleared her throat as if she was going to recite in grade school. "I thought about what you said, and I realized I took the wrong tack with those women. I laid myself open to exactly what I got from you. There are plenty of reasons for people to support my auntie's order. I didn't need to put down the precious Sisters of the Holy Trinity to make that point and I especially didn't need to make my aunt vulnerable by attacking the sisters' slave-holding."

A little part of Heaven wanted to stick her tongue out and say, "I told you so." Instead she tried to sound sympathetic. "I've gone out on longer limbs than that. I think if you remind these society Catholics that your aunt's order could use some help in giving out scholarships, they would respond. They seem like they're good-hearted."

"I hate saying anything close to 'I'm sorry,' so I'm glad that's out of the way," Amelia said. "Now I want to ask you something in my capacity as a reporter."

Heaven assumed Amelia was going to ask her about last night's attack on the Moonwalk, not that she could figure out how Amelia would know about it. Did the German joggers call the police and tell them a woman had been attacked on the Moonwalk? But how would that lead anyone to Heaven? Could it be Will giving Amelia a news tip?

"And what could that be?" Heaven said innocently.

"Have you received any threatening mail, any poison-pen letters, hate mail, extortion?"

To say Heaven was surprised by this turn would be understating it a great deal. "What are you talking about?"

"When someone writes to you and says defamatory things or asks for money not to reveal certain things. Usually unsigned," Amelia answered patiently, as if Heaven were too dense to understand the definition of her words.

"Why?"

"Usually because the person is mentally unstable or

has criminal intent," she said, continuing her answers in the same smart-ass vein.

Heaven wanted to slap her. She lulled me into thinking this was a peace visit, then she hits me with this, Heaven thought. "Amelia, now why would you ask me such a question?"

"Why won't you answer me without all these questions back?"

"Because I don't understand what . . . Has this got something to do with the vandalism against the convent?"

"Then I take it I should report that Heaven Lee refused to comment?"

"Fine with me. You're going to have to give me a reason for this line of questioning before I say a thing," Heaven said, and turned and went back to the kitchen.

The women chefs and their sous-chefs were sitting in the courtyard at Bayona. They had run through the schedule for the dinner and each chef had talked about their course, how it should be plated and how many people it would take to get that done. Heaven had remained quiet throughout the briefing, except when she presented her course. Now that they were nearing the end of their business she made up her mind and stood up. "Now that we know how organized we are, can I ask you all a very personal question?"

Someone made a crack about sex, and everyone laughed.

"I received a terrible letter at my restaurant. It was unsigned and it said some very bad things about the restaurant and my employees. Not only did I get a copy but the newspaper in Kansas City received the same letter and so did the health department. I've been very upset and I've been trying to figure out who in Kansas City might have it in for me. That wasn't exactly a small list." She paused for the laugh and got it. "Now I've come to wonder if it might have something to do with the vandalism at the convent. And I wondered if any of you had received any hate mail. And I would ask that, either way, you not repeat what I've told you tonight. The reputation of a restaurant is very fragile, as you all know."

It didn't take long for a response. "Good work, Heaven. I would have never figured out that that piece of trash had anything to do with this," Lidia said. "I got one two weeks ago and so did the New York City health department. I can't tell you what it said, it was so disgusting."

"I'm so relieved. I thought someone was going to blow my cafe up because my letter said Bacchanalia should be a parking lot," Annie Quantero from Atlanta said.

"Since I don't have a restaurant, I got one saying Hitler was right and why didn't I have recipes for cooking Jews," Rozanne Gold said.

There was shocked silence for a moment. Then, one by one, the whole group confessed to some kind of an unsigned written assault on their businesses and sometimes on them personally.

Heaven felt like a great weight had been lifted from her shoulders. From the looks on the faces of the other women chefs, everyone had harbored the same fears, that unfounded accusations would be the death of the businesses into which they put their hearts and souls.

"This doesn't mean that there isn't still some nut who wrote all the letters," Heaven pointed out.

"Yes, but probably it's the nut who is trying to sabotage the Sisters of the Holy Trinity and wanted to cast the chefs in the worst possible light, hoping it might make the news somewhere," Susan Spicer said. "What do you say we hire a guard to be at the food tent at all times and each of us chip in to pay for it?"

That idea was met with enthusiastic response and they sealed the deal with a few bottles of Dom Perignon.

Heaven looked around the table. They were at Upperline, a wonderful uptown restaurant near Truely and Mary's. The four of them, Mary, Truely, Will and Heaven, had formed an easy alliance. Their evenings were comfortable, as if they'd been dining together for years. All four were quick-witted, slightly sarcastic, and good storytellers. Heaven thought of Hank. It would be a totally different dynamic with him at the table, much sweeter.

Sometimes it was fun to hang out with people your own age.

"So not only did you get chased all over New Orleans last night, you admit that you've been getting hate mail and so have all the other chefs, and you call this a good day?" Truely shook his head and poured more wine, a bottle of Flora Springs Cabernet Sauvignon.

"It came as a great relief to all of us that this was a group problem, not someone singling us out. I was worried sick," Heaven said.

"And you hadn't told us a thing about it," Mary said, scolding her.

"The fewer people that know about something like that, the better. I would never have taken the chance to tell my tale to the other chefs if Amelia hadn't come over and questioned me about it. That bitch," Heaven added with a chuckle.

"Who do you suppose told Amelia?" Will asked.

"Maybe Amelia knew about it because she did it," Mary offered.

Heaven shook her head. "I don't think so, but I don't have any reason except a weird fondness I've acquired for Amelia. I think the person who did all this, the vandalism, the cross, the letters, sent copies to Amelia at the television station. But I couldn't ask her that today because I wasn't admitting that I received a letter."

"What will happen tomorrow night, will the fish give us all a tummy ache?" Will said, still not taking the threats to the nuns very seriously.

"The chefs decided to all chip in and pay for a guard for the food tent," Heaven reported.

"Good plan," Truely said. "I wouldn't want anyone to mess with the coffee. It's a single estate bean from Kenya that kicks ass."

"Thanks for donating expensive coffee, Truely," Heaven said.

"Mary would kill me if I didn't." He gave his wife a pat on her hand. "And it can't compare to what you've given, in time and money."

"Let's get back to last night. I can't believe you didn't call the police. Will was wrong," Mary said, looking severely across the table at both Heaven and Will.

"I can't believe I didn't either. So this morning I called up the French Quarter station and they sent someone over to Peristyle to take my statement. I don't know if they believed me. It was pretty farfetched, what with the casino and two streetcars and the Moonwalk and the Camellia Grill. But at least now if I'm strangled again, I'll be on record," Heaven said, watching Will for a reaction.

She thought he shifted uncomfortably and his eyes darted around the table, meeting Truely's for just a breath too long. It only lasted two seconds. What were those two trying to tell each other? Maybe Heaven was just reading things into Will's reactions tonight because they had that on-the-lips kiss the night before. It was probably nothing more than two friends trying to react the same way to some woman and her ravings.

"Heaven has survived another harrowing day in the life of Super Chef. I think this calls for champagne," Will said, with a trademark wink and a smile. He waved a hand to the waiter across the room.

"I hope we're lucky," Heaven said to no one in particular as she dealt empty plates out on the long serving tables they were using to organize the dinner.

The cocktail hour was over and guests were looking for their table assignments. The weather was perfect and so was the setting; a slight breeze blowing the ribbons the decoration committee had tied on the tent stakes, the smell of roses wafting from the garden walls, fat white candles nestled safely in glass hurricane lamps that reflected the twinkling candlelight. Cocktails had been in the formal garden on the street side, what Heaven now knew was the back of the convent. The entire inner courtyard, facing the river, had been tented. Now people were making their way through the entryway, from the back to the front of the convent, to dinner. A brass band was leading the way.

The women chefs had decided not to list the chef

responsible for each course on the menu, as most celebrity chef dinners did. They preferred to show solidarity and just list their names at the top of the menu, trusting that their fellow cooks would not sully anyone else's reputation with something less than spectacular. So far all the starters had been devoured with gusto, although Heaven was sure the onion soup beignets were the biggest hit of all.

The first course was already on the table, a cold English green pea soup with a shrimp-filled fried won-ton on the side. Heaven had learned long ago in her catering days that if a cold soup could be on the table, in place when the guests sat down, it really helped get the dinner rolling. You needed every bit of help when you were serving a coursed dinner in the middle of nowhere, kitchenwise.

Earlier, Heaven had poked around the convent grounds to check out the rest of their set-up. It was an organized production. The dish-washing tent was set up right next to one of the maintenance sheds with running water. There were hoses running to big metal tubs on stands, like people used to use to wash clothes. Next to each tub were two big trash containers for busing food off the plates and bowls. On the other side of the tubs were long tables with the empty boxes from the rental company. The dishes were scraped, rinsed in the tubs and then repacked in the boxes. The rental company would rewash and sterilize them at their plant.

Now, it was time to plate the fish course, an octopus salad that was one of Lidia's dishes, plus a mini fritto misto, that Italian combination of fried seafood that was so popular in Venice. To do that, the cooks had several of the outdoor propane tanks and stock pots that were so popular in New Orleans to fry whole turkeys or boil crayfish. In this case they had been converted into deep fat fryers. There was delicious grouper, soft-shell crab and zucchini blossoms, all in a delicate batter that reminded Heaven of an Asian tempura batter.

The chefs had made diagrams of the way each plate should look on butcher paper and taped these diagrams up on the inside of the tent siding. This plate had a small mound of the octopus salad on one side, a piece of grouper and a half a soft-shelled crab on the other, with two squash blossoms in the middle, their blooms facing opposite directions. The last touch was a light dressing for the fritto misto, olive oil and aged basalmic vinegar with some anchovy blended in.

That was Heaven's job, along with three other volunteers—drizzling the dressing after other chefs and volunteers had placed the other salad elements.

As one group of servers picked up the soup bowls, the second group started serving the fish.

Since it was spring, the meat course was lamb. The chefs had long grills set up and some of the volunteers had taken the tedious job of grilling twelve hundred baby lamb chops. They were just keeping them on the grill a minute, then turning them over for another minute, as they had to be put in the electric warmers after they were grilled and would keep cooking. There was no way to have rare lamb at an event like this, but they were hoping for a little pink left in the center. These were being served around a baby-artichoke-and-potato gallette that had been baked at Bayona and brought over in warming boxes. There was also another side dish on the plate that Heaven intended to copy, a crawfish spoonbread. A little mound of it was decorated with a crawfish and placed at the twelve o'clock position on the plate. The guest sits at the six o'clock position.

The talk in the food tent was minimal. Everyone had their assignments for every dish ahead of time. On this course, Heaven was placing the three chops around the potato-and-artichoke galette. She walked slowly down the aisles of tables with plates, going behind the two people doing the potatoes.

Although it wasn't the hardest physical labor in the world, plating for a big party was intense work. You were a part of a team fighting the clock. It was hard enough getting out food reasonably hot and still edible for a large party in a hotel situation, as anyone who has eaten at a banquet knows. Doing it in an outdoor setting with no kitchen required lots of organization. Heaven was glad she had so much catering experience to fall back on.

When the lamb went out, the kitchen started drinking. It wasn't that the next courses weren't as important. To the diner, the cheese and salad, and the desserts, were just as important in how the whole dinner worked together. But the crew was glad they had the hot stuff out of the way and that nothing bad had happened in relation to the many incidents that had occurred before the dinner. So, the Veuve Cliquot was broken out and everyone raised their glasses. So far, so good, someone quipped as a toast and then they quickly went back to work.

The salad course was simple. A local grower had supplied baby Lalla Rosa lettuce. Some blueberries and toasted pecans were tossed on top and a light dressing with blueberry vinegar and hazelnut oil was lightly drizzled on the lettuce. But because New Orleanians weren't afraid to eat, after the salad was served, platters of French and American cheeses would be passed, along with dense walnut bread and crackers. The cheese trays had been arranged by the cheese wholesaler, who came to the dinner to fuss over his prize triple creams. He didn't want anyone to mishandle his goods as he had been carefully aging cheese for the evening. Heaven's assignment was to slice the walnut bread with a volunteer. She waited until the salads were ready to go out, then they sliced furiously so the bread would be fresh when it was presented. Heaven hated being offered bread that had become even a bit dry to the touch.

She left the volunteer to put the bread in baskets. The next course was her Nola Pie.

Heaven went to the first empty table, where someone was already putting down empty luncheon-sized plates. She had asked for a slightly larger plate because cutting into a tart on a dessert-size plate could result in food flying onto the table. A clean bus tub was piled with the cookie crusts, still in their pie shells. Heaven and Pauline had added some pecans to the shortbread dough. Heaven showed a volunteer where to place the pastry shell, at the top of the plate. "Be careful taking these out of the aluminum. They're fragile and we only have twenty-five extras. Five broke in the shipping," she explained.

Heaven retrieved the rest of the ingredients. It was the job of the lead chef on every course to make the first plate so everyone had a pattern to follow. In the empty crust, Heaven placed some pieces of broken up pralines. She had ordered them from one of the local praline makers, the one at the French Market, and asked them to break the large rounds in small pieces just before they delivered them to the site so the sugar wouldn't have time to crystallize. Heaven was afraid the smaller pieces would crystallize faster than a whole praline. Sugar was so tricky. She bit into one and it was still creamy, not grainy.

After the praline bits, Heaven spooned in some Louisiana strawberries that had been sliced and macerated in just a little sugar and Grand Marnier. In Peristyle's kitchen, Heaven had baked custard in hotel pans and burned sugar on the top to create pans of crème brûlée. A volunteer had taken one of the biscuit cutters and cut rounds out of the custard in the afternoon, before the sugar was burned on it. Heaven carefully slid a spatula under one of the custard rounds and set it on top of the strawberries. "It's all right if the surface of the brûlée is cracked. It can't be helped."

Then she opened a big cake box full of cookies from Crossaint D'Or. Pauline had wanted to do these but, because of her bad wrist, Heaven had enlisted the French Quarter's favorite pastry bakery. Now Heaven placed a dab of strawberry puree on the plate in front of the tart, and on it placed a cookie in the shape of the sisters' lost cross, a cookie that had been decorated with the appropriate curlicues so it looked authentic.

"The puree should fix the cookie on the plate, but the servers need to be careful so the whole thing doesn't shift," she said to the assembly around her. Appreciative murmurs followed. It was a very New Orleans dessert and the cross made it right for the occasion. Heaven picked up the bowl of praline bits. "Thanks, but this was a team effort since several of the parts were produced right here in the Quarter. I just thought it up. I'm on praline. Let's go," she said, and started down the line of plates.

Only the sorbet course remained. Heaven took a long drink of Veuve and smiled to herself, relieved. The last tart had just gone out of the tent. She took a deep breath and walked into the narrow area behind the kitchen tent and in front of the dish-washing tent. The kitchen tent only had its canvas walls down on the side facing the diners. The back side was open so the chefs could get some air. The side facing the river was also open, and was the location of the grill and the propane tanks with their iron tripods and pots of grease. Heaven could see six or seven people in chefs' coats coming up the drive lugging coolers filled with various flavors of sorbet they had just retrieved from the freezer at Bayona.

It was almost over. A jazz band had played during dinner and there was a dance floor set up on the flat part of the courtyard that was usually a parking lot. A Cajun band was going to play soon and Heaven saw someone with an accordion walking up the drive behind the sorbet. She turned toward the dining area and spotted Truely and Mary and Will. There was a beautiful blonde beside Will, obviously his date for the night. Good, Heaven said to herself. The four of us were getting too cozy. On Monday I'll be gone back to Kansas City and all of us will go on with our lives. And whatever damage the nun-hater was after will be history, except for losing the cross.

All of a sudden, a roar, then a whoosh of air, broke through the festive party sounds, followed by an explosion. It seemed to be coming from Chartres Street, right in front of the convent. The whole crew in the kitchen tent started down the driveway to the street, including their guard. When Heaven got to Chartres, she saw flames shooting out of a location about a half block away on Ursulines.

Everyone in the French Quarter lives in fear of fire. Fire had decimated this part of the city several times over its long history. The closeness of the buildings to each other meant a whole block could burn quickly.

People were running from all directions toward the flames. Heaven and most of the chefs stood on the corner by the convent, not walking any closer. The fire department trucks were winding through the narrow streets honking horns, with firefighters already off the trucks securing hoses to fire hydrants. A pumper truck backed into place and the chef's guard, who was an off-duty policeman, helped with traffic control.

Heaven was relieved that whatever blew up down the street wasn't meant for the party. So was everyone else. Giddy with excitement and champagne and the knowledge that they were on the last course, the cooks headed back up the drive. As Heaven turned she saw Will Tibbetts come to the convent entrance and look intently in the direction of the fire. Heaven thought he must have been in a pretty hot conversation with the blonde if he was just now getting up to see what the hell was going on.

As Heaven reached the kitchen tent a great hue and cry came from the opposite direction, the dishwashing tent.

"Oh, no."

"Oh, my God."

"Who is it?"

Heaven pushed up to the front of the crowd. There, wedged in one of the tubs for rinsing dishes, his legs dangling over the side, was Truely Whitten with a Global knife stuck in his chest, a hose running water into the tub and washing away any evidence. Placed between Truely's legs so it was resting on his torso, was the stolen cross of the Sisters of the Holy Trinity.

Heaven couldn't believe her eyes. "I bet that's my

knife," she said without thinking of the consequences of that admission.

Suddenly Nancy Blair was standing right beside Heaven. "And that's my cross," she said to everyone's surprise.

Heaven looked up from the body just in time to see Will catch Mary as she fainted.

Chicken Crepes

For the crepes:

1 ⅓ cups milk
1 cup all-purpose flour
3 large eggs
3 T. unsalted butter, melted
1 T. sugar
dash kosher salt
canola oil or vegetable oil spray for your crepe pan

Mix all ingredients but oil together with an electric mixer or blender. Let set at least an hour at room temperature. Heat a crepe or sauté pan and spray or moisten with a small amount of oil. If you have a 1 oz. ladle, use that, or just pour a small amount of the batter in your pan and quickly swirl to coat the pan thinly with the batter. Cook about a minute and then carefully turn with a spatula. Cook another minute and turn out on wax paper. Cover with a towel or paper towel. Repeat process. Makes about 20 crepes. In some cities crepes are available pre-made at fancy food stores. You can make these the day before and refrigerate. Bring to room temperature before you try to use them.

For the filling:

5–7 lbs. bone in chicken breasts
5 stalks celery, sliced thin

1 small can water chestnuts, chopped fine
1 cup sliced almonds, toasted
1 cup Monterey Jack cheese
1 cup sour cream
kosher salt
white pepper
paprika
celery salt
dried dill weed
juice of one lemon

Preheat oven to 350 degrees. Cover the breasts with water and bring to a boil in a large saucepan. I usually add the tops and bottoms of my celery, at least half an onion with the skin still on, and a carrot if I have one. You can throw in some fresh herbs if you have them around although I don't recommend rosemary. Reduce heat, skim, and simmer for 20–30 minutes until the breasts are cooked through. Drain and cool.

Pull meat from the bones and dice. Add all the other ingredients and combine, seasoning to taste. Place a spoonful on the top third of each crepe and roll up. Bake in a shallow baking dish for 30 minutes. Before the last ten minutes, spoon on some sauce Royal and a little grated Parmesan cheese to brown. Or you can omit the sauce and these will be good in an old-fashioned, country club food way.

For the sauce Royal:

2 T. butter
2 T. all-purpose flour
1 ½ cups cream or half and half
1 ½ cups chicken stock
½ cup grated Parmesan plus some for the top

In a heavy saucepan, melt butter and add flour to make a light roux. Let cook over low heat a minute or two, then add liquids and bring to a simmer. When the mixture starts to thicken add the cheese. Cook another 3–5 minutes and remove from heat.

Seven

Heaven never would have believed an hour earlier that the night would end like this, sitting in Lafitte's Blacksmith Shop having a drink with Nancy Blair and Amelia Hart, of all unlikely people. She felt she should be with Mary, but she and Will and Will's date, who turned out to be named Charlynn, had gone to the police station to give their statements. They didn't know how long it would be, so Heaven promised to see Mary the next day.

Lafitte's was famous for being one of the oldest buildings still standing in New Orleans and the darkest bar in a city full of dark bars. A plaque by the door said it was built in 1780. Since then, pirates had sold their treasures in the back rooms and slaves were bought and sold there long after the practice had been legally abolished by the European government of Louisiana territory.

Tonight, the piano player at the piano bar in the corner of the back room was entertaining a group of conventioneers with Louis Armstrong imitations.

Heaven and the other women were sitting in the front at a table by the open windows, the night life of lower Bourbon on parade not three feet away, music in the air. Heaven felt strangely comfortable. The vibe of the bar, welcoming and dangerous at the same time, was appropriate for this particular night. Murders had no doubt been plotted inside these walls. Tennessee Williams had done some drinking in Lafitte's. Had he ever sat where she was sitting now, Heaven wondered. Did he look out this window with unseeing alcoholic eyes at his neighborhood? She glanced around at the dilapidated room. Was a slave bought and sold right here, like a sack of cotton seed?

Heaven tried to focus on the two women at her table and snap herself back to the present, realizing she had a bone to pick with Amelia. In all the excitement, she'd not asked about Amelia's source of information for the poison-pen letters. "Amelia, before you start in on Nancy, how did you find out about the letters to the chefs?"

"I could say I don't have to reveal sources but after tonight I don't feel like playing cat and mouse. I got a copy of every letter in the mail. Plain envelope, New Orleans postmark."

"And ours were all postmarked with the city the chef lived in. I wonder how the creep accomplished that," Heaven mused.

"Mailing service," Amelia said impatiently. "Now, can I conduct a little interview here, please?" Amelia turned her attention to Nancy. "Nancy, let me get this straight. You found the cross through the antique underground and were going to return it to the sisters."

"And paid a pretty penny for it, too. I have connections in those circles, as I've always loved beautiful things. My houses were full of antiques. I asked some old friends, they came through." There was no apology in her voice, only pride.

"Who did you call to find the cross?"

Nancy snorted. "When I told you I'd be interviewed only if we went for a drink, I didn't say I was going to run my mouth like a fool. I wouldn't tell the police, told them they could haul an old lady off to jail if they wanted to. I'm sure not going to tell you, Ms. Hart."

"Tonight why don't you call me Amelia?"

Their cognac arrived in real glasses. The first time it had been served in plastic cups and Nancy sent it back. The three women held up their glasses for a toast. "Salud," Heaven said solemnly.

"Okay, somehow you got the cross. Why didn't you call up the sisters and simply return it then?" Amelia asked.

Nancy snorted dismissively. "A woman has to use her strength for her own advantage. I'll put this question on the table and then you two tell me which sounds better. I return the cross and it's back in its rightful place at the dinner. The sisters thank me and everyone yawns. Or, I bring the cross with me, stash it in the storage shed until the speeches start and then stop the whole proceedings by walking up with the cross in my hands, triumphant."

Amelia and Heaven looked at each other. "Excellent point," Heaven said.

"How was I to know someone would stab ol' Truely with your knife and then set the damn cross on him like a dead pope?" Nancy said, irritated. No diva liked to have her plans ruined.

"So, now that we have that out of the way, what do you two think?" Heaven asked.

Amelia turned to Heaven. "What do we think about what?"

"Who killed Truely, of course," Heaven said impatiently. "Do either one of you know any dirt on him?"

"You're the one who stayed at their house," Nancy pointed out. "You're closer to them than we are."

"Yes, but I don't know the big picture. I only saw them every few years. What I can tell you is Mary and Truely seemed like a regular married couple around the house. I never saw them fight."

"And you call that regular?" Amelia asked with sarcasm.

Nancy Blair got up. "It's almost three in the morning, ladies. I think I'd better turn in. Would you two do me the honor of walking me home? Its not far, that big house back from the sidewalk up on Governor Nicholls."

"You live there?" Amelia Hart was impressed. "I always wondered who lived there." She threw down some money. "This is on the station. After all, I was conducting an interview."

The three woman joined the street traffic on lower Bourbon. Nancy put an arm through each of theirs, walking in the middle and limping slightly. "If you play your cards right," she said, "you can both have a tour. But not tonight. I'm pooped."

"How about if I come over about ten in the morning with a camera to get a little sound bite? You can say just what you said to me tonight," Amelia propositioned, not done working her angle yet.

"All right. Now hush," Nancy barked. They walked along in silence, each of them trying to make sense out of what had happened, letting the disco beat fight with the zydeco rhythms of Bourbon Street. The music propelled them in the night.

*   *   *

Heaven got up about eight, early for when she had gone to bed, and packed, the lack of sleep balanced with nervous energy.

Last night she had offered to move over to Mary's until the funeral and Mary had accepted her offer. Heaven had called as soon as she got up and arranged for a rental car. She was sure there were plenty of cars at the Whittens' but she wanted the independence of her own vehicle.

Next Heaven called home. She needed to let Hank and Murray know she wouldn't be home on Monday as planned. Hank didn't answer at her house and she considered calling his mother's. Even though they technically lived together, Hank still had clothes and other belongings at his mother's house. His mother didn't approve of Hank having a girlfriend twenty years older than he, so as long as he still had stuff in his childhood room, it was easier for his mother to think of Heaven as temporary. Heaven thought of herself as temporary. She refused to believe that Hank wouldn't eventually want to marry someone his own age and have a family. Hank was the only one who didn't think of their relationship that way. He was very happy with things as they were.

She decided not to call Hank's mother. If Hank wasn't at the hospital, he was probably going to church with his mom, then on to lunch with her. Heaven just left him a message on her home phone, telling him about Truely and leaving the phone number at Mary's house.

Murray was home. He picked up on the second ring and Heaven told him briefly about the dinner and the murder.

"Can you live without me a few more days?" she asked.

"You know we'll be fine. It was an easy weekend. No problems in the kitchen. And Jack was in again and seemed almost normal, not just normal for him, but really normal," Murray said. "What would you think of him working some in the kitchen?"

"Well, I'd be willing to give it a try. Does Jack think he wants to cook?"

"He's mentioned it a couple of times. It'll wait until you come home."

"I have some good news," Heaven said, and told him about the hate mail being connected to New Orleans and the sisters.

"You're kidding. All the other chefs got them too?"

"Yeah, but no one wanted to bring it up because they all thought, just like I did, that it was a disgruntled employee or a local maniac. It was a big relief to us all when we discovered that it was simply a plot to discredit us because we were cooking for the sisters."

"I don't know, Heaven. When that qualifies as good news, it's time to get out of Dodge. I wish you'd just come home." She could hear the anxiety in Murray's voice.

"I'd love to, but I can't leave Mary like this. Truely and Mary have no children and I'm not sure about Truely's family, whether anyone still lives in town. There may be some elderly aunts. I know his parents are dead. I think Mary's originally from Minnesota or something."

"And what about the fact that he was stabbed with your knife?" Murray said, still thinking of things to worry about.

"What I said to the police was that there were dozens of chef's knifes around and it was just a coincidence that the killers chose the knife of someone who actually knew the victim. It was my Global and they're such cool-looking knives, it probably caught the killer's eye. That's what I said but I'm not even sure I believe it."

"Why?"

"Because I'm sure my knives were put away in their case under the table. We were all careful to keep track of our knives and I'd put mine away just after we served the Nola Pie. I didn't think I'd need them to scoop sorbet."

"I'm telling you, I don't feel good about this. When's the funeral?" Murray asked.

"Tuesday, I think, but it could be held up by the autopsy. If I'm not coming home on Wednesday, I'll call you. And you call me if you need me."

Heaven gave Murray the phone number at Mary's and they hung up, promising to get in touch with each other at the first inkling of a disaster on the horizon, either in Kansas City or New Orleans.

Heaven heard them before she saw them.

She'd arrived at the Whittens' twenty minutes before. The maid let her in, her usual pink uniform replaced with a black one. Perhaps, when you were employed as a maid in New Orleans, they gave you a set of uniforms, one for regular days and one for mourning occasions. Already the place had the look of a funeral home. Flowers crowded the hall. Heaven went right upstairs and put her things away in the bedroom she'd used a few weeks earlier. That seemed so long ago now.

Heaven was convinced she should say something to Mary about the big man in Truely's office, for Mary's own good. This was no time to worry about whether Truely was mixed up with the wrong crowd. As she went downstairs to find Mary she heard another familiar voice.

"Don't you have an ounce of sense?" Will Tibbetts barked sternly.

Heaven thought that was a strange way to tell a widow to buck up.

"This is really an insult. The coffee business isn't on my mind right now," Mary said, her voice sounding as though she was close to tears.

What was that about? Heaven would have listened outside the door, but they spotted her coming through the dining room on her way to the glassed-in porch where they were sitting drinking Bloody Marys. I guess this is the Southern way to mourn, she thought, then scolded herself. If you can't drink a Bloody Mary on the Sunday morning after your husband gets stabbed on Saturday night, when can you?

"Heaven, when did you get here?" Will crossed the room swiftly and gave her a kiss on the cheek.

Now that she could see as well as hear, she realized both Mary and Will were speaking to a third person, the one pacing nervously from one side of the porch to the other. It was the man who had been talking to Truely in the hotel bar, the man who owned the other coffee importing business in New Orleans. Heaven cleared her throat. "Just a few minutes ago. I put my bags upstairs. Mary, how are you?" She gave her old friend a hug and sat down on the wicker love seat beside her.

Mary looked like hell. She glanced up at Will before answering. "I'm still in shock."

Will looked at her sympathetically. "Yes, and then ol' Leon here comes marching in here like he owned the place, demanding Mary sell the business to him."

Leon Davis adjusted his tie for the second or third time since Heaven entered the room. "He promised me first right of refusal. Just name your price."

Quickly Mary got up. "You must act like a gentleman, Leon, and let me bury my husband. You understand, don't you?"

Nonplused by that tactic, Leon Davis halted his nervous pacing. Will swooped at him and put a hand on his back, guiding him toward the hall. "Name your price," Leon yelled over his shoulder. Heaven and Mary watched silently. When Will returned to the room, he went straight to the bar.

"He's gone. Sorry about that, Mary. We'll have to tell everyone in the house no more visitors today." And he changed the subject firmly. "Heaven, I meant to ask the police last night, but I forgot. Where the hell was that guard you said the chefs hired?" Will handed Heaven a Bloody Mary he'd mixed for her.

"The explosion. He went down to help with traffic control on Ursulines. I think he, and the rest of us, thought the dinner had been pulled off without a hitch. It didn't occur to anyone that the explosion might be a diversionary tactic."

Mary looked alarmed. "Is that what you think now?"

"I didn't hear the police say anything about the two being related," Will said, with his usual skepticism at Heaven's theories.

Heaven explained. "The police aren't dumb. It must have crossed their minds, even if they didn't mention it yet. They know the convent has had a lot of trouble. Then, just when the sisters are having their big benefit, an explosion occurs just a half block away and creates all kinds of chaos, someone comes up dead at the dinner and no one saw a thing because they were all distracted by the explosion. Sounds fishy to me."

"But why Truely as the victim? He had nothing to do with the sisters except for helping me with this benefit.

He didn't even go to the Holy Trinity Academy growing up." Mary was getting upset again.

Heaven warmed to her subject. "Think, Mary. Maybe it had something to do with Truely's business. You work in international law and your husband was an international importer. Surely, you must have some idea about the coffee importing business. It can't just be a bunch of kindly farmers like Juan Valdez."

Mary shook her head. "No one would want to kill Truely. I think he was just the innocent victim of the maniac that's been terrorizing the sisters and their old convent. The victim could have been anyone. They just wanted a dead body."

Heaven stopped trying to get her point across. It was easier for Mary to believe that than the other alternative, the one that Heaven was suggesting. "And that's a good explanation too. I'm sure the police are working on all the angles," she said.

The phone rang, and soon the maid rang them on the intercom and announced it was for Will. He picked it up and talked briefly with his back turned to Heaven and Mary. Then he spun around and shook his finger at Heaven. "Well, sugar, one of your conspiracy theories has just been shot down."

The houseman came around the corner with plates on a tea cart. They had good-smelling crepes filled with some kind of a cheesy chicken mixture on them. Everyone grabbed a plate. Heaven was glad to see Mary had an appetite.

Heaven flopped down on a big white rattan chair with flowered chintz pillows and dug into the crepes. "Which one?" she said and sipped her drink.

"One of my neighbors on Governor Nicholls is a reporter at the *Times-Picauyne*," Will said. "I slipped him a hundred bucks this morning to go in on his day off and see what was shakin' with this case. That was him saying that the police just released the information that the explosion was caused by a methamphetamine lab blowing up. It was just some punks who didn't know their chemistry, not someone planning a 'diversionary tactic,' as you put it."

Heaven started to argue with Will but looked at her friend Mary's face and thought better of it. Mary was holding her temples and pressing in, like she was having a terrible headache. "You know, Kansas City is one of the meth capitals of the country," Heaven said conversationally. "We have those explosions every weekend, when some idiot who's already been high for days tries to cook up a batch for the weekend customers. It's a dangerous activity. Mary, can I do some phone calls for you? It would be so much easier for me."

A tear slid down Mary's face. "I was hoping you would do that. Truely has lots of second and third cousins around the country. I don't expect many of them to come to the service but I should let them know. Will called Truely's auntie, who lives out in Meterie, early this morning. He and I, of course, didn't want her to see it in the paper first. She's eighty." Mary's voice trailed off.

Heaven reached over and touched her friend's arm. "Do you by any chance have a list, or should we go through your address book?"

"I made a list last night, or this morning I guess it was, when I was wide awake. It worked. When I saw all the people who should be notified, there's Truely's business associates as well as the family, I became exhausted and was able to sleep for a couple of hours. Heaven, are you sure you want to do this?"

Heaven had put her drink glass down on a beautiful round oak table, then thought better of it and picked it up again. "I'll just go in to the kitchen and sit at the table in there. When's the . . . " she lost the ability to say the word funeral.

Will, who had been standing up since his phone call, circling the room, gave Heaven her answer over his shoulder. "Wednesday at eleven at the cathedral. They couldn't guarantee the medical examiner would be done in time for Tuesday services." He continued circling, not aware of the grizzly images of autopsy he had planted in both women's heads.

Heaven paused at the door. "Oh, by the way, Will, I have to be gone this evening for a couple of hours, from six to eight, say. Can you be here then so Mary won't have to be alone?"

Will turned and smiled. He looked terrible and Heaven realized he must be devastated by his friend's death. "I'm here for the duration, darlin'," he said sadly.

Heaven backed out of the Whittens' driveway, pausing before she pulled into the street to check her directions. She'd considered calling Hank's relatives and canceling their meeting, but after spending several hours on the phone delivering the bad news about Truely, she was anxious to get out of the house.

She picked up Highway 90 and drove for several miles, then she noticed the road was now called Chef Mentuer Highway. It was a down-at-the-heels part of town, but certainly not abandoned. The mix of muffler shops and warehouses, beer joints and storefront churches was all still in use.

Soon undeveloped land appeared on the sides of the road and Heaven knew she must be out of New Orleans. It wasn't long before she saw the first building with a sign announcing a Vietnamese grocery. And soon on both sides of the highway there were strip malls from the 1970s, abandoned by their original owners, with Vietnamese symbols and names. Many of the signs advertised restaurants and groceries, but there were also lawyers, doctors and accountants.

Heaven spotted a yellow sign on a storefront that advertised FAMILY MEDICAL PRACTICE AND DENTISTRY in both English and Vietnamese. She pulled into the parking lot, which was still about half full of cars. The restaurants and offices all seemed to be open, families going in and out, and young Vietnamese men were standing in front of a pool hall laughing and exchanging a version of high fives. It was a typical American Sunday evening, except all the faces were Asian.

Heaven put her head on the steering wheel and tried to breathe deeply. She was nervous about meeting Hank's cousins. She was tired from the day at Mary's. She took her hands and pulled the skin of her face tight, hoping she didn't look as old and beat-up as she felt. Hank's favorite cousin was very polite on the phone, but Heaven had been a little hurt that he had suggested meeting at the office, instead of at home. Now she understood. Mothers with small children and men with their older mothers in tow were going in and out of the doctor's office. The cousins obviously had Sunday office hours. Heaven shook out her hands, put on some lipstick and got out of the car. Before she could get four steps, a boy of about ten came running out of the office to her.

"Are you Uncle Hank's girlfriend?" he asked cheerfully.

"I'm your man. I mean, I'm your woman," Heaven said with a smile, trying to ignore her own shaky start. She'd forgotten all the packages, so she went back to the car and opened the trunk. "I've brought some things from your Uncle Hank."

The boy, eyes snapping with intelligence and interest in the loot, politely held out his hands. "Do you want me to carry something?" he asked.

"Yes, will you take this shopping bag, please?" Heaven said as they walked toward the offices. "I know your uncle found that new Game Boy game you've been wanting."

"Uncle Hank's the best. I miss him. He never comes to visit anymore."

She felt a pang of guilt. Hank was a busy doctor. She knew she wasn't the only reason he couldn't go on family visits too often. But she also knew any spare time he'd had lately had been spent with her instead of his family. "Hank told me to tell you he's bringing his mother and they're coming to visit when you're off for summer vacation this year and can take him around."

The boy's eyes lit up with pleasure. "I'm George."

"I'm Heaven, George. Nice to meet you."

A man older than Hank but with his same striking good looks came out of the back of the office and extended his hand quickly to Heaven. There were still a few people in the waiting room. "I'm so glad to meet you, Heaven. Hank has told us so much about you. I'm Tran Wing, and I guess you've already met my son, George."

"For some reason, George picked me right out of the crowd and has been my escort," Heaven said, deciding this was no time to stop using irony.

"Uncle Hank told me to look for the brightest red

hair," George explained solemnly, as if he'd had several shades of redheaded women to choose from.

"My wife, who is a pediatrician, and my brother, who's a dentist, still have patients, but I've finished up. Let's go next door so you can meet our mother and George's little sister."

They stepped into another part of the offices, a big comfortable room with a small kitchen and sofas and toys. A television was humming in the background with *60 Minutes* tuned in. There must have been ten people in the room; the matriarch, the spouses and the children of this branch of Hank's family. Heaven hoped she had gifts for them all. They fell silent when Heaven walked in. Very formally, Tran took Heaven up to each person and introduced her, explaining the relationship they held to Hank.

Then Heaven quickly opened up the shopping bags full of remembrances from Kansas City. There was something for everyone plus three or four gifts for relatives that hadn't been able to make it to this viewing of the girlfriend. It was a mini version of Christmas and Hank had written each person a note. From what Heaven could tell from the bits and pieces that the cousins read aloud, each note was personal and elegant, just like Hank himself. By the time this gift giving was completed, the other two doctors had joined the rest of the family in this adjunct rec room.

Tran, as the spokesperson for the family, rose and started putting the gifts back in the shopping bags to be taken home. "I'm sorry we couldn't invite you to our house. It isn't far from here but since Sunday is a very busy day in our practice, we thought we could all go next door and have some supper together and it would be more convenient."

"I don't cook on Sundays," Tran's wife said, not apologetic, just matter-of-fact. She was stretching her back, like someone who had been on their feet a long time.

"I think it's great that you have office hours on Sunday. It must help your patients a great deal."

Tran nodded. "There's still a great many shrimp boat owners in our community, that and people working in the hospitality industry of course. The shrimpers aren't home much during the week and hospitality workers have irregular hours. And many of our children go to parochial schools and don't get back here until evening. There's no time for them to go to the doctor or the dentist until the weekend."

"Yes, but that's true of most busy families all around America. Not too many professionals adjust their hours to meet the needs of their constituents," Heaven said as they all trooped out of the offices and headed for a Pho restaurant just a couple doors away.

Soon the long table at which they were seated was loaded with dishes: summer and spring rolls, crispy shrimp and sweet-potato fritters, chicken wings that had been braised in caramel sauce. Everyone had ordered a version of pho noodles in broth, some with chicken, some with duck or pork or dumplings. There were big platters of the condiments traditional with pho: basil, cilantro and mint leaves, lime wedges, bean sprouts, slices of raw jalapeno. Tran sat Heaven in the middle of one side of the table so she could interact with as many people as possible. Everyone was kind, interested in Heaven, curious about the already televised news of murder at the convent and her involvement, and generally great about making her feel comfortable. The exception to this was Tran's mother, the sister of Hank's mother. Heaven could see she absolutely couldn't bring herself to even generic politeness to Heaven out of respect for her sister. She grunted when Heaven tried to engage her in conversation and soon Heaven gave up trying. It was a lost cause.

The dining room was beginning to clear of the other diners, most of them families like this one. She glanced at her watch and saw it was after 8:30. How could she pay for dinner? Say Hank had insisted? Maybe she should just be a gracious guest. She turned to Tran. "I have to go soon. I promised my friend Mary I'd be back around nine. She is in distress, as you can imagine."

Tran nodded. "Of course, and please don't even think about paying for this—Hank said you would try. But I have a trade out with this family. We eat. They get checkups."

"Thank you. It was delicious and so was the company," Heaven said and made a general good-bye to the table, and a special one to George. "George, I expect you to come visit in Kansas City as soon as your parents think you can fly on an airplane by yourself."

"When I'm twelve," George said firmly. This obviously had already been discussed in the family.

"I'll walk you to your car," Tran said softly, taking Heaven by the elbow in a courtly gesture. "I'm sorry about my mother's unfriendliness."

"Don't think a thing of it. If I didn't know what a nice older woman I am, I wouldn't like me either."

"Well, you understand that even if she thought you were terrific, which the rest of us did, by the way, she couldn't act like it because of her sister's feeling about your relationship."

"I do understand," Heaven said, wanting to explain.

"I keep telling Hank to go find someone his own age. When I see your family, your wonderful children, I think that's what Hank should have and that's something I can't give him."

"Hank understands that planning for a perfect life is worth nothing. If you love someone, you must act like that love is going to disappear tomorrow. And it can."

Heaven thought of Hank's father being shot at the end of the Vietnam War for helping the Americans. She wondered how many others in this family were victims of that time. "Hank is the wisest person I know. I really do love him," she said as she got in the car.

"And he loves you. Enjoy it," Tran said with a smile, and gently closed the car door.

Heaven gave a little wave and quickly pulled away. The tears were welling up and she certainly didn't want to start blubbering in front of Tran. She turned out on the highway choking back sobs. Meeting Hank's family had been a big drain and, even though it had gone well, Heaven felt like she'd been through the wringer.

She drove deep in thought for a few minutes, the impulse to cry dissipated, just letting the evening catch up with her, remembering as many details as she could to relate to Hank when she got home.

Then roadside signs began to catch her eye, signs that she didn't remember from the trip out. There were houses on stilts that she didn't recall either, just barely visible back from the road as her headlights hit their outlines. It was dark out here. Each house had apparently been named something that appeared on a sign by the mailbox. Heaven slowed down and read some of the signs. TA-TA was followed by GREEN ACRES, then PAW-PAW'S DREAM then THE OTHER WOMAN. Cute. Heaven saw the blackness of water on each side and boats overturned in the yards. These were possibly weekend houses, fishing camps as she'd heard Truely and Will call them.

She must have gone the wrong way when she left Versailles, heading into the lake country instead of back toward New Orleans proper.

Just as Heaven started to look for a place to turn around, bright lights in her rearview mirror blinded her and she felt the back of her car bumped. She realized she'd been driving slowly but this was ridiculous. Bang, another bump. It was a two-lane highway and it seemed deserted. Why didn't the asshole just pass her if he was in such a hurry? Heaven slowed down further to force a pass. She could tell it was a big pickup truck. She was in a smallish four-door car of some kind; she hadn't paid any attention to the make when she picked it up at Enterprise Rentals. The front of the truck loomed over the rear of Heaven's car. It was rather like a German Shepherd mounting a Cocker Spaniel. Bang. This time the two vehicles were locked together temporarily, then the truck backed off enough to disentangle itself from Heaven's car.

Heaven saw a driveway ahead with a steep slope on each side. She'd just turn into the driveway and hope that someone was home, although the chances of that didn't look good. All along the road, the houses were silent and dark, another reason she figured them for weekend places. It was Sunday night. Everyone with any sense had gone back to New Orleans, unlike Heaven, who had headed for the middle of Lake Pontchartrain or wherever she was.

She had to get away from this maniac behind her, and she turned sharply into a drive just as the truck gave her another hard bump. It was enough to send the little car straight down the side of the drive into the ditch. Heaven heard and felt the front tires sink into water. She jerked the car into reverse but it was no use. She was at an awkward angle in swampy land with her front end in a drainage ditch. The car whined and shimmied, but didn't move. Heaven turned off the ignition but left the headlights on. What difference would it make if the battery ran down?

The lights of the truck were bright behind her and it was then that Heaven realized her biggest problem might not be finding a tow truck. But she did have her cell phone with her and she reached into the backseat, grabbing for her purse. At the same time she locked her driver's side car door and made sure the other doors were locked as well. As she fished frantically through her purse for the phone, someone with something, a tire iron or a baseball bat, smashed the back windshield of the car. Glass flew in Heaven's direction because of the angle the vehicle was tilting. She ducked under the steering wheel and held her breath, waiting for the next blow. Any minute now, the window next to me is going to be smashed and some hand will come in and strangle me, she thought. Or worse, maybe that was a shotgun blast. Now they're going to finish me off.

Instead, Heaven heard the squealing of tires and the sound of the truck pulling away. It was dark suddenly, except for her car's lights pointing down the ravine. She took a while to come out of the duck-and-cover position. While she cowered, she thought over all the different scenarios. Maybe they'd left one of their crew there, out in the darkness, to finish her off and they would be back to pick him up later. No reason for that. They could have finished her off now and not have to make a second trip. Maybe someone was coming down the highway so they took off but were coming right back.

Heaven didn't hear the sound of another car speeding to her rescue. It was very quiet, dark and quiet. She finally decided not to stay huddled under the steering wheel of the car, no matter what was waiting for her. She peeked up. A pile of safety glass slid off her shoulders. She felt around her face and neck and didn't find any blood, just a couple of nicks and what would be a bump on her forehead in a few minutes where she'd banged into the steering wheel. The car wasn't as lucky. She was glad her car insurance covered rentals. Heaven resumed her rummaging for the phone, found it and dialed 911. She knew how to identify her location to the police. The signpost for this fishing camp was right in front of her car. It said, DO OR DIE.

Barbecue Shrimp

8–10 lbs. large shrimp, unpeeled, or heads on *and*
    unpeeled if you can find them. These should be in
    the 20 count per lb. size.
½–1 lb. pound butter
1 cup olive oil
juice of 2 lemons plus 3 lemons sliced thin
6 cloves of garlic, minced
1 T. Tabasco or other Louisiana hot sauce
3 T. Worcestershire sauce
½ cup Thai sweet chili sauce or Vietnamese rooster
    sauce
2 tsp. paprika, sweet or hot
any fresh herbs (basil or thyme or oregano would be
    good)
kosher salt
black pepper
½ cup fresh parsley to finish the dish

Heat everything but the shrimp and parsley together.
Simmer a minute then cool and pour over shrimp and
marinate in the refrigerator for a couple of hours, stirring
occasionally so all shrimp are covered. Place shrimp in a
shallow baking dish and bake at 375 degrees for about 20
minutes, turning shrimp often. The time will depend on
the size of your shrimp, of course. When shrimp shells
have turned pink and the meat white, remove from the
oven and serve in a soup bowl with parsley on top and

lots of French bread to sop up the sauce. My version adds the Asian sauce, which you would never see in New Orleans, so if you are a purist, leave it out. It does offer a nice heat that is different from the Louisiana hot sauce heat.

Eight

Heaven put down the phone. "My new best friend at Enterprise Rental says he'll pick me up in an hour. He said the last car wasn't completely totaled and they'd give me another chance. He just laughed and laughed. Only in New Orleans."

Mary looked up from her cup of coffee and smiled weakly. "What a pair we are. My husband was murdered, practically right in front of my eyes. You, for some reason, are a running target for a vendetta that keeps getting you chased. Are you sure you're okay?"

Heaven rubbed her neck. "Sore, that's all. Mary, there isn't just 'some' reason. There's a reason. Just like there's a reason that Truely was killed. We just have to figure it out. Have you heard anything from the police?"

"The detectives came and questioned me last night. They said they were still interviewing the guests and I guess all of you chefs, too. But the bottom line so far is that out of four hundred bloody people plus all the waiters and the musicians, no one saw anything of value. No one remembers Truely talking to anyone, walking away with anyone. He got up from sitting beside me to check out the explosion, said for the rest of us to stay there, and that was the last anyone saw of him. There was too much confusion."

Heaven poured herself coffee. "I hate to sound cynical, but how can anyone, and I'm talking about Will now, think that the explosion wasn't a diversion? Is there any doubt in your mind? I mean, if it weren't for the explosion everyone would have been sitting in the courtyard having sorbet. Do you think someone would have just walked up to the table and stuck my Global in Truely? Hardly."

"No, I don't think that. But there could be other explanations. Maybe someone was following Truely, looking for the chance to take him out, or maybe someone at the party had a grudge against him. When the explosion occurred they saw an opportunity and took it."

Heaven was alarmed. "Mary, did someone at that party have a grudge against Truely?"

Mary shook her head. "Not that I know of. I know what you say about the explosion makes sense. I'm just trying to find another solution that isn't so premeditated."

"Yes, I know what you mean. I don't like the idea of someone following me around town jumping on me and trying to run my car off the road every other day. That all takes planning. I guess I thought the first attack had something to do with the nuns. But last night has me puzzled. The dinner for the Sisters of the Holy Trinity is over."

"Heaven, will you help me do something?"

Heaven shuddered inwardly at the possibilities. "Yes, of course. But I'm more of an urn person myself. I don't know much about coffins and I assume as Truely was a Catholic a coffin will be involved."

Mary ducked her head, rubbing her brow. "No, I've already done that. Yesterday evening, after you left. Will told me I should get it over with and he was right, of course. But it made this whole crazy thing too real." Mary stopped and gulped, quiet for a moment. "No, Heaven, I'm asking about something else. I guess I'm the new owner of a coffee importing business. This whole thing with Leon is making me nervous. He's being very . . ."

"Aggressive?" Heaven suggested.

"I need to see what's up and I wondered if you'd go with me down there, for moral support. I really know very little about Truely's business. And all Truely's papers, the insurance policies and such, are in a safe at the office. I guess I could ask the office manager to send them over with someone, but I think it would be good to go there personally. They must be stunned too."

Heaven was thrilled. She had been planning to figure out an excuse to go to the coffee warehouse. Now she wouldn't have to; one had been handed to her. "I'll be glad to do that with you. But I must have a biscuit and another cup of coffee first. Mary, how are you holding up?"

"I'm still numb. I can't for the life of me figure this out. You saw Truely in action. Everyone loves him. Loved him."

Heaven got up and patted her friend on the top of the head, stacking a biscuit and a slice of ham on top of her coffee cup. "I'm going up to get my clothes on. You do the same. Then we'll go to Truely's office. Your law firm is sending over dinner tonight and several of the actual lawyers are coming to pay their respects."

"Where did you get that information?"

"From the maid, who gave me the rundown when she came up with my first cup of coffee. I guess after the way I looked when I came home last night she thought I needed a jump start."

"Please tell me again what happened," Mary insisted. "You were pretty vague last night."

"I got turned around when I left the cousins and I headed the wrong direction and someone followed me and bumped the rear of my car and I drove down into a ditch and then they came over and knocked the back window out of the car and then they left. No big deal."

Mary shook her head. "I can't believe this. It's a nightmare."

Heaven headed for the door. "We'll figure this all out. Don't you worry," she said, leaving her friend sitting there, her head in her hands.

As Heaven showered, she switched from thinking about Mary's loss to thinking about saving her own skin. The truck had obviously followed her to the Vietnamese neighborhood. Then, when she left and turned the wrong way, maybe whoever it was thought she was out there doing something else. Or not. Maybe they could care less which way she drove; they were going to mess with her, east or west. Maybe they thought the stop at Hank's cousins was just a ploy. What if the bad guys went to the cousins and tortured them or something? What if Hank's aunt paid someone to kill the redheaded witch as a gift to her sister back in Kansas City? Heaven had to laugh at that one. She was getting a little paranoid. But she would feel totally responsible if anything happened to Hank's relatives because of her. She'd call Hank later and talk the whole thing through with him.

*   *   *

When Mary and Heaven got to the coffee warehouse, one of the secretaries was smoking a cigarette in the parking lot. She looked excited when she spotted Mary.

"Oh, Miz Whitten, you don't know how glad I am to see you. You'll never guess who showed up a few minutes ago and is in there trying to sweet-talk his way into Mr. Whitten's office. Not that anyone would let him do such a thing. But he says Mr. Whitten promised to sell him the business. Will I still have a job, Miz Whitten?"

Mary stopped. "Who are you talking about? Who's here?"

"I'm sorry, Miz Whitten. I thought you knew it was Mr. Leon Davis I was talking about."

Mary tried to smile at the young woman. "I'll take care of Mr. Davis. He's got a lot of nerve, coming over here and upsetting you like this."

Heaven marched in to do battle, Mary right behind her. She spotted a knot of workers over by the lunchroom, across the warehouse. Silently the two women joined the crowd.

Heaven took the lead. She walked up to Leon Davis and grabbed his arm roughly. She was sure she had the advantage of surprise. He didn't know her from Adam, having just seen her once or twice when he had other things on his mind. She turned him toward her and poked his stomach with her hand. "Didn't you hear a thing Mrs. Whitten said to you yesterday? Butt out."

Leon Davis stepped back and fanned his arms at Heaven as if to ward off a pest. "I don't know you," he sniffed, spotting Mary over Heaven's shoulder.

"Leon. I asked you yesterday to let me have my time to mourn my husband," Mary said in a steely voice.

"I wasn't bothering you," he countered. He clearly never dreamed Mary would show up here today.

"I just had a feeling you weren't going to respect my wishes, Leon, and sure enough, here you are, trying to get information that's none of your business. If I were to decide to sell this business, after the way you're acting, it sure wouldn't be to you."

Leon Davis flared at that. "I had an agreement with your husband. I'll sue."

"Get out, Leon, or I'll call the police and have you arrested." Mary folded her arms. The small group of workers stared at the intruder. Leon Davis started to say something, then thought better of it, turned, and walked across the warehouse and out the open doors.

Mary turned to the group. "Please don't worry about what I said to Leon. As far as I'm concerned, this company isn't for sale. Now I'm going to find my husband's insurance policy. Heaven?"

"Take your time. I'm going to look around," Heaven replied. "You were great."

Mary smiled weakly and she and the group headed down the hall toward the offices.

Heaven tried to act casual. She moseyed around the warehouse looking for just the right target. It had to be a man, of course, and preferably someone who looked like he knew what he was doing. She wanted to get a feel for how the people who worked here were taking the death of their boss. If Heaven was right and Truely was killed because of some problem in his coffee importing business, then maybe the employees had noticed something.

A man was walking on top of the burlap sacks of

coffee beans, ten or twelve feet off the ground. He was tall, very dark-skinned and intent on his work. His arms rippled with muscles that didn't come from the gym, but from hard physical work. Heaven couldn't figure out what he was doing, though. He had a cone of metal in his hand and with the pointed end of the cone he was stabbing the sacks of beans. His back was turned to the room.

Heaven yelled up at him. "Hey, you, on top of the coffee sacks. What's that you're doing?"

The man swung around and looked at Heaven, not understanding the question at first. Civilians must not wander in here very often, Heaven thought as she watched the man processing the situation. "Who're you?" he asked politely but without giving anything away.

"I'm Heaven Lee. I'm a friend of Mary and Truely's. Mary is in the office now and I came down to keep her company."

The man had been working all the time. He had slipped a plastic baggy out of his shirt pocket and was tilting the metal cone into the bag. Green coffee beans ran out in the bag and he locked the top of the baggy and slipped it in his other shirt pocket. "I remember you. You were here with Truely a month ago."

"It's the red hair. I can't get away with anything," Heaven said coyly, trying to loosen the man up a bit. "So what is that thing?"

"This is called a trier. You can 'try' the beans with it, see what's what without opening the whole sack." He jumped over onto a stack of bags that were marked ETHIOPIA. He pulled a sack from the middle of the pile; how, Heaven couldn't imagine, as they were hundred-pound sacks at least. Upper-body strength. Then he stabbed the trier into the sack with a violence that gave

Heaven the creeps. She got a better look at the tool and saw that the metal cone wasn't complete. There was a quarter inch of air where the two sides didn't meet. She could see the coffee beans inside the tube. With smooth gestures, the man tipped the cone toward the wide end and the beans ran into a baggy. Heaven noticed him pull a marker out of his hip pocket and mark the baggy "Ethiopia/Ebanks/single estate."

"The trier closes the bag back up too, so you don't have a hole," the man said.

"Then what will you do with those beans that you collected?" Heaven asked in her most interested voice. She was interested, of course.

"They test them. Water content and acidity and such. So when they get to the roasting, those that do the roasting will know how long and such."

"Where do they do the roasting?" Heaven walked along on the ground, following the man above her.

"Out in Saint Bernard Parish. They got lots of folks workin' out there."

"How do you like working here in the warehouse?" Heaven was starting to sound like a junior investigative reporter.

The big man jumped down right in front of Heaven, giving her a start. She wasn't used to someone invading her personal space from above. "It's a job," he said with some amount of scorn in his voice, like it was the dumbest question anyone had ever asked him.

"It's too bad about Truely isn't it?"

"Chickens always come to roost sometime," the man said cryptically. "Truely was all right though, not like some of 'em."

"Any ideas who killed him? Was he ever fighting with

anyone around here? I remember seeing a great big guy in Truely's office. Who was that?"

The man just stared at her for a few seconds. Heaven could tell he thought she was an idiot. Then he shook his head. "I got to get these samples to be tested."

As he started to walk away, Heaven called out, "I'm sorry. I didn't ask you your name."

The big man kept on walking.

Heaven hung up the phone. She had just talked to Hank about her mishap coming home from his relatives. She'd spent ten minutes regaling him with how wonderful everyone was, except his aunt of course. Then she told him what had happened when she left and asked him if he thought she should warn the cousins. Hank was worried about her, but thought warning the cousins was unnecessary. "After all, I've been around for lots of your brushes with death. No one has ever bothered me," he said matter-of-factly.

Heaven wasn't sure Hank was right. It still creeped her out that whoever had run her off the road had been watching and waiting outside the cousins' offices. But what would the bad guys do, go in to a doctor's and ask what the redhead had been doing there? Search the place for something Heaven might have left there? As far as she knew, none of these threats were toward anything but her big mouth and her inquiring mind. No one thought she was holding the crown jewels. The problem started with her being in New Orleans. That was pissing someone off.

Heaven went over and laid down on the bed, closing her eyes. The law firm would be here in a minute. She would go down and try to help Mary with her colleagues. Will had arrived twenty minutes ago and Heaven took that opportunity to go change her clothes and call Hank. She wasn't tired or even sleepy. Her mind was going a mile a minute. This Leon Davis must be a total idiot. He was looking so good for Truely's murder. Heaven's eyes closed.

She must have dozed off for a minute, despite her belief that she wasn't tired. She awoke with a start when voices from the first floor turned harsh. It was Mary and Will, not quite yelling but sharp, strident. Heaven quickly rolled off the bed and had every intention of sneaking down a floor and listening in the stairwell. But before she got to the second step, she heard a second man's voice, followed by a woman's. The lawyers had arrived. Will was greeting them, his voice warm again, full of compassion and southern hospitality. What a con he was, and how appealing it was. Heaven straightened her clothes, mussed her hair and went downstairs.

"That's the last of them," Heaven said as she walked back from the front hall. She had just seen the last three callers to the door.

It was a little past eleven. The house had been full. Not only did Mary's legal partners come, bringing dinner from Pascale Manale's, most of the staff of the law office came as well. Then many of the neighbors had seen all the cars and decided a full-blown home visitation was in progress and they dropped by. The house was full of cigar smoke and empty whiskey glasses. Bowls of shrimp peels from Manale's famous barbecued shrimp were everywhere. Heaven had tried to help the staff keep up for a while, fetching drinks and taking dirty plates to the kitchen. She'd given up about an hour before. Now she started arranging all the dirty glasses she could find on the wicker library table on the enclosed porch where Will and Mary were sitting, nursing a nightcap.

"Heaven, stop that. We have extra help coming tomorrow for the next few days. I should have realized this would be a strain on the staff," Mary said almost dreamily.

Mary readily confessed earlier that she had a prescription of something from the tranquilizer family that her doctor had given her to get her through the week. During the evening, as she watched Mary pound back gin and tonics, Heaven hadn't bothered to mention you usually shouldn't mix those kinds of pills with lots of alcohol. Mary was a big girl and the hospital wasn't that far away. Heaven herself enjoyed the feeling of a Valium and a bottle of wine served together on occasion. Grownups and heartache, that was the real lethal combination.

Heaven made a quick sweep of the dining room and brought in five more empty glasses to add to her collection. She put them with the rest and joined Will and Mary. "That was certainly an evening Truely would have loved. It had the flavor of an Irish wake mixed with French Catholic political intrigue."

"Don't forget the Germans. There's some of those first German settlers in the mix there," Will offered.

"Oh, they're no fun when it comes to a funeral. Let's forget them," Mary said with a little hiccup.

"Well, Heaven girl, if you think that was a good wake, wait till Saturday. Boy, does Truely have something special planned for Saturday."

Saturday. Heaven planned to be in her restaurant in

Kansas City plating homemade ravioli on Saturday. She bit. "What are you referring to, Will dear?"

"That's right. It's in the will," Mary said.

"What's in the will?" Heaven asked, thinking this could easily turn into a Three Stooges routine.

Will explained. "Truely stipulates in his will how he wants his death to be celebrated. I prefer to think of it as a celebration of his life. He had a party out at the roasting facility once every few years. It was always a big blowout. Last time the theme was, 'Will Work for Sex.' You should have seen the costumes at that one."

Heaven was a bit surprised. Truely seemed a little too proper to have a party with everyone tricked out like hookers. She tried to picture what Mary had worn. Her corporate suits? By some standards they would be appropriate as a uniform of someone for sale. "What did you wear, Will?"

"1970s polyester pimp suit, powder blue, with platform shoes," Will said without hesitation.

"So Truely wants a party for his wake?" Heaven asked cautiously. She couldn't stay through Saturday. No way.

Will went over to the library table and pulled out the drawer. He picked up a rolled-up scroll and tossed it on Heaven's lap. "Tomorrow a couple hundred of these go out all over New Orleans."

Heaven supposed the idea of the invitations' design was a scroll at the gate of paradise, where Truely hopefully was. The invitation said, "In honor of Truely Whitten, Red Beans and Rice, Dress as your favorite Vice. Saturday, Eight o'clock at the roasting plant," in elaborate gold script. Down at the bottom of the invitation it mentioned: "The Iguanas, Kermit Ruffin, Charmaine Neville will perform." "Now don't tell me all these famous New Orleans musicians are dropping their

Saturday-night gigs to play at Truely's wake?" Heaven said skeptically.

Mary nodded. "Truely set aside enough money to take care of it. He'd already made arrangements with the musicians' managers and there was extra money to hire replacements for whatever gigs they were supposed to play."

Which led Heaven to her next question. "Did Truely have some premonition he was going to be murdered?"

Mary and Will both shook their heads. "Absolutely not," Mary said, stumbling over the word absolutely a little. "He just enjoyed organizing this part of his death. He thought it would happen when we were old. He got a kick out of the thought of a bunch of old coots dressing up like hookers and gamblers."

"Truely had a family plot. He knew that his funeral would be at the cathedral. There wasn't much to plan concerning his demise so he went for the party," Will said.

"Mary, I just don't think I can stay," Heaven said.

"No way," Will responded quickly.

"You have to," Mary said.

"I need to get back to the restaurant. I missed last weekend and I shouldn't miss next weekend."

Mary leaned forward and sloshed her drink slightly. The liquid spilled on her foot and she stared down at her one wet shoe, a demure low-heeled pump. "Oops." She tried to focus on Heaven. "I know this is a terrible imposition. But there's money to pay someone to replace you."

"That's not the point. I just—"

"The point is I need you here. I need you to find out who was messing with the nuns. If you can find out who it is, I know it will solve Truely's murder," Mary pleaded.

"The police—"

Now it was Will's turn to plead. "Heaven, honey. At least you're gonna stay for the funeral, right?"

"Of course."

"Then the soonest you could get home would be Thursday. I don't, and I'm sure Mary Beth doesn't, expect you to stay around forever until this thing is solved. But if you just stay until next Monday you could make Mary Beth feel better about the investigation. That's just three extra days, more or less. And it would make Truely happy if we threw lots of money at you, just to cover your expenses back in Kansas City. And then you'd be here for the party."

Heaven got up and poured herself a cognac out of a cut crystal decanter. She noticed the bottle was almost empty. Truely's friends weren't seeing him to the next life with punch and cookies. "I'll have to talk to Murray and see what he thinks. If the kitchen is holding up, I'll stay. But don't think for a minute I'm going to figure out all these crimes."

Will came over and gave Heaven a hug. "Just do your best, sugar. That's all we ask."

Mary Whitten was barely with them. She nodded at Heaven through eyes that were slits. "Thanks," she said, slurring.

Will went over to Mary and pulled her to her feet, removing the glass from her hands as she stood up. He placed it on the library table. "Now I'm gonna get Miss Mary Beth here upstairs. I think I'll spend the night in the guest room on the second floor. See you in the morning, Heaven."

As the two lurched around the corner, Will only slightly more sober than Mary, Heaven started turning out lights. She was thinking about Mary Beth. Heaven couldn't remember if Will had always called her Mary Beth, or if he was affecting Truely's name for his wife. It sounded so foreign to Heaven's ears, still.

The dark was comforting and, although she had intended to go right upstairs and go to bed, Heaven sat down on a big comfy wicker chaise lounge and sipped her drink. What a mess. She was homesick for Kansas City and the restaurant and the waiters and the cooks and Hank. She couldn't think of a thing to do that would shed light on any of this. The only thing she knew for sure was that someone badly wanted her to go home and Mary needed her to stay.

Heaven didn't know how long she'd been asleep, but all of a sudden she was wide awake, still sitting on the porch with her legs stretched out on the chaise lounge and the empty cognac snifter in her hands. She listened. Nothing. What had made her start like that? She continued to sit quietly, looking around at the windows that made up the glassed-in porch. She had to turn her head hard right to see, but she finally spotted him. The shadow of a large man was out on the gallery, right in front of the French doors. Heaven immediately knew it was the man she'd seen at the coffee warehouse. She felt it in her bones. He was jimmying the door, trying to break in. Was he Truely's murderer, now coming to kill Mary, too?

Heaven screamed as loud as she could. The silhouette outside the door straightened up and turned quickly. She heard the thud when the big man jumped off the gallery. Heaven screamed again and got up, figuring that the intruder couldn't possibly shoot at her as he high-tailed it down the sidewalk. She fumbled for the light on the porch, turned it on, and then went into the dining room and turned on the lights in there too. Will Tibbetts stumbled down the stairs in his boxer shorts. "Heaven, are you all right?" he called.

"Someone was trying to break in."

"Where?" Will asked.

"The French doors on the porch. I fell asleep out there. It was the man I saw at Truely's office last month."

"What man?"

"Don't you remember? Oh, never mind. I don't know if it was him. I just know a large man, tall and heavy and strong-looking, was outside the door, trying to get into the house," Heaven said.

Will went out on the porch and jiggled the French doors. They opened easily. He stepped out on the gallery and looked down at the door handles. "Yep. The wood's splintered. I guess your big man didn't have any lock picks. Some kinda amateur?"

Heaven was done. She was tired and scared and hurt by Will's skepticism about everything she said. "He's not my big man, you asshole. You act like I just make this stuff up to amuse you. I'm sick of your smug attitude. I want nothing more than to go home to Kansas City. Right now I care very little about who is messing with the Sisters of the Holy Trinity and only a tiny bit more about who killed Truely. I'm going up to bed and I don't care if someone breaks in and steals every item in this house, not that I think for a minute that it was a regular, run-of-the-mill burglar. Don't say another thing to me." With that Heaven swept up the stairs. Will knew not to make a peep.

*   *   *

164

"Heaven, I'm so sorry. Please tell me Will hasn't run you off," Mary said pleadingly.

This morning, the tranquilizers and booze from the night before had taken their toll on Mary. She looked puffy in the wrong places. She was standing in the doorway to Heaven's room. Heaven was still in bed. Now she pulled the sheet over her face, not ready for the day.

"I lost it last night but it won't happen again, I promise. I was so out of it on alcohol and pills, I didn't even hear you scream."

Heaven still didn't speak. She could act like she was really angry and pack and leave. It might mean the end of a friendship but she and Mary hadn't been that close since she moved to New Orleans. What the hell.

"Mary, someone needs to take me seriously. A man that I think could be the same man I saw at Truely's office last month tried to break into your house last night." Heaven's voice was muffled by the covers.

"I know. Will told me. He said you were furious with him."

"I'm just tired of all this crap. Whatever or whoever killed Truely and stole the sisters' cross and vandalized the convent is not done yet. And I'm not admitting I think it's the same whatever or whoever that did all these things because I'm not sure it is. Mary, you could be in danger."

"Heaven, maybe it was you they were after. After all, you're the one that's been assaulted twice in the last week," Mary pointed out.

Heaven pulled the sheet off her face and glared at her friend. "Don't remind me. And knowing that I've been assaulted twice you're still asking me to stay here longer?"

Tears started sliding down Mary's cheeks. "Yes. I need a friend."

"You have Will," Heaven said crossly.

Mary wiped at her face with the sleeve of her pajamas. "I don't blame you, I really don't," she said as she walked out of the bedroom.

Heaven flopped from side to side in bed for a while, then grabbed the phone and dialed Murray. "Your voice sounds so good to me," she cooed when he answered.

"What is this, some sex call?" Murray said a bit nervously. Murray wasn't much for sex talk.

"I wish. Here's what's happening down here. The funeral won't be until tomorrow and I have a seat on the evening flight to Kansas City. You can't know how much I want to be on that airplane. But Mary has asked me to stay until Monday and try to sort out what is happening with Truely's murder and the problems at the convent."

"Well, do you want me to tell you that you have to come home? I will, you know, but it would be a lie," Murray said, catching on right away to Heaven's mood.

"Part of me wants to stay and poke around a little more. Part of me wants to get out of town while I'm still in one piece." Heaven gave Murray the short version of what had happened to her on Sunday.

"Hank already called and told me about it," Murray said with a touch of pride that he'd been Hank's confidant.

"And then last night I fell asleep on the porch. Someone tried to break in through some French doors right where I was snoozing. I realize thieves read the obits to get ideas but I don't think that's the kind of break-in this guy was planning. There had been a hundred people in and out of Mary's house that night. It didn't look like a deserted dead person's house at all."

"You think it had something to do with Truely's murder?" Murray was getting interested now.

"Yes. So what should I do? Stay down here until someone finally injures me, or come home while the gettin' is good?"

"The gettin' was good when you came home from New Orleans last month. It's all been downhill since then, babe. What if you do this—tell them you'll stay if I can find someone to replace you in the kitchen, which you know I can. But if it doesn't feel right, come home on Friday."

"Good plan, Murray. A bald-faced lie, but with a touch of truth. After all, anything can happen in the restaurant world. You really could need me by Friday."

"The thing to do is try and do some investigating that doesn't involve being alone in dark places, okay, babe?"

"Daytime work, eh?" Heaven was sitting up now. Talking to Murray had brought her back. How could she think of leaving when there was so much to do? He was right, she could leave any day, citing an emergency. She felt much better.

"Just do me a big favor and call in every so often. You know how Sal will worry." Murray could blame Sal for being the worrywart when they all knew Murray was much worse.

"It will be the highlight of the day. Hopefully tomorrow I'll have something to run by you. Something I discovered in the daylight in a crowded place."

"There you go," Murray said. "I'll hold down the fort. Don't worry about us. Oh, by the way, I told Jack."

"Told him what?"

"That you'd talk to him about working in the kitchen when you got home."

"Are you sure you didn't say it was a sure thing because I'm such a softy?"

"No, nothing like that," Murray said in a soothing voice.

"Until tomorrow then," Heaven said, hung up and bounded for the shower.

In twenty minutes flat she was dressed and downstairs pouring a cup of coffee. Mary and Will looked up from their ham and eggs expectantly.

"Want some breakfast?"

"I'd love some breakfast. I can't eat those messy shrimp with the skill that you New Orleanians do so I quit dinner early," Heaven said cheerily. She walked over to the business end of the kitchen and talked to the woman manning the stove, a new person Heaven figured for one of the temps Mary had hired.

"Heaven," Will began, "I'm sure sorry I didn't take the matter with the burglar seriously last night. I apologize." He sounded fairly sincere.

Heaven ignored him. "I talked to Murray, and he's going to work on covering me in the kitchen. I still may have to leave, but at least I'm not going home on Wednesday."

Mary held out her hand toward Heaven. "Thank you."

Will tried again. "Yes, Heaven, thank you. Does this cold shoulder mean the last words I'll ever hear you say to me is that good old-fashioned ass-chewing you gave me last night?"

Heaven turned grandly toward Will and smiled. "Apology accepted, Mr. Tibbetts. Now jump back, you two. I'm going to go do some investigating. Can you draw me a map to the new convent of the Sisters of the

Holy Trinity, the one they actually use?" A huge omelette appeared and she dug in.

Heaven didn't mess around. In just a few more minutes she was in the car with the map that Mary had drawn for her. After several wrong turns she located the neighborhood the convent was in. New Orleans was so damned hard to navigate because the city wound around right beside the river. There wasn't a grid anywhere except the French Quarter. All the rest of it turned back on itself. She drove slowly around the area where the convent was located, then parked her car on a side street and pulled out her cell phone and dialed. "Amelia?"

Heaven smiled at Amelia's hello. "Thanks for giving me your personal cell phone number. I guess since I'm always in the middle of trouble, it was a way for you to angle for an exclusive."

Amelia's response made Heaven get out of the car and start walking toward the corner. "I'll get to the point," Heaven said. "I'm sure you're ready to go on the air soon. Do you have a researcher that you could throw a job to?"

Heaven walked farther out in the road, scrinching her eyes to see down the street. "Will you have them find out who owns the condominiums named the Chalfant? And also a complex named Annunciation, and then Creole Cove. Can you meet me later for a drink? Napoleon House is fine. After the six o'clock news, about six thirty. Don't let me forget to tell you what happened to me Sunday," she said and clicked off the phone.

Heaven got back in the car and headed for the the other side of town. She needed to retrace her steps from Sunday night in the daylight. For one thing, it might help her find a reason for the truck hit-and-run. For another, she needed to see that she was on a perfectly normal stretch of highway, not the southern equivalent of Sleepy Hollow, where that headless horseman ran up and down the road. The images in her mind were less concrete than they would be after she saw the fishing camps and lakes in the daylight. When she reached Versailles, the Vietnamese enclave, she considered stopping at the cousins' but decided against it. If she told them what had happened on Sunday they would feel responsible. If she didn't tell them, she would feel uncomfortable, lying by omission. Hank was right. It was better not to include them in her sordid affairs unless they had to know.

Heaven slowed down after she passed the last Vietnamese shopping area. She was curious and detoured down a side road; seeing neat brick houses, a school, an old woman walking on the side of the road with the traditional peaked straw hat on her head. This must be the neighborhood where the cousins lived. She drove down to the end of the main road through the residential area and turned around, back to the highway continuing east.

Pretty soon Heaven saw the first sign that announced the fishing camps, this one named JOLLY ROGER. Will and Mary had explained that this strip of Highway 90 was between Lake Pontchartrain and Lake Borgne. The Gulf of Mexico was up ahead somewhere, it and Lake Borgne seeping into each other.

Heaven had always been a little scared of Lake Pontchartrain. The brackish water looked so lifeless when you flew over it, and the lake itself was so big. Once, years ago, Heaven had driven across the the long bridge, the Lake Pontchartrain Causeway, that took so many New Orleans workers home each night to largely white suburbs like Mandeville and Covington. She vowed she would never do it again, it shook her so badly. She imagined all kinds of automotive emergencies that would be impossible to handle on the narrow strip of highway shooting down the middle of the lake. Now she shuddered thinking about her attackers in the pickup truck and how much worse their assault would have been if she'd been driving on the causeway.

When Heaven saw the house sign DO OR DIE, she pulled off and stopped the car. The deep tire tracks were still there, where the tow truck had pulled her car up from the ditch. No one seemed to be home, the fishing boat was still safely tucked under the stilts of the house where it had been on Sunday night. Heaven noticed a freshly painted plaster rendition of the Seven Dwarfs on the lawn. Where was Snow White? Heaven walked up the drive, poked around under the house, not really looking for anything, walked back to the car. She made a pretense of checking out the other tire tracks, the truck's. They were bigger and heavier. She was sure an evidence technician could take a plaster cast and tell exactly what make of truck and tire had pushed her in the ditch. And if there had been a fatality, they would have done that. As it was, the police didn't have the resources to do that kind of work for a bump and run without a real injury to Heaven.

She got back in the car and continued east, not really having a plan. She was glad she'd made the trip, for her own mental health. The area was almost comical in its hominess. It wasn't the scary place it had seemed when Heaven had discovered that she'd taken a wrong turn in the dark.

She drove on. She remembered once going to a charming little town that she was pretty sure was just up ahead. Sure enough in twenty minutes Heaven was walking down the street in Bay St. Louis. She had lunch in a little joint, ordering the recommendation of the waitress, chili cheese fries and a shrimp po'boy. It was a fine fried-food establishment. She spent the early afternoon visiting several little shops, bought a little piece of folk art, a painting of dancing crawfish, then started back toward the city.

All day, without letting it overtake her, she'd been trying to be conscious of whether someone was following her. By this time, about three in the afternoon, she was relaxed and certain that no one was tailing her today.

On the way back to New Orleans Heaven spotted a sign that said Bayou Sauvage National Wildlife Refuge. A little wildlife would make this day complete. She turned in. On one side was the bayou, water still and dark green, with a bicycle path next to it. On the other side was a hiking path that struck off into the woods. There didn't seem to be anyone else around. No other cars were in the parking lot. There was a covered gazebo-like structure with picnic tables and pamphlets on the wildlife area. It was empty.

Heaven got out of the car and headed toward the bayou. These incredible trees—she supposed they were live oak, tall with curved branches—were dripping with Spanish moss. There wasn't much of a breeze, but the weight of the moss was so slight that it swayed gracefully every time there was the slightest ripple of air currents. There was nothing like it in the Midwest, that was for sure. She was mesmerized. She walked down the bicycle path, watching the herons and other waterfowl speed through the air over the water.

Heaven was not a nature girl. Her exercise was lifting large pots of boiling chicken stock, not jogging or any other outdoor sports. She had skied with one husband, played golf with another, but usually she would go antiquing while the man played sports. At this point in her life, she lived in a commercial space without benefit of a yard or garden and she liked it that way. When she did walk, it was at the gym on an elevated indoor track.

But for the moment, Heaven thoroughly enjoyed ambling beside the winding strip of water, listening to the calls of various other living creatures, admiring the trees and watching closely for an alligator to come charging out of the bayou. Heaven liked being outdoors with no other people around for a change. There'd been enough crowds lately. She slowed down so she wouldn't frighten a snowy egret that was walking on the side of the bank, staring intently at something in the water.

Then it happened. The first shot rang through the air, splitting the serenity of the moment. It took Heaven a second to recognize it as a gun shot. When it registered, she ducked down in the tall grass, her movement and the noise scaring the egret. It started flapping its wings for a take-off, rising awkwardly off the bank. But the second shot hit the big bird and it collapsed right on top of Heaven with wings flapping wildly.

She shrieked in spite of herself, but instead of jumping up, getting the bird off of her, and running like a madwoman for the car, she made herself lie still, the dying bird convulsing on her head and shoulders. She stayed like that for ten minutes, afraid to move for fear she would be a target for the marksman. Finally, she decided to throw the poor dead bird up in the air. If the shooter was still out there, that should draw a shot.

She flung the body as hard as she could and it made a clumsy trajectory up and back down, landing beside Heaven with a soft thud. No gunshots. After another five minutes of relative silence, no yelling, no footfalls, Heaven got up, grabbed the dead bird by its leg, and ran to the car.

"So what happened then?" Amelia Hart asked.

"You mean, what did they say when I went walking in the Vieux Carre police station with a dead bird and told them it was evidence?" Heaven polished off her Pimm's Cup and waved to the waiter for another. She had made it to her six thirty date at the Napoleon House only a few minutes late. "Well, they didn't cart me off to the loony bin, but I don't think they were very impressed with my line of logic. I realized at some point that no one in this whole mess has been shot at before. It's a first."

Amelia started ticking things off on her fingers. "Let's see. There was graffiti, termites, a cross stolen, you were chased through town, Truely was stabbed, you were run off the road, and now either someone was trying to scare you, kill you, or they were poaching egret feathers and you got in the way. It is the first gunshot."

"And don't forget the hate mail. Put that on the list. But there are no other bullets to compare the one in the bird to. I figured that out after I'd already arrived at the police station, thrilled that I had a clue."

"So are they going to dig the bullet out of the bird anyway, do an autopsy?" Amelia asked, a small grin appearing on her face despite her attempts to remain serious. The image of Heaven taking a dead bird to the police station was choice.

"I'm sure I wasn't out the front door before the poor bird was in the Dumpster," Heaven said. "I tried to tell them there was probably a law against killing wildlife in a preserve like that. They said it was against the law to kill wildlife in the projects, too, but that never stopped anyone. They got a big kick out of that."

"Heaven, I wouldn't usually suggest a retreat, but after what you've just told me, the bump and run on Sunday and this thing today, why don't you go back to Kansas City while you still can?"

Heaven sighed and wondered why Amelia wanted to get rid of her. "I plan to do that soon. But the funeral is tomorrow . . ." She took a long drink. "Anyway, did your researcher have any luck finding out who owned those condos around the convent?"

Amelia nodded. "Of course, honey. We know how to get information out of the city." She held out a list of names. "But I have to tell you, none of these names rang a bell with me."

Heaven looked at the printout. "I was hoping they were all owned by the same person or corporation. Damn." She folded up the sheet of paper and stuck it in her purse. "Well, thank you anyway."

"I know where you were going. Greedy real estate developers. But why would they pick on the old convent if they wanted the newer one?" Amelia asked.

"Good question, but one that isn't pertinent if there isn't an owner in common to some of this real estate. I'm just trying to do some busywork to keep Mary satisfied. She thinks that Truely was killed as part of the plot against the nuns, that he was just unlucky, that the bad guys would have taken anyone."

"And what do you think?"

"I think that's possible. I also think it's possible that someone wanted to kill Truely, staged that explosion down the street so there would be confusion and slipped my Global in between his ribs when the rest of us were out on the sidewalk."

"On purpose," Amelia said quietly as she thought over the two possibilities.

"Very much on purpose," Heaven said. "Enough. Do you want to split a muffalata?"

"I'd like that," Amelia replied.

Tiramisu

2 ½ cups strong espresso, lukewarm
30–40 ladyfingers, depending on the size of your bowl
6 egg yolks or pasteurized yolks
¾ cup plus ⅓ cup sugar
1 ½ lb. Mascarpone cheese (Before Mascarpone was widely available, I would fake it with a mixture of half cream cheese and half ricotta. It's not bad. You may want to add a little sugar.)
2 cups whipping cream
¼ cup dark rum
½ cup chopped up chocolate, semisweet or sweet, but the best you can afford. Divide this in thirds. If you need a little more, don't be bashful.

Use a glass trifle bowl or a 13-by-9-inch glass baking dish. Dip ladyfingers in the espresso and line the bottom and the sides of your dish. Sprinkle a third of the chopped chocolate on the ladyfingers. Combine the yolks and the ¾ cup sugar in a bowl and with an electric mixer mix on high for quite a while, until it is frothy and lemon colored. Then fold in the Mascarpone cheese and rum and blend until smooth. In another bowl, whip the cream and when peaks are starting to form, add the ⅓ cup sugar and beat to stiff peak stage. Fold the Mascarpone and the whipped cream together.

Spread half of the filling over the ladyfingers. Throw the next third of chopped chocolate on there and add another layer of soaked ladyfingers. Spread the remaining filling over the ladyfingers and sprinkle with the remaining chocolate. Chill for four to six hours. If you are using a fancy glass bowl with a much smaller surface, just make more layers—ladyfingers, filling, chocolate.

Nine

A hand shot out of the crowd and touched Heaven's arm. "I hear this is one of your concoctions." It was Nancy Blair. "It sure is good. What's it called?"

"Nancy, I bet you've had this before. It's an Italian dessert called Tiramisu, which means 'lift me up.' The caffeine in the coffee and the chocolate does the lifting, I guess. I thought we needed a dish made with coffee, in honor of Truely."

"Poor old Truely. You don't believe that crap about Truely being just a random victim of whoever was harassing the nuns, do you?"

Heaven's heart leaped. "No, I don't. Do you know something I don't?"

"I know bullshit when I hear it. I don't for a minute think someone just picked Truely out of the crowd. In fact, whatever is going on with the sisters, it hasn't been violent if we don't count Truely, and I don't."

Heaven looked around at the crowded room. They were back at the Whittens' for the after-funeral meal.

"Two things. It may not have been violence per se, but whoever wrote all those hate letters just to shake up the chefs was a very sick individual. I think a person like that could kill someone. Second thing: I agree with you. I don't think Truely's murder had anything to do with the place he was killed."

Nancy Blair shook her head. "You're wrong there, Heaven. I think the culprit did kill Truely at that party on purpose because they knew it would be ascribed to whoever was causing the trouble for the nuns."

Heaven smiled. "Good point. But why are we the only ones that seem to be tracking with this thing?"

Nancy looked around the room nonchalantly as she talked, her eyes darting from group to group. "The police department is made up mostly of men, even today. It was always a great boon to my business that my customers were men because it's so much easier to hoodwink them than women. And the police have had several murders since Truely's on Saturday night. We only have to think about this one."

"I'd love to talk to you about this some more," Heaven said.

"Lunch tomorrow at Commander's Palace. Shall we say one?" Nancy Blair glided on to the next collection of well-coiffed, well-lit, mourners.

The funeral had been grand and long. Heaven had excused herself from the chore of going to the cemetery by volunteering to come back to the house and make sure everything was ready for the hordes, that they had plenty of booze available and the food out on the table. She was getting the idea that in New Orleans, funerals and all the events surrounding them were perfectly legitimate social occasions. St. Louis Cathedral had been full of people dressed to the nines. Now the house was vibrating with only slightly subdued voices telling tales about Truely and gossip about each other.

Heaven was impressed with the generosity of Truely and Mary's friends. The food had started pouring in the day before the funeral. A whole country ham would just appear on the porch with a note. Turkeys and briskets, the linchpin of Midwestern funeral meals, were nowhere to be found on the long dining room table. In their place were big platters of Jambalaya and crawfish. Shrimp creole, a dish that Heaven had almost forgotten about, was emitting a wonderful aroma from a big silver chafing dish. A bowl of South Carolina rice sat beside it, each kernel separated perfectly from the next. Stacks of muffalata sandwiches had been delivered from Central Grocery early that morning. The entire sideboard was filled with sweet things: pralines and sweet potato pie and chocolate cake and Heaven's Tiramisu. Elegant china and heavy silver flatware had been laid out. It was no wonder they'd needed extra staff to get ready. Everything sparkled. Heaven had to remind herself that someone had been killed to bring all these party lovers together.

All of a sudden, Will Tibbets had Heaven by the elbow and was steering her out the open French doors onto the gallery. There were plenty of people out there as well, sitting on all the beautiful wicker furniture, eating and drinking. Will slipped his arm around Heaven's waist and squeezed her. "Thank you."

Heaven rested her hand on Will's shoulder for a minute. When she realized what she was doing she jerked her hand quickly away, like she'd been burned. "For what?"

"For being here for Mary Beth, or Mary as you like to call her. As long as she's been living here, I think she still feels like the outsider."

Heaven stepped back and found a chair to sink into. Will sat down effortlessly on the porch beside her, crossing his legs and not spilling a drop of his drink. "Will, you all think folks who came here way before the Civil War are newcomers to the area. Of course Mary would feel like an outsider after a mere eighteen or twenty years," Heaven said. "By the way, now that Truely is buried, we have to talk."

"I can feel another attack of the detective coming on," Will said, pulling at the edge of Heaven's very short black skirt. "Can't you take somethin' for this problem of yours?"

"What problem is that, wanting to find out the truth about Truely's death?" Heaven pulled his hand away from her skirt.

Will grinned and wrapped his arm around Heaven's leg. "I sure do love these black stockings you got on today. You have good legs, sugar."

Heaven pushed his hand off. "Go ahead. Change the subject. But you must have some ideas about who killed your friend."

Will stood up just as gracefully as he'd gotten down. "When I say that Truely had no known enemies, I really mean it. That's why I keep thinking it had something to do with the sisters. I'm not talking that way just to make you irritated, sugar."

Heaven waved her hands at him dismissively. "Oh, you know you love irritating me. Now go away. I need to think."

"Yes, ma'am," Will said as he patted Heaven's head and went back through the French doors.

Heaven sat and listened to snatches of conversation swirling from each side of the open doors. Laughter sounded on the other side of the porch. A fork clanged, falling on the wooden floor in the dining room. You would have thought Truely had passed quietly in his sleep for all the concern she heard about his violent end from this crowd. The benefit for the art museum next week was much more of a topic of conversation. Did these people have no interest in finding out what had happened? Perhaps there was some unwritten code that murder was not to be discussed until after the victim had been interred twenty-four hours. There certainly was plenty of codified behavior in the South, and New Orleans was so special, so unique, it wouldn't surprise Heaven at all if everyone in there drinking Truely's booze already knew who did it and they were just waiting until the "correct" moment to clue in the police and maybe, if she was good, Heaven, too.

The only problem was that Heaven just couldn't wait. She got up and ran up the stairs to her room, grabbed her purse, her raincoat, and her cell phone, and slipped out without saying anything to Mary.

In just a few minutes she was standing by the fence that surrounded the outdoor loading area of the Pan-American Coffee Company. The warehouse and the plant were closed today to honor Truely. On her visit here the day before with Mary, Heaven had noticed a loose piece of fencing when she'd been talking to the man taking the samples from the bags of coffee. The chain link wasn't connected properly down at the bottom where the fence turned a corner. She'd meant to tell Mary to have it repaired, and she would, after she was done using it.

Heaven took one more look around. The warehouse

next to Truely's was facing the opposite direction. The parking lot of that warehouse was on the other side of the building as well, so without the coffee employees around, there was no one in sight, except people on ships on the river and they surely wouldn't be paying attention to her. She put on the raincoat, lay down on the ground, pushed the loose metal fencing up, threw her purse through the opening, and rolled herself under in an almost neat, fluid movement. One of her high heels got caught in the holes of the fence but it was easily retrieved, and she got a hole in her dark stockings, thigh high, but it didn't seem to be spreading. Heaven took off the raincoat and shook it. She hadn't changed out of her funeral clothes for fear of attracting attention leaving the house in tights and a tee shirt. She was in a short black skirt, black knit top, black leather jacket and the opaque black stockings and Italian high heels. It was more of a New York outfit than a New Orleans one, but it was all the black clothes she had with her and she had stupidly thought black would be the dress of the day. Little did she know that the locals wear their pastels to a funeral. She dusted herself off, put her shoe back on, and headed inside with the coat over her shoulder; if she was lucky that is, and could get inside.

Heaven had briefly considered going into Mary's purse and stealing her keys. But who knew if she was carrying around the keys to Truely's business? She might have stuck them in a drawer somewhere. They could still be on Truely's dresser. Mix all those possibilities with the fact that Heaven wouldn't know the keys to the warehouse from a hole in the ground, and she'd decided to wing it.

Beside the large sliding doors that were usually open to the inside of the warehouse, there was a standard-sized door for use going in and out during inclement weather, when the big doors were closed. Heaven thought there was a chance that smaller door might be unlocked. It wasn't. She stood and jiggled it for a minute.

She and Mary had talked about the fact that the place didn't have an alarm system, that they left big piles of coffee beans out in the yard, as they called this covered outdoor wharf area. Theft had never been a problem for Truely as the burglars of New Orleans didn't seem to be into roasting their own coffee beans. Now Heaven was sorry she'd fussed at Mary about tighter security. Mary must have said something to the work crew about locking the place up tight.

Heaven dug around in her purse. She knew there was a bent paper clip down in the bottom somewhere that she used on her computer when it froze up. She found it, and also a credit card and a hairpin. She fiddled around and discovered, to her delight, that picking a simple lock like this one wasn't so hard. It wasn't a dead bolt. Heaven stepped inside the warehouse and dropped her coat by the door.

She had no idea why she'd been compelled to come here today or what exactly she was looking for. But she'd been thinking about what people killed for and it was money and hurt feelings most of the time. What combination of those two had done Truely in?

She now had a half-baked theory. After all, coffee beans came from exotic places that also grew other more illegal plants. Although she couldn't imagine that the United States Customs Service wasn't totally hip to the geographical relationship between Colombian coffee and Colombian cocaine, maybe there was something else that could be smuggled in that wouldn't be quite so obvious. She knew they had lots of emeralds in Columbia. Maybe Truely was involved in the gem smuggling game.

Heaven pushed and pried bags apart so she could read their origins. She found some labeled ORGANIC BOLIVIA and others saying COLUMBIA ESTATE. That seemed like a good place to start. Now she had to find one of those tools, the trier. She knew that the time clock was in the room with the fancy coffeepot and the tables and chairs for employees to eat their lunch. She went there and sure enough, a whole row of triers hung on hooks on the wall by leather loops, along with the long lab coats she had seen some workers wearing. She grabbed one of the triers and went back to the bags.

She was looking forward to this part. It had looked like fun stabbing into the coffee bags. Heaven slipped off her heels and climbed up on a small stack of the Bolivian beans. She was awkward with the tool at first, tearing a hole in the first burlap sack by not having a smooth in-and-out motion. Someone would curse when they moved this bag and it leaked beans all over the place. The person doing the cursing would most likely be the surly man who hadn't revealed his name the day before. Oh, well. After a few attempts, Heaven got the trier down pat. She could stab down into the bag deep enough to be sure there wasn't a bag of emeralds hiding in there. She methodically stabbed each bag in three different places, then moved on. Soon she was out of Bolivia and almost done with Columbia. She briefly considered diamonds from Africa and almost started over to the African coffee, then gave up. This wasn't getting her anywhere. She sat down on the edge of the pallets and looked at the mess she'd made. Because she wasn't armed with the baggies that were needed to store the beans that came out of the burlap bags in the trier tube, she had just tossed them on the floor. All around the pallets of bags she'd been poking in, there were coffee beans. They stuck out like a sore thumb in an otherwise neat environment. Heaven considered finding a broom and cleaning up after herself. She decided against it. If she hadn't found anything in the sacks of coffee beans, maybe she'd learn something from the reaction to a break-in at the warehouse. It might scare someone into making a mistake and she might notice that mistake.

With that decision, she walked back to the lunchroom and hung up the trier. Then she walked down the hall and opened every door. Most of them were for offices, full of invoices and computers and fax machines. But down at the end of the hall, several doors past Truely's office, she found a room that puzzled her. It looked as though a brand-new sewing machine had just been moved into the room; the box for it was still lying on the floor. A chair had been pulled up to a table and the sewing machine was plugged in and set up. On the floor beside the chair was a stack of coffee bags, their seams carefully opened so they were flat. Heaven looked through the pile. Costa Rica, Venezuela, Mexico, Ethiopia. Not a Bolivia or Columbia in sight. What Heaven couldn't understand was why the sewing machine? Was Mary going into the coffee bag fashion business? Since she wasn't supposed to be here, it wasn't a question Heaven could just ask when she got home, but she definitely would have to find out.

Heaven tackled Truely's office last. After ten minutes of determined digging, she was almost ready to give up on it. She couldn't take the time to go through the file cabinets and the desk didn't seem to have one personal item in it, not one. It was a massive oak number with a wide middle drawer, a lot like the desk her Mom had used in the barn for her antique business. Heaven remembered things getting caught in that middle drawer, so she pulled it out again and wiggled the drawer up and down, putting her hand back as far as she could. There was something wedged in between the drawer and the side of the desk at the back of the drawer. Heaven gently pried at it until it fell out the other direction on the floor. It was a photograph. She reached down and picked it up.

"Oh, shit," she said out loud. It was a photo of Amelia Hart wearing a revealing piece of lingerie, a teddy. Heaven supposed you could call that little bit of lace a teddy. Amelia was blowing a big kiss at whoever was holding the camera. Heaven slipped the photo in her purse and tried to put the desk back in the same disarray it had been in when she started her search, wondering if someone else had been there before her, removing the private stuff but missing that photo. Maybe Mary looked through it when they'd been there the day before, trying to find all of Truely's papers. Or maybe it had been tossed today, while all were gone. She took off for the warehouse.

When she got back to the door she'd entered, she put on the raincoat, went out and purposely left the door slightly ajar. It wasn't enough to attract the attention of a vagrant looking for a home for the night, but it would tell the warehouse crew that someone had been there. That and all the coffee beans she'd left on the floor should shake someone up.

Heaven went out under the fence, this time taking her shoes off and shoving them to the other side of the fence first along with her purse. She was getting better at this breaking-and-entering stuff.

*　*　*

The house was quiet when Heaven got back. They must have run out of scotch. Quickly, she went up to her room and now changed her clothes into tights and a big white linen men's shirt. She went back downstairs looking for Mary, quickly trying to figure out what she was going to say about her whereabouts. Blending back in with the crowd wasn't an option.

She found Mary sitting by herself on the enclosed porch, obviously one of her favorite places. "Heaven, where have you been?"

She lied. "I didn't know hardly anyone and after the first hour I had run out of niceties. I don't know how you Southerners do it. I went over to Audubon Park. Ended up at the zoo. It was great. But what I want to know is how did you get rid of the hordes of people that were here?"

"When the food was gone, they left. Also, I think Will told them it was time to go."

"Where's Will?"

"I told him it was also time for him to go home and get some rest. I know he's crushed about Truely and he just hasn't had a chance to let go."

"What about you? It seems like we haven't had any time to talk about this stuff. Have you bawled your eyes out yet?"

"That first night I did. But the medication is making everything hazy now. I'm still numb."

"Just remember, give yourself a time limit on taking the pills. They can creep up on you."

"Right now I don't care if I ever come out of this fog."

Heaven started to say something trite about time changing the way we felt about tragedy, but she decided to keep her homilies to herself. "So what are you going to do tomorrow?"

"I've asked for a month off from the law firm so I can attend to Truely's business, decide if I want to keep it or sell it. In the morning two lawyers who are taking my cases for the month are coming over so we can go through them. Luckily, I don't have anything ready to go to court right now."

"Good, then I'll work on my project in the morning while you're busy."

"What project?"

Heaven smiled innocently. "You know, who has it in for the nuns." And what Truely was doing with a naughty photo of Amelia Hart in his desk, she thought to herself with a sinking feeling.

Heaven stood outside the restaurant Bayona and let her eyes adjust to the bright sunlight. She'd stopped there to check with Susan Spicer on where the labor for the benefit dinner had come from. Heaven hadn't given it much thought at the time. She'd supposed that employees of the many restaurants and cafes in the French Quarter had somehow been summoned. But in the cold light of day she realized nothing happens without someone making the phone calls and having access to temporary labor. Susan's manager had confirmed this. They had used a temporary staffing agency in the food service field. The service sent waiters and dishwashers to hotels when they had a big convention and their own staff couldn't handle it, or an offsite party for a restaurant. They also worked with the local caterers to supply workers for them.

The office of the employment agency was on Burgundy so Heaven walked over there. The young man behind the desk was very polite; tall, with a shaved head and a nose ring. No, he didn't mind showing her the list of workers from the night of the chef's dinner. After all, the police had that list already.

"Thank you so much," Heaven said sweetly. "As I said, I'm one of the chefs that cooked that night, and there were two or three people that I thought I might want to hire again, although I'm not sure what their names were. Do you think I could take a copy of the list with me so I could call folks from my own phone?"

The man behind the desk guessed it would be okay. These people wanted temporary work. But what would happen to the fee that the agency was supposed to collect, if Heaven were to hire these people independently, he asked slyly.

Heaven dug around in her purse and came up with her business card and fifty dollars. She scribbled her cell phone number on the card and handed it and the cash to the man. "This is my old card, from when I lived in Kansas City, but that's my cell phone number on the back. And here is a little good-faith money, so you know I'm not trying to cheat your firm. If I hire any of them I'll call you and have them report to you as well."

The young man considered this for a second and swept the cash off the desk into his pocket with a nod. The deal was done.

"Would you help me with just one more thing? Could you go down the list with me and comment on the people you know? You can tell the servers from the dish people better than I." Heaven had spotted a lone straight-back chair pushed against the wall. The place was a pretty bare-bones operation. She quickly grabbed it and carried it over to the young man's post, knowing that unless he was totally unlike most people in the food business, he wouldn't refuse to give his opinions on the crew.

In twenty minutes or so, Heaven was standing outside the employment offices having learned more than she wanted to about the temporary servers of New Orleans; which ones were addicted to cocaine, which were reliable, which showed up late but at least showed up. There were only five names the deskman wasn't familiar with. Three of the names were Hispanic with no addresses and Heaven figured they would be the hardest to track down. One was a woman and Heaven didn't know what to think about that. Sure, a woman could shove a knife in Truely with enough force to kill him. But could she then position his body in a tub of running water, complete with the cross? It was possible, but it was much more likely the killer was a man. The fifth unfamiliar name was generic, James Smith, and that rang Heaven's bell. If you were a hired hit man, you'd want to be anonymous, Heaven supposed. James Smith didn't have a phone number on the list, just the words Verti Mart. That's where Heaven was headed now.

Verti Mart was a French Quarter institution. Heaven supposed it had once been a corner grocery store. And it still had soft drinks and liquor and milk in the front. But mainly it was a deli with a huge prepared food business. Mass quantities of food were prepared there every day for the workers and residents of the Quarter to consume. The variety was astounding. Meat loaf, baked chicken, meatballs and spaghetti, scalloped potatoes, all the po'boy sandwich combinations, every salad known to a deli, vegetables dressed and cheesed up were behind the counter. The place was open twenty-four hours a day and had teams of delivery bicycles running all over the Quarter with their wares.

Heaven had been in the Verti Mart last week, walking back to her hotel from prepping at Peristyle restaurant. She had gone in for some bottled water and stayed for twenty minutes talking about all the food they offered. Today the same team of workers was behind the counter, a young man with purple hair and one with tattoos all over his arms and what Heaven could see of his torso. Although these guys did not wear chef's jackets—cut off jeans, tee shirts and dirty white aprons seemed to be the standard uniform—they did have their armpits covered, and they had hip head scarfs holding their hair away from the food. Just one shock of purple curls stuck out in the front of the head rag of the one boy.

Heaven talked to their backs as they worked. "Hey, I know you don't remember me. I was in here last week."

The two moved as one, turning toward Heaven and then turning back to the Styrofoam containers they were filling. "Yeah, I remember your hair," the purple-haired boy said. "Can I get you something?"

"I was looking for someone, and I'd love some macaroni and cheese," Heaven said, knowing she had to order something to keep their interest. "Do you have an employee named James Smith?"

"We did. Hasn't showed," the tattoo man said as he pulled the macaroni and cheese container out of the cooler and piled what must have been five pounds of the stuff in a container for Heaven. He put it in the microwave and turned the switch.

"Did he work here long? Any idea where I can find him?" Heaven asked.

They both shook their heads in unison. "Only about

two weeks. He hasn't been here this week. Slacker," purple hair declared solemnly.

"By the way, what did he look like? Was there anything unusual about him?" Heaven asked.

"Yeah, he only had one tattoo," the tattoo boy said disapprovingly. "An arm bracelet," touching his upper arm.

Heaven was excited as she left Verti Mart. She stuffed the macaroni and cheese in the nearest trash container and headed over to the police precinct to give them the news that she'd tracked down the hired killer who killed Truely. Sort of.

"So this is the second time in twenty-four hours that I visited the local police station and they were less than happy to see me."

Nancy Blair handed Heaven the French bread. "I love the bird story. But you forget, the Quarter police are used to dealing with eccentrics. You're probably not even the only person to come in there with a dead bird this week, or with a tip on a murderer, as far as that goes."

"You think?" Heaven pondered what it would be like to have the French Quarter as your beat. "I will say that the detectives admitted they had focused on the so-called James Smith as a possible suspect. But they haven't had any luck finding him so far. I think he's long gone. Back in New Jersey by now."

Nancy's eyebrows went up. "New Jersey? Oh, Heaven, really. Are you trying to imply a gangster hit man?"

Heaven shrugged. "I know. It's probably just my imagination. I've been thinking that maybe Truely was smuggling something into this country in his coffee. Jewels. Drugs. Something that might have gotten him killed."

"That makes some sense, except for the fact that the customs officers down here are a pretty shrewd bunch. And they are Federal. Not as easy to bribe as you might think."

Heaven shook her finger at the older woman. "That sounds like it comes from experience. But enough of my wild imagination. Can we move on to another topic?"

"Of course. How do you like your gumbo?" Nancy asked.

"Oh, it's great," Heaven said absentmindedly. They were sitting in the courtyard at Commander's Palace. Heaven could see a birthday party taking place in a glassed-in room to one side of the main house. A passel of twentysomething women with blond hair were drinking mimosas and watching one of their own unwrap presents. There were clumps of purple and pink balloons tied on the birthday girl's chair, waving cheerily in the air currents caused by the air conditioner ducts. "Nancy, have you ever heard of Truely having an affair?"

"You mean with Amelia Hart?" Nancy said slyly, pleased with herself.

"You dog. Why didn't you tell me if you knew?"

"I don't know for sure. Rumors are mother's milk in this town, child. I never saw them together."

"But?" Heaven said impatiently.

"About a year ago it was the talk. Then, two or three months ago, word was that Truely had broken it off."

"You mean that right before I came to town for the first meeting, when Amelia showed up and pitched a fit—right before that, Truely broke up with her?"

Nancy wagged her finger. "All just rumors, but yes, it was a couple of weeks before that meeting, if my memory serves me right, and it doesn't always."

Heaven thought of the photo burning a hole in her purse. "So Amelia might think that getting rid of Truely at the nun's party could kill two birds with one stone."

"But, as I recall, Amelia didn't show up with her cameraman until after the explosion and after we found Truely," Nancy said, squinting her eyes as she tried to bring up the sequence of events.

"But think about what I just told you about the guy from Verti Mart who worked the party and now has disappeared. Amelia didn't have to stab Truely herself to be responsible."

"I wouldn't want Amelia mad at me. But she's a big girl. When you go out with a married man, chances are it will end with him saying 'see ya.' "

"Were any of your lovers married, Nancy?"

"Honey, you forget what I did for a living. Before I was a landlady, I was a whore. Every John was married, or almost every John."

"Speaking of married, you haven't heard from your current husband, have you?"

Nancy looked down as the waiter came and brought their entrees, soft-shell crabs for Heaven and a Cobb salad with crabmeat for Nancy, and poured the wine. A bus-boy refreshed their water. When the servers were gone, she said quietly, "Not a word."

"I think now is the time to tell me about those other five husbands." Heaven tore a crispy leg off a crab and ate it.

Nancy shook her head and looked off in the distance. "I can barely remember their names," she lied. "Andy Blair and I married when I was fifteen. He was the cutest boy in Memphis. We lived in a shack with no indoor plumbing. It was the only time I was happy."

"So you kept his name?"

"I became a working girl while I was still married to him. It was my business name and it just made sense to keep it."

Heaven figured that Nancy kept the name Blair because it symbolized something to her, a more innocent, happier time. But she wouldn't dream of calling her on it. "Did you move to New Orleans with Andy?" she asked.

"No, to get away from him," Nancy said, her face clouding up. "Next I married my business partner, Pete Herman. He owned a club over on Conti and I had girls in the rooms above." She took a sip of wine. "Then a gangster from Chicago, Sam Hunt. Sam died in a shoot-out outside a bank in Detroit."

"While you were married?"

"No, years later. In the early sixties." Nancy's voice had taken on a dreamy quality.

"Next?"

"Charles McCoy. A cop. We moved across the lake and I tried to go straight. I put up preserves and green beans and Charles tried to raise cattle. What a joke that was."

"Each of these husbands sounds like he'd be good for a whole book. Keep going, though. I want the full slate."

"The next one hardly counts. We were only married for three months. Wayne Bernard was his name and he was a gambler. Horses were his thing. We met at a track and he won big and we flew off to Las Vegas. Then he went back to the East Coast and I went back to work. That was it."

"And then Jimmy, isn't that his name?"

"Jimmy Stouffert. He turned my head almost as bad as Andy Blair. An old woman's foolishness," Nancy murmured.

Heaven wanted to ask a million questions. She could see why the woman from the university was going to write a book about Nancy's life. "You know, Nancy, you don't have to be old to make bad decisions about men. I'll tell you about my husbands sometime. But now, do you mind if I don't stay for coffee?"

"Not at all and I'll hold you to that about your men. I bet you've had some good ones too. What's your hurry?"

"Well, I had a list of things to get done today and so far all I've crossed off is tracking down a missing dishwasher, or not tracking him down. I want to go to the library and find out about what caused that explosion down the street from the convent Saturday night, the meth thing. And I think I need to talk to Amelia Hart. I'll tell you one thing. If she did have something to do with Truely's death, she sure was as cool as a cucumber when the three of us went out for a drink that night. Not a tear in sight."

"There are plenty of men in their graves because of women they underestimated, Heaven. It wouldn't be the first time." Nancy took Heaven's hand in hers for a moment.

Heaven covered the older woman's hands with her free one and patted. "Are you coming to Truely's party Saturday night?"

"I wouldn't miss it for the world. Then next week I'm going to New York."

Heaven had slipped the waiter her credit card when they came in. She had motioned to him a minute ago and he appeared with the slip for her to sign.

"Thank you for lunch but I think it was my turn," Nancy said, frowning at the waiter.

"What's going on in New York?" Heaven asked.

"I'm going to an auction at Sotheby's. A couple of my antique dealer chums are going with me. There's some nice religious articles in the sale."

What an unusual thing for a former madam to collect. "Do you have much religious art?"

"Oh, a few pieces. I've always been fond of the Russian triptychs from the tenth and eleventh centuries."

"Were you religious even when you were . . ."

"A landlady? Goodness, no. But you get old and you figure you need a back-up position, just in case."

"So you reformed and started writing checks to the Catholic Church. That's just what they count on." Heaven grinned as she got up from the table.

"Be careful with Amelia. I'll see you Saturday night," Nancy said.

"Wish me luck," Heaven said as she slipped out of the courtyard gate.

Heaven thought she was going to the library in the Central Business District. But her car drove right to the television station instead. "Then let's get this over with," Heaven said out loud as she buzzed the outer door. This time when Amelia Hart learned it was Heaven, she told the receptionist to let her come back by herself. Just as she's getting to trust me, Heaven thought. She picked her way through the warren of cables and lights and found Amelia in her office, sitting in front of her computer. She looked up and smiled a friendly smile. "Hey, Heaven," she called.

Heaven pulled out the photo and threw it on Amelia's keyboard. "You really had me fooled. I thought we were becoming buddies. And all the time you hadn't bothered to tell me you were fucking my friend's husband, the same husband who just happened to end up dead last week."

"Where'd you get this?" Amelia said sharply, holding the snapshot.

"Hidden away in Truely's desk."

"Mary didn't see this, did she?"

"No way. But should I be looking for more photos around the house so she never does?"

"I had no idea he kept that. What do you want, Heaven?"

"I want to know about you and Truely. And don't lie to me, please. Don't insult me further."

"You're a smart girl. Surely you understand why I wouldn't mention this to you, you being Mary's friend and all. Then, after Truely was killed, I sure wasn't gonna say a thing, no way," Amelia said defiantly. "Truely already tore my life apart once. I wasn't about to let him do it again in death."

"Was it over, or was it still going on?"

"Over four months ago. Truely told me it had to end. Before that, he'd never said anything about leaving Mary Beth, never made any promises. But I know he did love me. So I was shocked. I tried to get him to tell me why. He said his business needed his attention. That something strange was going on with it."

"Are you just saying this to divert my attention back to Truely's business and away from you as a murder suspect?"

Amelia's eyes flashed with anger. "Do you think I liked losing my boyfriend over his *business*? How insulting. 'I love my wife.' 'I can't do it to my children'—a girl can understand those lines. But, 'I have to take care of my business?' Heaven, I sure wouldn't tell you this pitiful tale unless it was the truth."

"You didn't tell me anything until I came in here with

evidence. In my book, you just became suspect number one. You hated the Sisters of the Holy Trinity, and you'd been scorned by Truely. Why not take him out and make it look like a plot against the sisters?"

"Heaven, I'm sorry you had to find out about our relationship, but I didn't kill Truely. You know I couldn't sneak anywhere in this town. I'm too well known. And I didn't pay someone else to kill Truely either. It was over and my feelings were hurt, that's all. The whole affair was so typical of this town. The Uptown white guy in the seersucker suit comes callin' at the beautiful colored girl's bed, not the coal black girl's bed you understand, but the one with skin the color of cafe au lait. I was mad at myself for falling for it."

"You just keep revealing more motive for murder," Heaven said and got up from the side of the desk where she'd been perched. She reached down, picked up the photo, and turned for the door.

"Heaven, don't do anything stupid, like showing that to Mary. Please, give me that."

Heaven put the photo in her purse and held the purse behind her back. "Don't threaten me, Amelia. If I find out that you're lying to me about anything else, forget about Mary, I'm going to the police with this. I may go to the police with it anyway," she said and ran down the hall and out into the reception area. But Amelia didn't follow.

Heaven had one more thing to do while she was in the Quarter. She walked over to the convent, trying to sort out what Amelia had said and done. Did Amelia have enough of a dark mind, or a broken heart, that she could be behind all this mayhem after all?

Heaven felt betrayed. She thought she was making

friends with Amelia, but it only went so far. Then the lying started. It was true that it would have been difficult for Amelia to bring up her affair with Truely to Heaven. Amelia knew Heaven only as a friend of Mary's. But Heaven was sure Amelia wasn't telling her everything about her relationship with Truely. She was sick at heart because now she'd have to lie, too. Mary didn't need to hear this.

Heaven slipped into the convent at the Chartres Street entrance. She passed the bookstore quickly while the volunteer who worked there was selling some tour tickets to a couple.

She had an idea. It had hatched when Nancy Blair mentioned her interest in religious art. It would only take a minute to eliminate a nasty possibility that was bothering her. She hoped it would be eliminated, that is.

Heaven walked over to the side of the courtyard where the cross had been reinstalled on a raised brick dais. It looked like this time they had sunk it in concrete. Heaven knelt in front of it, hoping lightning wouldn't strike her down. She bowed her head and dug around in her purse at the same time to find the key to the rental car, then she leaned forward, threw her arms around the cross and kissed it, while scratching the back side of it near the base with her car key. She peeked around at the tiny gash she'd made. Under the rust and patina there was something wrong. Bright, shiny, new metal sparkled at her. She got up quickly and made a little curtsy at the cross, then went out the way she'd come.

The volunteer was standing in the door, smiling approvingly at Heaven for her piousness. "Yes, we're all so glad to have the sisters' cross back where it belongs."

*   *   *

When Heaven got to Mary's house, she saw Will's car in the driveway. She parked on the street so he could get out, relieved he was there. She wouldn't want to be weak and spill the beans about Amelia. With Will around there was no chance she'd bring up that subject to Mary. Of course, there was the possibility that Will knew about the affair. After all, he was Truely's best friend.

"Yoo-hoo," she yelled inside the big front hallway. "Where are you two?"

"Heaven, we're in the library," Mary called.

When Heaven entered the lovely old paneled room, Mary was sitting at Truely's desk and Will was on the floor with one of the desk drawers in front of him, carefully taking out papers and reading them. "What are you two up to?" she asked.

Will smiled. "Pardon me if I don't get up. Mary has a bottle of Sancerre open over on the bar."

"I asked Will if he'd help me go through Truely's desk. I think he's almost ready to believe you, Heaven."

Heaven felt her heart beating faster. On the way home she'd made plans to go through that desk after Mary went to bed, looking for incriminating photos of Amelia, and anything else she could find. Now they'd beaten her to the punch. Damn.

"Believe me about what?" Heaven glanced at her watch. It was almost seven, certainly in the right time zone for a glass of wine. The day had flown by and she hadn't gone to the library. That would have to be on the list for tomorrow. She went over and poured herself a glass of wine.

Mary's voice sounded tense as she talked to Heaven.

She must have not taken her Xanax or whatever she'd been on. "Yesterday, during the funeral when no one was around, someone broke into the warehouse."

Heaven caught her breath and looked concerned. "Oh, no. Did they take anything?"

Mary shook her head. "Not that I could tell. They opened some bags of coffee beans and the warehouse manager thought they'd searched Truely's office. I went down there and I thought the office looked like it always did. But the manager knows the place better than I do. He said the desk was a mess. I could have left it that way because I wasn't tracking very clearly when I went down there with you. I really couldn't tell if anything was missing. The safe hadn't been opened."

"So I'll concede Truely may have something somebody is wantin' to get back," Will said without looking up from the pile of papers on his lap. Heaven walked over to where he was sitting and saw a folder marked household insurance that Will was working from. There were a couple of photos lying on the floor but they looked like pieces of jewelry that probably had an additional insurance rider on them. Thank goodness, no near-naked Amelia. She reached down and picked up a photo of a diamond pin in the shape of a bouquet of flowers.

"What a beautiful pin," she said.

Mary looked up and Heaven flashed the snapshot in her direction. "That was Truely's mother's and she gave it to me before she died, the old bag."

Will chuckled and Mary even grinned a little.

"I thought it was too big, too showy. I hardly ever took it out of the safety-deposit box," Mary continued. "Of course, it may have to do with the fact that Truely's mother always treated me like I was a carpetbagger. Any pin she'd give me, I guess I felt wasn't worth much."

"Now, Mary Beth, that pin is worth fifty thousand dollars if it's worth a nickel. That old lady liked you."

"She sure had a strange way of showing it," Mary said stubbornly.

The maid, the regular one on staff, came to the door of the library and announced dinner was ready.

As Will got up off the floor he snapped his fingers. "Oh, I forgot to tell you, Amelia Hart called for you."

"Great," Heaven answered shortly.

"Aren't you going to call her back?" he asked.

"Not now. We're going to eat." Heaven had no intention of talking to Amelia tonight. Let her stew over whether I'm telling Mary about her and Truely. She deserves to be miserable for a while.

Will and Mary gave up their search and the three of them went to sit at the big table in the dining room. It was rather dreary, Heaven thought. "Why don't we eat in the kitchen instead. It's just us, isn't it? This seems too formal."

Mary brightened. "Better yet, let's fill our plates in the kitchen and take them out to the porch. There's a bridge table out there and we can eat on that."

When they were settled, Heaven tried to figure out what she could tell them about her day and realized she hadn't told them everything about the day before the funeral. "I have lots of news. Do you remember the day I went out on Highway 90 again and someone took a shot at me or maybe at an endangered bird?"

Mary and Will nodded, their mouths full of very dry roast beef.

"Well, because that was so sensational and because the next day was the funeral, I never got around to telling you that I had this idea that somehow maybe the real estate that the sisters owned was what someone was after. That's why I had you draw me a map and I went up there."

"And?" Mary asked.

"And I had Amelia Hart check it out through her sources at city hall. There wasn't one person that owned a bunch of property up there. No big dummy corporation. I've got the names of the owners. You two might know some of them. Can I show you?" She looked at Mary out of the corner of her eye to see if she reacted to Amelia's name. Now that Heaven knew about Truely and Amelia, she couldn't imagine she didn't say the name like it was spelled, "Adulteress." But Mary remained the same.

"I know everyone in the real estate biz, Heaven, remember?" Will said, as if Heaven had forgotten he did real estate transactions. She had. Quickly, she ran to the library to get her purse with the list.

Mary and Will scanned the list of property owners together while Heaven choked down some of the overcooked roast, carrots and potatoes. It reminded her of Midwestern cooking. She looked at their faces for some sign of recognition.

Will handed the list back to Heaven and she stuck it back in her purse. "I'm amazed I don't know one soul on that list. They must be speculators from out of town."

"Me either. Sorry," Mary said.

"So do you want to hear what I did today?"

Will reached over and patted Heaven's arm. "This is just like having a teenager around. What trouble did you get in today, sugar?"

"Don't be condescending," Heaven snapped, jerking her arm away from his touch. "I tracked down the company that provided the labor for the benefit at the convent. It's a company that provides temps for caterers and

special events. I thought maybe there would be someone who had only worked for them the one time, who
just happened to show up at that gig to kill Truely. Sorry,
Mary."

"But how would you know whether they were a regular or not?" Will asked in his usual skeptical manner.

"I wouldn't, but for a small bribe, the guy at the employment agency shared what he knew. Don't doubt me,
Mr. Smarty Pants."

Will threw up his hands in mock surrender. "Sorry,
sorry. Well, what did you find?"

"There were several people that didn't usually work
for the agency but one in particular got my attention. He
had a real bogus name, something like John Doe, and he
worked at Verti Mart only he hasn't been at work since
the benefit. I think he's a hit man from New Jersey."

Heaven could tell both Mary and Will were intrigued,
but the hit man from New Jersey was a little hard for
them to take. They looked at each other and back to
Heaven, almost rolling their eyes.

"Oh, come on Heaven," Mary said. "That makes no
sense. Why would someone from New Jersey come down
here to kill Truely?"

"I think Heaven was just using New Jersey as short-
hand for someone from organized crime, Mary. The coffee Cosa Nostra," Will said with a smirk.

"Well, I went to the police station and mentioned all
this to them and they weren't so cavalier."

Now Will's smirk disappeared. "What did they say?"

"You mean after they asked me if I had any more dead
pelicans with me? They insisted on calling the egret a
pelican," Heaven said huffily. "They said that they had
also been trying to locate that person, James Smith, it
was. So, I think I'm on to something."

"According to your theory, James Smith is back in Hoboken by now," Will reminded her.

"They have phones and faxes in Hoboken. The world is a small place now, Will. You have to go farther than the East Coast to get away with anything."

Mary took a sip of wine. "Why is it that you think organized crime might be, might have been, after Truely?"

Heaven smiled faintly at her friend. "Now, this is not a reflection on you, or Truely for that matter. I'm in business and I know how rough it can get. What if Truely was smuggling something into the country in the coffee beans?"

"Like what?" Will asked, smirking again.

"Drugs, diamonds, emeralds. I don't know. Stuff they have in those coffee-growing countries that people in the United States want."

"I can't believe that," Mary said. "The customs people here in New Orleans are the best in the country. Because I deal with international clients, I know about customs. Truely wouldn't take that kind of a chance with his business. He could have lost everything."

Heaven got up. "I hate to remind you, but he did lose everything, his life. Someone killed Truely and I still don't think it was because he was at the benefit for the Sisters of the Holy Trinity. I'm beat. I'll see you in the morning." Heaven was too weary to tell them about the cross tonight, and she sure wasn't going to talk about Truely's affair. Let them live in ignorance a while longer, or maybe forever.

When she got to her room, she used her cell phone to call Iris's number in England. She wrote down the phone number in Brazil that was on Iris's machine, then held the phone close to her face without hanging up for a minute. Hearing her daughter's voice helped. She was feeling increasingly disconnected, from Kansas City and her life. She had to get out of here soon. When she called the number in Brazil, the hotel operator told her Iris McGuinne was out and did she want to leave a message.

"Tell her her mother called and I'm still in New Orleans."

Fried Green Tomatoes with Shrimp Remoulade

For the tomatoes:

beer
all-purpose flour
1 tsp. ground cumin
canola oil for frying
green tomatoes

Green tomatoes are easy to find from July to October in many places where you have access to a famer's market. Just ask one of the farmers to bring them to you green. You can also ask your produce man at the grocery store, as often the commercial tomatoes are shipped unripe and then ripened at a wholesale produce place.

Make a batter with equal parts beer and flour, say 1 cup to 1 cup. How much you need will depend on how many tomatoes you are fixing. Add a little ground cumin to the batter but I normally don't add salt. Let your batter sit at least an hour at room temperature, then heat about an inch of oil in a cast iron or other heavy pan and slice your tomatoes in ½ inch slices. When the oil is medium hot, dip the tomatoes in the batter and fry, draining on a paper towel and sprinkling with kosher salt. At Ugles-ich's they serve about three tomatoes topped with a mound of shrimp per serving.

For the Shrimp Remoulade:

2 lbs. large shrimp, cooked, cleaned, and chopped
1 cup green olives, chopped
2 each red and yellow peppers, roasted and diced
½–1 cup mayonnaise
¼ cup Creole style or spicy mustard
¼ Dijon mustard
2 T. horseradish
1 bunch green onions, sliced just into the greens
juice of a lemon
paprika and cayenne to taste
kosher salt
black pepper

To roast the peppers: Seed and quarter the peppers. Put in a shallow baking dish and drizzle with olive oil. Sprinkle with kosher salt as this draws out the sugars and really changes the flavor. Cover with foil and bake at 350 degrees for 40 minutes, checking once and turning the peppers.

To make the remoulade salad, combine all ingredients and mix well; chill for at least an hour. Serve a scoop of salad with a serving of fried green tomatoes.

In New Orleans, you would never find olives and peppers in a remoulade salad. They are my addition and I love the sweetness of the peppers with the mustard and horseradish spice. This is a good lunch salad with or without the tomatoes. You can serve it on fresh spinach, as I have, or chopped iceberg lettuce or those ever popular field greens.

Ten

Before she left the house the next morning, Heaven wanted to see if her hunch about the location of the real cross was correct.

Mary was already leaving, out to run errands for the party.

Heaven first dialed information and then Sotheby's the minute Mary's car pulled out of the drive. "I'm interested in your sale next week of religious artifacts," she said when her call was answered. "Yes, I'd love for you to send me the catalog, but specifically I collect crosses, and I heard you might have one from the eighteenth century. Is it large? Twelve feet? Could you do something for me? I just can't wait for that silly catalog to get here to see that cross. It sounds luscious. Is it . . . oh, French, well, I do love the Spanish ones but would you mind faxing me a photo of the cross right away?"

Heaven was in the library and she found the number of the fax machine on its keyboard. Then she gave

Mary's name and address and asked them to overnight the catalog.

It was only a few minutes until the fax machine began its familiar hum of transmission.

She grabbed the paper and, even through the grainy reproduction of the catalog photograph, she could see it was the cross of the Sisters of the Holy Trinity. She sat down to think, rubbing her temples. She suddenly had a headache. It was one of those times when she wished she'd been wrong. It would make things so much simpler.

Heaven supposed there were dozens of explanations. But two seemed the most probable.

When Nancy Blair had let it be known she was interested in the stolen cross, some of her antique dealer friends could have tricked her, creating an imitation cross to sell to Nancy. Then they'd placed the real cross in the auction in New York, confident that no one in New Orleans would be the wiser.

But why would they encourage Nancy Blair to go to New York and attend the very auction the real cross would be sold in?

That led to the second explanation: that Nancy Blair herself had paid to have an imitation made, knowing the nuns would be so glad to get their cross back they wouldn't check its authenticity. Then she'd made plans to sell the authentic cross in New York. If that was the case, did she have it stolen in the first place, or was she just capitalizing on the hand that came her way when she was able to retrieve the real cross? Heaven picked up the fax of the cross and stuffed it in her handbag.

She was going to have to think about this.

In the meantime she dialed Amelia Hart's cell phone.

"Amelia, now listen to me," she started. "I didn't tell Mary so don't worry about that. But I still could. And the best way for you to convince me you're not Truely's murderer is for you to help me find the person who is."

Heaven started shaking her head at the phone. "I don't want to hear about it. Tell me sometime over lots of cocktails at Lafitte's. Right now I want you to check the morgue for any John Does. One of the people who worked the party Saturday night has been missing since then. This one has a tattoo around his upper arm. That's all I know. I don't think I've ever seen him. Call me back on my cell phone if you find anything." Heaven gave Amelia her cell phone number, clicked off and headed out the door to visit the French Quarter once more.

In a few minutes she was standing out in front of the apartments where the explosion had taken place on Saturday night. It wasn't easy to figure out these New Orleans dwellings, where one ended and the next began. It looked to her like there were two buildings facing each other with a courtyard in between and enough room for cars to be parked inside. The garage door flush to the sidewalk was closed. Up above that door was a balcony with ferns hanging and a table and four chairs. No damage showed on the street side. If windows had been broken, they were replaced. There were no black fire marks on the brick.

Heaven looked at the regular-sized door next to the garage door. There were four brass slots for name tags next to four buzzers. Three of the buzzers had names next to them and one slot was vacant. Heaven rang all three of the buzzers with names. Nothing happened. She rang again.

All of a sudden, the normal-sized people door opened and an apparition appeared. Heaven was pretty sure she had lucked out. She could work with this. An older woman stood there, a suspicious look on her face. She was dressed in ballet shoes, a long muumuulike dress in an exotic African print, and around her neck there were two or three pounds of Mardi Gras beads in the traditional green and purple, along with some silver and gold. Her gray hair was long and wild. "What do you want?"

Heaven smiled her best smile and stuck out her hand. "I'm Heaven Lee. I'm a chef from Kansas City and I was cooking at the benefit for the Sisters of the Holy Trinity on Saturday night. You had that terrible explosion over here and it just about scared the bejesus out of me. All this week I kept thinking, gosh, I hope everyone in that house is okay, that no one was injured. So, I just decided to come on over and see for myself."

The woman didn't shake Heaven's hand but she didn't slam the door in her face either. She pulled up her muumuu to reveal a bandage around one of her calves. "Flying glass," she said by way of an explanation.

Heaven leaned into the woman's personal space and peeked around her into the door opening. "How terrible," she said sweetly. "Was your apartment damaged?"

The woman backed up slightly and indicated her apartment to the left. "Lost all my windows. I was watching TV. All of a sudden I was covered with glass."

Heaven stepped just inside the door sill. "Oh, I'm so glad the fire didn't spread. What in the world happened? Was someone frying and their oil got too hot?"

The woman snorted. She had been teetering between alarm and the desire to tell the whole story. Now that

Heaven was planted inside the courtyard door, she decided to talk. "Hell, no. It happened in the vacant apartment, right across from mine. Those two boys live on the first floor over there. Been there for ten years. Below me is a nurse. Course she wasn't home when we needed her. Works nights a lot."

Heaven looked across the courtyard. If this was the place Will had driven out of, the pretty table and chairs were gone, but they could be behind a tarp she spotted in the corner of the open space. There was room for two or three cars in the middle of the two buildings but only a Honda was parked there now. Lots of the greenery around the perimeter was trampled. Heaven presumed the firemen had done some damage with their equipment. At the upper apartment the door frame was charred and plastic covered the actual entry. Two of the windows were still covered with boards.

"They're fixing that one last, since no one lives there right now. Got ours done right away 'cause they were keeping us at the Holiday Inn here in the Quarter till we could get back in."

"Do the firemen have any idea what caused that terrible explosion?" Heaven asked innocently.

The woman looked around and whispered to Heaven, "Drugs."

"Really? How did drugs cause an explosion? Was someone on drugs and they forgot to turn off the stove? Was it an electrical thing?"

"No, no. Its some kind of a speed drug. Someone must have broke in there and they were making it right up there. A meth lab, the firemen said. It doesn't take much equipment to make the stuff. There've been police in there for days, picking up all the pieces of things and putting them in plastic bags. I guess it's cheap," she said conspiratorially, "at least compared to cocaine."

"You don't think the boys on the first floor were involved, do you? Or the nurse?"

Heaven had crossed the line. The women put her hands on her hips, ready to defend her neighbors against this outrageous idea. "Why would you say that? Some crack addict came in here, that's all. I wasn't feeling well and hadn't been out of the apartment all day and everyone else was gone. They just set up shop for the evening in the vacant apartment. Probably thought they'd be gone by morning."

Heaven was confused. The way this woman kept using the word "they" made Heaven think she had seen the culprits, or at least knew how many of them there were. "I'm sorry. The whole thing was so traumatic for me. I just haven't been able to sleep. I keep hearing that explosion. So I just thought if I came over here, I could see that everything was . . . No one was in the apartment, were they?"

"Not that they found," the muumuu lady said, keeping the possibility open for dramatic effect. "Police said the perps must have gone out to get something and they had combustibles too close to each other." The woman fluffed her hair a little, proud of using the slang "perps" in a sentence.

"Well, I feel better now. I'm so glad no one was hurt seriously. But you better get off that leg. Keep it up as much as possible," she said like she knew what she was talking about.

"What did you say your name was?"

"Heaven Lee. Oh, earlier, when you said 'they' kept you at the Holiday Inn, was that the insurance company?" She figured it wouldn't hurt to ask one more question.

"No, it's our landlord. Tompkins Tibbets. He's a real gentleman. Said he'd deal with the insurance company, and even if they wouldn't pay he wanted us to be comfortable."

Heaven nodded. "You don't find 'em like that much anymore. Thank you and bye now." She slipped out onto the busy street.

Heaven headed for Croissant d'Or for a café au lait and an almond croissant. So she *had* seen Will coming out of that drive on her first trip here. It was his fucking building that had blown up and he hadn't so much as mentioned it this whole week. Was he trying to spare Mary more details than she needed right now? Was he trying to keep Heaven from putting two and two together? He was insistent that the explosion had nothing to do with Truely's death, that it was a coincidence. How did he know that for sure? Because he'd been aware of what was going on in his apartment?

As Heaven sat down and sipped her coffee, even she, with her wild hypothesis, couldn't believe Will was behind some drug-cooking ring of meth addicts. Why? If it was his drug ring, he wouldn't use his own property, surely. No, Heaven still didn't think Will was the mastermind of anything. But why had he kept such a pertinent piece of information to himself? She could find that out soon, hopefully. She was meeting Will for lunch at Uglesich's in an hour. Just enough time to stop by the library and get some information on manufacturing methamphetamine.

The main library was in the Central Business District, conveniently located between the French Quarter and the restaurant she was due at soon. She found a parking place on the street and reached for some quarters for the meter. She slipped into the library and asked for the computer section. In a minute, she was online. She went to ask.com with the question, How do you manufacture methamphetamine? Several sites showed up and she skimmed them, printing out one from the Koch Crime Institute that seemed comprehensive. She paid for her copies and was back out in the car with ten minutes left on the meter.

As she drove over to Baronne Street for lunch, she tried to figure out her strategy with Will. Would she just burst out with the fact that he owned the building where the explosion had occurred? Or should she try to trick him into, what, lying about his connection? What would that accomplish?

Uglesich's was housed in a plain cottage in a not-so-good part of town. It was open only for lunch, and New Orleanians say one of the worst things that ever happened was when folks from out of town discovered Uglesich's. The owners had family connections with Croatian oyster farmers so the oysters were always fresh and delicious. Heaven loved their barbecued oysters, sauteed in hot sauce and butter and served with new potatoes.

There was always a wait and she poked her head in the door to make sure Will wasn't inside, then got in line. The owners, Anthony and Gail Uglesich, worked the front counter and took orders and money. Then as a table came up you sat down and somehow you and your food caught up to each other. Before she got to the ordering part, Will slipped his arm around her. "Hi, sugar. Good timing," he said as they slid up to the old bar. "Gail, honey, I think we need a dozen raw ones to start. And I know this little gal can't go back to Kansas

City without some fried green tomatoes. And I'll have the trout. What else you want, Heaven?"

Heaven tried to hold her temper. How presumptuous of Will to order for her without asking. "And some barbecue oysters, please," she said. "A Barq's root beer to drink."

Will didn't even notice he was in trouble. "And I'll have some of that good Belgium ale, Chimay, is it?"

Just then, a party of eight got up, freeing up two tables in the small lunchroom. After a couple of minutes of busing and pushing the tables apart, rearranging chairs, Heaven and Will were told to sit down.

Heaven couldn't wait. "You asshole. Why didn't you tell me that you owned the building where that explosion occurred?"

"Whoa, now. Calm down, little lady," Will said as their raw oysters arrived, freshly shucked, from a tiny oyster bar near the kitchen. Will jumped up and gave the shucker, a handsome black man wearing a head rag, a five-dollar bill.

"Heaven, I don't even have to tell you why, do I? Your imagination runs wild, girl. You didn't need any more fuel for the fire. I've owned that building for twenty years. I didn't think twice about it. When all that commotion occurred at the benefit, by the time I got to the street and saw it was my building, the fire trucks were there. I have a property management company that runs my buildings in the Quarter, but still I had every intention of going back in and asking Truely to watch my date for a few minutes so I could check it out. Truely knew I owned that place. Well, you know what happened then. I could give a rat's ass about that building after we found Truely."

"She was pretty, your date. I forgot to tell you that.

Did you happen to mention to Mary later in the week that it was your building?"

"Well, for all I knew, Mary was aware that it was my building. But when she never brought it up, I didn't either. Why give her another thing to worry about?" Will had been eating his oysters with gusto through this explanation. Now he pushed back his plate of shells. "And before you say another word, do I look stupid? If I was trying to kick up a ruckus so someone could kill my best friend easier, do you think I'd use my own property to do so?"

"What about if you were the one running the meth lab out of your empty apartment?" Heaven said half-heartedly.

Will laughed. "Until this week, you could have put all I knew about that crank stuff in a thimble, Heaven, honey. Now talkin' to the police and the insurance investigators I know a little more. Seems like a terrible drug to me. It's cheap, it makes folks mean, and you don't need a botanical to make it. No waiting for the next poppy crop to bloom. That means an unlimited supply, as long as you can score some asthma medications and a few other things."

The rest of their food came. "You don't sound ignorant. You sound very knowledgeable," Heaven observed.

"I told you I asked the cops about it, since it sure messed up my property. Now, how did you find out I'm the landlord?"

"I went over there and met one of your tenants. An eccentric dresser. She told me about that nice Tompkins Tibbets who owns the building and sent them all to stay at the Holiday Inn while their windows were being replaced."

"Well, I am nice, something I just can't get you to see. It could have rained so we boarded up the windows and that makes a place so dark. And I do have insurance." Will offered Heaven a bite of his trout. Heaven took it. She might be angry with him but not so angry she wouldn't eat his food. It was delicious. "Heaven, I should have known better than to try keepin' something from you. You're good, honey."

"Flattery will get you nowhere. You're not out of the doghouse yet. How come you didn't tell me about Amelia and Truely?"

Will blushed. "You don't expect me to rat on a fellow Southern gentleman, do you? After the fact and after his death? Get serious, girl. But I am impressed with you. In one day you found out about Truely and Amelia and that I'm the unlucky landlord of the building that blew up. Are you gonna tell me how you do it?"

"Will, I don't like uncovering all this hidden stuff. I found a photo of Amelia in a teddy. Well, something like a teddy. And it was in Truely's . . ." she realized she was going to tell on her own unlawful search if she didn't watch out, "desk at home. I was using it today and I looked for a piece of paper and the photo of Amelia was stuck up in the drawer."

"Do you think Mary Beth saw it? She was going through there last night," Will asked with worry in his voice. "Surely she would have said something."

Heaven, knowing the photo wasn't really in the home desk said confidently, "No, it was stuck good between the drawer and the side of the desk. I just happened to feel it when I was looking for an eraser."

"Eraser, sure. Don't tell me another lie," Will said with a grin. "You were nosing around in Truely's desk.

I'm glad it was you and not Mary Beth. There's no reason for her to worry about something that was over and done with."

"So that leads me to ask. Was it really over and done with, because if it was, then maybe Amelia was mad enough to seek some kind of vengeance. I've seen her temper before."

"Yes, the affair was definitely over. Not that Truely and I discussed it very much. But I knew he was seeing her, so he told me when he'd cut it off. He said she never thought it was going to be a permanent thing, that she was a little hurt, but he'd bought her something nice to remember him by."

"What?"

"I didn't ask, sugar. Now as to your friend Mary Beth. I'm as sure as I can be that she didn't know a thing about it. Truely never showed off with Amelia. Although I'm shocked he was so careless with that photo. Heaven, you sure have been a busy girl. Why don't you just slow down a little, get your blood pressure cooled off."

Heaven got up and threw some money on the table. "Besides your former best friend, who's dead, I'm the person who's had the roughest time of it. I've been threatened, chased, shot at, and run off the road. It's personal, Will."

"Where are you going in such a hurry?" Will said as he tried to give Heaven her money back. She was already halfway to the door.

"I've got homework to read," she said and waved over her shoulder.

When Heaven got to Mary's house, it was empty. The maid was gone and so were Mary and the part-time help. Maybe all of them were helping get ready for the party out at the roasting plant. Heaven was glad to have a moment of privacy. She took the paper on meth to the porch and spread out on the chaise lounge. When she finished reading it, she called Murray. He was steamed.

"I thought you said you'd call in every morning," he said in lieu of hello.

"Murray, is something wrong? You have the number down here. Why didn't you call me if something was wrong?"

"Nothing's wrong. You just promised you'd keep in touch. It's Friday. Are you coming home?"

"I'm staying until Monday, like I promised, or kinda promised Mary. Unless you need me."

"We're just fine. Has anything else happened?"

Heaven thought about the dead bird and breaking into the coffee warehouse. No need to bother him with that. "Nothing major. But the plot is getting thicker." She told Murray about Will owning the house that had exploded last Saturday, about Amelia and Truely having an affair, and about the fake cross. "So what do you think I should do about this cross business? I can't let Nancy Blair scam the nuns. Or, if it's not her, her antique dealer friends."

"Nancy has to know about it because she said she was going to New York for the auction. If she was totally innocent, her antique dealer friends wouldn't let her come along to a sale of something she thought was safe and sound at the convent," Murray said patiently, like he was talking to a novice reporter.

"You're right, of course. I knew it would help to talk to you. Even if she didn't start it, she's going to get a cut of it now. So do I call the cops?"

"Well, you said she was a pretty cool old gal. Why not give her a chance to withdraw the cross from the sale before you go calling the NYPD?"

"You mean confront her?" That idea gave Heaven a nervous stomach. It was hard to imagine being a hard-ass with someone over seventy. Especially someone like Nancy Blair.

"You wouldn't have to mention that you tracked down the real cross in New York. You could say you went over and looked at the cross and compared it with the old photographs and you're sure it's not the same, but do it completely straight, like you never in a million years thought she had anything to do with it," Murray suggested.

"Good idea. But that's not what I called to talk to you about. Are the waiters all there, by the way? How are reservations for tonight?"

"The early crew is here working on the dining room. We have two hundred reservations but all is well. Now what did you call about?"

"What do you know about methamphetamine?" Heaven asked, thumbing through the pages on her lap.

"That they make it in motel rooms all around the Kansas City metropolitan area."

"Can you remember any big stories about it at all? I've got the list of ingredients here. I went to the library. They use paint thinner or battery acid to make the stuff, for God's sake, and iodine."

"You can take the active ingredient out of cold medicine and use that, I think," Murray added.

"Yes, because you can turn the pseudoephedrine that's in cold pills into ephedrine, which is a controlled substance."

"I remember!" Murray shouted into the phone.

"Remember what?"

"I remember them seizing ten tons of that pseudo-ephedrine in Los Angeles last year. Even though it's not a controlled substance, the DEA tracks big sales of it and they got 'em on a conspiracy beef."

"Conspiracy to manufacture meth?" Heaven asked.

"Yeah," Murray said, "which was a better collar than just possessing the pseudo stuff."

"Where did it come from, do you remember?"

"Yeah. Mexico."

"Murray, I knew your memory banks would have something. You remember all kinds of news stories. Thank you."

"Why all the questions about meth?"

"Supposedly a meth lab exploded down the street from the convent just as Truely was getting dead."

"That stuff is very volatile. Don't get blown up," Murray said jokingly, hoping Heaven would tell him there wasn't a chance of that.

"Don't worry, you have to mix it together wrong to get it to blow up. Bye, now." Heaven hung up quickly, not wanting a lecture from Murray. She shuffled the papers around on her lap absentmindedly, deep in thought.

All of a sudden she realized the doorbell was ringing. She had so slipped into the ways of a house with servants, it hadn't dawned on her that she should get the door. She rushed through the house and to her surprise it was the big man from the warehouse, the coffee tester, standing on the other side of the glass panes. She hesitated. In all the time she'd spent with Mary and Truely, which wasn't all that much in the big picture, no one from the coffee business had come to the house. It was too late now. She couldn't hide in the dining room or run upstairs. He surely had seen her coming down the hall toward the front door. And why did he give her the heebie-jeebies anyway?

Heaven opened the door. This time she was determined to get his name. "Oh, hello there. We talked at the warehouse. I'm Heaven Lee. What's your name?" She had given this speech without indicating the guy should step into the house. She hoped her body language showed she was in charge.

"Durant la Pointe," he said without a hint of a smile. Heaven could feel the hostility emanating from him. "Is Miz Whitten here?"

"No, she's not. Is there a problem at the warehouse?"

Durant tilted his head. "If there was, would you be the solution to it, or the cause of it?"

Heaven was taken aback. Did he know she'd burgled the place? "What's that supposed to mean?"

"You sure had plenty of questions the other day. Too many."

Heaven tried a coquettish smile, although her heart wasn't in it. This guy was scaring her. "I'm like that. As to Mary's whereabouts, I just got home myself and I'm not sure when she'll get here. Do you want her to call you? Is there a message?"

Durant looked around at the beautiful wicker furniture on the gallery. "I'll wait," he said and perched on the very edge of the nearest chair. It was like he hated the thought of sitting on that big, comfortable chair on that big, comfortable gallery.

Heaven opened the door wider. "Mr. la Pointe, would you like to wait for Mary in the library?" The minute it was out of her mouth, she felt foolish. It sounded like a line from a Tennessee Williams play. Mr. la Pointe should have been followed by Mrs. Whitten. She should have called it the office instead of the library. More businesslike. How stupid. It would be a long time before she had the knack of Southern conversation. She was hoping not to be around long enough to cultivate it.

Durant la Pointe looked at her with barely concealed contempt. "I'm fine right here."

"But when Mary comes home, she'll pull her car into the back. She won't see you out here. Come on in." Heaven hoped there was a neutral but pleasant look on her face.

Reluctantly, Durant got up and followed her in the house. Maybe he was as scared of her as she was of him. She smiled and indicated the library, stepping inside the room and waving her arm in the direction of two leather club chairs. "Make yourself comfortable. Would you like something to drink?" Heaven stopped herself before she said "something like lemonade," which she had no idea if she could deliver.

"Nothing," Durant said and perched on a club chair as he'd done outside on the wicker.

"Well, then," Heaven said and swept out of the library, hoping her exit restored a little dignity to her persona. She wasn't quite sure what to do next, so she went to the kitchen.

When Mary bustled in the back door a few minutes later, Heaven was making cookies.

"What in the world?" Mary said, her hands full of shopping bags.

"I miss cooking so I thought I'd bake something. One of your employees is here waiting for you."

"One of my what?" Mary said as she unloaded her purchases on the kitchen table.

"One of Truely's employees from the coffee warehouse. Durant la Pointe. He's in the library," Heaven said.

"Is something wrong at the warehouse?"

"If it is he didn't want to share it with me."

"Thanks, Heaven. I better go see what he wants." Mary's voice trailed off as she hurried down the hall.

Heaven tried to remain focused on her project, but curiosity was one of her best traits. She creamed the sugar and butter together by hand using a big wooden spoon to burn up some energy. Then she turned on the oven and felt justified in sneaking down the hall while it was warming up. The voices in the library were muted, and Heaven couldn't detect any anger or hostility. It must just be that Durant didn't care for her. She started back to the kitchen, only to be busted by both Mary and Durant coming out of the library. All Heaven could do was ad-lib. "I was just coming to see if you needed a beverage," she said sweetly.

Mary indicated Heaven with her hands. "Durant, did you meet my friend from Kansas City?" she asked, looking at Heaven as if she couldn't remember her name.

"Kansas City, huh?" Durant said, rather impulsively friendly, Heaven thought.

"Yes, I'll be going back there next week," she said, wishing she could bite her tongue. What did he care about her travel schedule?

Mary took charge of this farce of a conversation. "Thank you for coming over, Durant. Let's try to get that shipment out tomorrow."

Durant la Pointe nodded and went down the long hall and out the front door without another word.

Why would Durant, who it had seemed to Heaven worked in incoming, be here at Mary's home talking about outgoing?

"Where's the cast of thousands that usually work here?" Heaven asked, trying to get them out of an awkward pause in the action here in the hall. Mary obviously didn't want to discuss Durant with Heaven.

Relief on her face, Mary put her arm around Heaven and they walked back toward the kitchen. "I transferred them to the plant for a couple of days. They're all out there fluffing the place up for the big party."

"I'm a little hurt. You haven't asked me to cook one thing for the party. Did my dish at the benefit make you lose confidence in my cooking?"

"Don't be silly. Truely had the whole menu listed in the codicil to the will."

"I guess red beans and rice are the main item?"

"Yes, from the Gumbo Shop. And Acme Oyster House is providing two oyster shuckers and the oysters and Uglesich's is sending over enough Shrimp Uggie for two hundred. Praline Connection is doing all the sides, the greens and black-eyed peas and sweet potatoes and two or three other things. Really, all I had to do was follow directions. Truely had it all figured out."

Heaven had found chocolate chips and pecans and was adding them to her cookie dough. She had no idea if these cookies would taste good or not and it didn't make any difference. It had soothed her to throw them together. It was Friday and she still had more questions than she had answers. She had to admit she might have to go home without solving any of them. "Did Truely have a bout with cancer or something?"

"No, why?"

"Most people don't have the menu to their wake written unless they have been face-to-face with the grim reaper."

Mary looked uncomfortable. "I told you, it amused

him." Tears started running down her cheeks. "I remember the night he did it. He tried to get me to write down my wishes." She was really crying now, gulping for air. "I told him it was ghoulish. I stomped upstairs."

Heaven hugged her friend, who was sobbing by this time. Without interrupting the tears she gently sat her down and got her a glass of water, then a glass of wine. "If you tell me where your tranquilizers are, I'll go get you one."

"My bathroom," Mary said softly. She put her head down. Heaven went up and despite her desire to search Mary and Truely's medicine chests, she just got the pills and went straight back down to the kitchen. Mary was standing at the kitchen sink, splashing water on her face. She took her pill bottle and shook out two.

Heaven cocked her head. "I'm all for recreational relaxation but you have a big party to put on tomorrow, so maybe we should just stick to one. I'll take the other one," she said and calmly took one of the pills and popped it in her mouth.

Mary giggled. "You don't even know what it is."

"I do too. Ten-miligram Valium. I left the Xanax upstairs. Now take your medicine."

Mary took her pill and sat back down, sniffling.

Heaven thought this was a good time to do a little digging. "Having that guy from the warehouse drop in reminded me. I've been wanting to ask you something. When I took the tour with Truely," she lied, "I saw this room with a sewing machine and a whole lot of coffee bags. It looked like they were making something out of them. What's that about?"

"Oh, sometimes these independent coffee houses want those bags to decorate with. Maybe they were repairing them to resell," Mary said reasonably.

That made sense. Heaven started looking through the drawers for the baking sheets. "I have to tell you something about the cross. You're gonna love this." She spooned cookie dough onto a baking sheet and put them in the oven as she told the tale of the phony cross. "So, Mary, you're a lawyer. What should I do? We have no real proof that Nancy Blair pulled a scam."

Mary laughed. "You're a lawyer, too. Just because you don't practice anymore doesn't mean you've forgotten all your lawyer tricks."

"That's a nice way of putting it. I fucked up and I can't practice anymore. But if that hadn't happened, I would never have found out how much I love cooking for people. So maybe it's for the best," Heaven said wistfully, knowing that wasn't all true. Nobody likes being kicked out of something.

"All right, as a lawyer, I don't think you should accuse her of a thing. You could call Sotheby's and tell them they're selling stolen artifacts. Or you could call the sisters and tell them to take a look under that faux finish on their cross. Anonymously, of course."

Heaven was impressed. "Not one, but two good ideas. You should be the one out on the mean streets doing the investigating."

The phone rang and Mary got it. She looked puzzled. "It's for you. I think it's Amelia."

"What does she want?" Heaven asked as she wiped her hands on a kitchen towel.

Mary held her hand over the phone. "She said it was concerning the John Doe you asked about."

Heaven grabbed the phone. She listened intently, said thank you, and then hung up.

"Heaven, what was that?"

"They found the body of James Smith just a little

while ago. He was dumped, I mean his body was dumped, right in front of the Convent of the Sisters of the Holy Trinity in the Quarter. But they said he'd been dead more than a day, or at least that's what the detective told Amelia."

"Heaven, for goodness sake, who is James Smith and why does that name sound familiar?"

"Because I talked about him yesterday. He was one of the people that worked the benefit that the employment agency had never used before. I'm sure his name isn't really James Smith. Maybe he has fingerprints on record. Mary, I think this dead person killed Truely. I thought he'd left town but I guess he didn't have the chance."

"How can you be so sure that this person killed Truely?" Mary stared blankly at the cell phone. The Valium was working.

Heaven took her dirty dishes over to the sink and found the soap. She filled the empty mixing bowl with soapy water and washed off the measuring cups as she talked. Her Valium was working too but she wasn't numb yet. "That's the sad part about this latest news, isn't it, Mary? Now we'll never know for sure."

The house was quiet and dark. Heaven had sent Mary up to bed and then finished up in the kitchen. She'd found a storage container for the cookies, ate a couple, and put them away. She dried her dishes and put them away. Then she turned off the lights and sat down at the kitchen table. She wished she'd felt surprised about the discovery of James Smith. But from the moment the boys at Verti Mart said he hadn't been to work since

Saturday, she knew he was either gone or dead. Just because she'd gone around town telling everyone she thought the suspect was back in New Jersey didn't mean she'd believed it.

Heaven had some worry about her culpability in James Smith's death. She'd gone all over the French Quarter looking for this kid. If she'd kept her mouth shut, would he still be alive? The fact that Heaven believed him to be a paid assassin didn't make her any more comfortable with the fact that she might have hastened his death with her big mouth.

She ran that around in her brain for a while, then got up to check the kitchen door. She had started talking to Mary as soon as she walked in and maybe she hadn't locked it behind her. It was locked, but it got Heaven thinking about the doors so she went around the whole first floor, checking the windows, jiggling to make sure everything was secure. When she got to the front door she stepped out on the porch.

The air was full of scent, heavy and moist. Shadows thrown by the streetlight played all over the gallery, but it was beautiful, not frightening. New Orleans had its own brand of enchantment, that was for sure. There was no other place like it. Heaven turned to go back in the house and saw him.

The big man. He was just standing across the street smoking a cigarette. Heaven knew he had seen her come out on the porch and that he was waiting for her to see him. But he didn't run away like he had the last time when she'd caught him on the porch. He very methodically stamped out his lit cigarette and got into a Lincoln town car and drove away.

He was obviously watching the house on a regular

basis. But why? Heaven locked up and went quickly up to bed before something else could happen.

She fell asleep almost as soon as her head hit the pillow, with only one question in mind. How could she talk to the big man?

Red Beans and Rice

1 smoked pork shank or ham hock
2 lbs. red beans, soaked at least two hours
1 whole jalapeño chili or a dried chili
2 bay leaves

Examine the beans for rocks, then soak in a large soup pot. Add more water and bring to a boil with the chili and the bay leaves. Reduce to simmer, skim, and cook to tender. After the first 30 minutes, add the shank. Don't add salt at this point. When the beans are tender, remove the shank to cool, and discard the pepper and bay leaves. Remove from heat.

2 qt. chicken stock
1 shallot, peeled and diced
1 onion, peeled and diced
1 yellow or red pepper, diced
1 green pepper, diced
3 stalks celery, sliced
1 fresh jalapeño, seeded and diced
4–6 cloves garlic, minced
¼ cup olive oil
3 cups uncooked rice
1 T. each Worcestershire sauce, Louisiana hot sauce,
    white vinegar
1 tsp. soy sauce
kosher salt and pepper to taste

2 lbs. assorted sausages (Polish, Italian, brats and real
    New Orleans andouille will work)
½ cup chopped fresh parsley

Without draining the beans, add a qt. of chicken stock
and the rice to the beans. Heat on a medium flame to
boil, then reduce to simmer. In a large sauté pan, heat
your oil and sauté the onion, shallot, peppers, celery and
garlic until they are soft. Add the vegetables and seasonings to the rice and bean mixture. Slice the sausages into
bite-sized chunks. Remove the meat from the smoked
shank or hock and add all the meats to your rice and
beans. Add more chicken stock as you need it. When the
rice is tender, it's done, about 40 minutes. Mix in parsley
and serve. This makes a big batch and you could halve it
but why not just invite some friends instead. Red beans
and rice is traditionally made on Mondays in New Orleans, when the household staff has had a day off. I think
it's a great party dish.

Eleven

It seems like we were sitting in this kitchen just an hour ago," Heaven said as she poured coffee for Mary.

"It was seven hours, but who's counting?" Mary said. She had one of her legal pads in front of her and she was already making lists.

"I don't have a vice costume yet. I thought it should have something to do with food. Gluttony, is that a vice or one of the seven sins?"

Mary smiled. "I think it's one of the seven sins and surely they qualify as a vice. What are you going to do, carry a turkey leg around and gnaw on it all night?"

"I hope I can come up with something more dramatic than that. Mary, I have to tell you something."

Mary's eyes clouded up. "Something besides the fact that a mysterious man was shot and dumped in front of the convent and you think it's Truely's killer?"

Heaven felt her pulse quicken. "Where'd you get the info that he was shot? I don't think Amelia mentioned how he'd died last night."

"I turned on the television early this morning. It was on the news. Little Miss Amelia herself. She said it was execution-style, two shots in the back of the neck."

There was some undercurrent in Mary's voice when she mentioned Amelia. Heaven thought for a moment that Mary knew about the affair. But she certainly wasn't going to bring it up. If she was wrong, if Mary didn't know, this was not the time to find out her dead husband had been cheating, when she was about to throw him the biggest wake of the century.

"Well, that may strengthen my theory that Truely was killed by a hired gun. But no, that's not it. Do you remember the second night I was staying here, I think it was the second, and I fell asleep down here and woke up and saw someone trying to get in the house?"

"That was the night I'd had too many pills and too much alcohol. But I remember you and Will fighting about it the next morning."

Heaven wanted to respond to that but decided to stay on message for a change. "Yes, well, last night I was checking all the doors to make sure they were locked and I stepped out on the front porch and the same man was across the street, just watching the house. I thought it was difficult to get on this street, what with the guard and all."

"It's supposed to be difficult. I'll stop at the gate when I leave and give someone hell. How do you know it was the same man?"

"Because this is the third time I've seen him. He was at Truely's office a month ago when I went down for my tour, he was on the porch trying to break in, I guess, and then last night. This is a big man, six foot five or so and two hundred fifty pounds at least. He's the kind of person who makes a visual impression."

"Do you think I should call the police?" Mary asked seriously. She, unlike Will, didn't disregard Heaven's opinions totally.

"Well, I think you should tell them that twice I've noticed this guy lurking around here. They'll probably take it better coming from the homeowner than the guest, who has been a pain in the butt to the police already."

Mary went right to the phone. Heaven grabbed a cookie from the plastic storage container she'd left on the table. "Do you want me to cook us something?"

Mary shook her head. "I'm sorry that the help is all out at the plant. I'm not hungry but I'll take you out for breakfast if you'd like."

"No," Heaven said, thinking she'd go sit at Café Du Monde, or go to Camellia Grill for breakfast. "I'm going to run up and take a shower. Tell the police I'll be glad to talk to them if they need me." She started up the stairs and remembered she wanted directions to the roasting plant, in case she and Mary arrived there separately. As she came back toward the kitchen she heard Mary saying, "I know, but it's the second time Heaven's seen him around the house. What are we going to do?" She had assumed that Mary had dialed the police. So she was surprised to hear her say next, "Will, I've got to go. I've got a million things to do before tonight. I'm going to tell Heaven I called the police and they're sending a car by every half hour. That should keep her mollified."

Heaven quickly went back up the stairs. She guessed she'd been too quick to think Mary believed her. Will had poisoned her mind about Heaven's theories, that was clear. Mary could be in danger because of that stupid Will and his attitude.

When Heaven got out of the shower she was determined to simply confront Mary and tell her she was listening to the wrong friend. She put on her robe and called down the stairwell. "Mary, where are you?" It didn't take long for Heaven to realize the house was empty. Her voice left a hollow echo in the air. It made her uneasy and she dressed quickly, wanting to get outside.

Then she remembered Mary's excellent suggestions about the cross problem. She sat down again at the kitchen table and picked up the phone, then put it right back down. So many people had caller ID now. She didn't want Sotheby's or the nuns bothering Mary about something she wasn't really in on. She probably shouldn't use her cell phone either.

She slipped out the back door to locate a pay phone. She found a whole bank of them outside the library on the Tulane campus. In just a few minutes she'd called Sotheby's and told some sleepy assistant curator who was pouty to be working on Saturday morning how he could save his company some embarrassment if he called the New Orleans Police Department and asked about the recent problems at the convent of the Sisters of the Holy Trinity. Because the young man seemed so dense, she spelled it out for him, yelling "That eighteenth-century French cross in your sale is stolen," right before she hung up.

Then she called the convent, and when one of the volunteers answered she told them their cross was a fake and that the real one was being auctioned off in New York at Sotheby's and that shouldn't happen to such nice folks who have helped so many poor New Orleanians. She said it with the worst Southern accent anyone had ever tried to fake but she figured the woman on the other end would be too flustered to be able to recount who had called with any accuracy.

"Well, that's one thing I can cross off the list," she muttered out loud as she went back to her illegally parked car. "Now for a costume." It seemed like a problem that could only be solved in the French Quarter.

When Heaven got home with the ingredients for her outfit, Mary was walking out the door with hers. She had a cigarette girl's box around her neck and a clothing bag in her arm.

"Are you going to give away cigarettes and Tiparellos to the crowd?" Heaven asked. "How decadent."

"Yes, as soon as I stop and get a few cartons of cigarettes. It's a vice now, isn't it?"

"Absolutely," Heaven answered. She was a little surprised that Mary was actually going to appear in costume at this affair. Shouldn't she be wearing a demure black mourning dress?

"I'm sorry I have to leave you to drive out by yourself. It's not far, just in Saint Bernard parish. I left you a map on the kitchen table."

"That's fine. Do you need any help?"

"Just come out when you get ready. I'm sure I'll find something for you to do," Mary said as she rushed to her car.

Heaven felt a tinge of paranoia. Mary certainly hadn't included Heaven in executing this party. Was she trying to keep Heaven away from the plant? That was nonsense, of course. She'd asked Heaven to go with her to the warehouse. Why would she not want her to go to the roasting plant? Heaven shook her head. She might be getting wacky with all her ideas. Will might be right.

For the next couple of hours, Heaven spent a relaxing time covering a black leotard with tiny plastic food of all kinds; vegetables, fruit, little cakes and cookies with the aid of a glue gun. It gave her imagination plenty of time to run wild over all the things that had happened to her and others this last week.

She even shed a few tears for Truely, sitting in his beautiful house. She was mad at herself for telling Mary about the big man. She should have just waited until tonight or tomorrow night and, when he showed up, snuck out to confront him herself. Mary hadn't mentioned calling the police and Heaven was pretty sure she hadn't, according to what she'd overheard Mary say to Will on the phone earlier. So, when she got home from the party, maybe the big man would be here waiting for her.

While she was finishing her get-up, Heaven thought about Nancy Blair and the cross. That sly old broad could very well have switched the crosses. Heaven knew that even with her new religious tendencies, Nancy was a scoundrel at heart. That was one of the things she liked about her. Heaven stopped short of thinking Nancy had the cross stolen in the first place. It seemed more likely she just couldn't help but take advantage of an opportunity when it came her way. Heaven hoped Nancy never found out that it was Heaven who had ratted the whole scheme out. She wanted to still be able to have lunch with Nancy when she came to town. She was so interesting.

Heaven looked at herself in the mirror. She hated

costume parties but today it had given her something diverting to think about. She had on the leotard covered with food. She had on fishnet stockings and black high heels. She had on her cutest chef's jacket, open. Then she had a big basket she'd bought cheap at the Farmers' Market, filled with vice-ish foodstuffs: pralines and chocolates and small bags of Zapp's potato chips and other salty snacks. She was the edible equivalent of Mary's cigarette girl and she planned to give out her vice food like party favors to whoever asked. Not that they'd be hungry with the menu Truely had planned for this event.

Heaven checked her watch. She still had a few minutes. Now that the cross was "solved" she'd like to tie up the explosion and Truely's death, her pet theory that no one else seemed to like.

She went into the library to see if there was a medical reference book. She saw a laptop computer on the desk that she hadn't noticed before. Maybe she could get on-line. She should be able to sign on using her password as a guest. In a minute, the screen was glowing and even though it wasn't a Mac, Heaven's computer of choice, she was able to stumble through turning the thing on.

She was scrolling around looking for the Internet connection when she saw a heading, "Recent Documents." Without thinking about the ethical implications, she moved the mouse toward it and took a look. There were several letters that looked like legal work from Mary. Maybe this was Mary's laptop from her office. There was a mailing list that Heaven figured Mary had used for the invitations. And there was a document titled "menu." Heaven figured it was Truely's last will and testament about his party, but why would it be under recent documents? She clicked on it and saw the date it had been created. It was the date of last Sunday, the day after Truely was killed. So did that mean Truely didn't really write the menu for his own wake, as Mary had insisted?

Heaven was stunned. She stared at the date on the screen for a while. Even with her vivid imagination she couldn't figure out why anyone would invent this elaborate party plan if it wasn't really what Truely wanted. Why bother? And that bullshit last night when Mary was crying and talking about remembering the very moment when Truely wrote the menu for his wake, what was that all about? Every time this party was mentioned, Mary and Will insisted it was Truely's big idea.

Heaven reluctantly turned off the laptop and left the house, grabbing her basket of junk food in the kitchen. There was probably a simple explanation. Truely had probably told Mary a hundred times about how he wanted a big party for his wake and she, being a lawyer, put it in black and white, like Truely should have but had never got around to doing. Maybe she felt that would justify the money this shindig was going to cost to the banks or the court or whoever might someday be looking over Truely's financial picture. Heaven relaxed a little. Yes, that was something an attorney would do, have back-up documents. And even if it wasn't technically ethical, Heaven could understand the why of it, even the lying to support the story. If that was what had happened.

She consulted the map Mary had left for her and drove out to Saint Bernard parish, located on the other side of town from the Whittens'. She saw the plant blocks before she got there. It was a former sugar refinery that had gone out of business in the early sixties.

246

Heaven wasn't sure when Truely's family had converted it for coffee roasting and shipping. The tall, old-fashioned smokestacks towered over an area of little, one-story houses. Heaven figured they were the houses of the sugar workers, who then became the coffee workers. There was a big Catholic church, a V.F.W. clubhouse, and then the street turned toward the gates of the plant. A chain-link fence around the perimeter of the place gave it a slightly ominous look. All the buildings were old and patined with the residue of years of burnt sugar and coffee ash. The road up to the plant now ran right by the river, the levee hiding the water from view except for occasional glimpses where a wharf and dock had been built. The fence gates were open. A guard in a gatehouse asked for her name and wrote it on his clipboard. Other cars were lined up to enter in front of her.

She followed the traffic and pulled up in front of a huge white house that looked like it belonged on a coffee plantation in Africa or Brazil. Palm trees had been planted in rows leading up to the house. A stately screened-in gallery lined the house on three sides on both the first and second stories. Heaven could see people strolling up on those porches. She imagined them promenading in their dress-your-favorite-vice apparel. The house itself was made surreal by being butted up against the ugly, plain plant. Heaven figured it for the offices of a sugar refinery owner who didn't want to admit he had to leave the plantation and do actual work.

It may have been offices at one time, but the Pan-American Coffee Company had turned the house into a lovely period postcard. It was a visitors' center with conference rooms. The history of coffee was presented in words and pictures on the walls. There were antique couches and chairs with a French flair, damask drapes, lots of small tables and chairs for cupping, as they called tasting coffee. It was a great party house. Heaven looked for Mary or Will or someone she knew but it was a room full of strangers.

She walked up the big staircase and out on the porch. The vice that seemed to be on most people's minds involved sex. There were lots of slutty outfits and some leather and bondage stuff going on. Heaven saw a man with a leather hood on and a golf ball taped in his mouth being led around on a dog leash held by a woman in six-inch stiletto-heeled boots who looked like she'd done this sort of thing before.

The night was perfect; less humidity than usual, and a breeze that was almost cool. The overriding aroma in the air wasn't magnolias, however, but the strong odor of roasted coffee. The sun had long gone down, but it wasn't true night yet, the sky a velvety blue that you felt on your skin. Over on the other side of the levee a huge freighter glided by, the top of its smokestacks showing over the rise of land that kept the Mississippi River in its banks. It was Felliniesque and disquieting to Heaven, tons of steel gracefully floating on unseen water.

Heaven enjoyed being out on the porch where she could watch newcomers come up the palm-lined walk. Riverboat gambler outfits were a favorite with the men, many of whom Heaven was sure had a predilection for that vice. A few had copped for the easy ones like sports fan or fisherman, costumes that didn't require any effort other than going to the basement. Being from Kansas City, Heaven knew lots of football fans who were addicted in a vicelike manner to the Chiefs.

Suddenly, there was yelling. Leon Davis was walking rapidly up to the house, cutting through the plant parking lot from the direction opposite that everyone else was coming from. A single security guard was trying to shout him down. He kept going. "Mary Whitten, I know you're in there," he yelled, waving his hat. Guests laughed, not taking anything seriously. This was Truely's wake. Of course the man who owned the other coffee importing company would be there. Quickly Will Tibbetts appeared out on the sidewalk and spoke to the guard, who reluctantly turned and went back to his post. Will talked right in Leon's ear for a while and then the two of them went in to the party together. Strange. Heaven wondered what Will had said to calm down Leon.

The walk was lit by sunken spotlights, giving every entrance a Hollywood vibe. Heaven noticed a woman entering in what Heaven was beginning to recognize as Uptown ladies' church fashion; a fancy suit and a big hat and gloves. Lace was involved. As was a huge diamond pin. Heaven was amused by the irony of the costume. Who among this group would admit the love of excessively fancy clothes was a vice? As the woman got nearer the house, Heaven was rocked by recognition of that diamond pin—and the woman wearing it. The pin was shaped like a bouquet of flowers. It was the pin that she'd seen a Polaroid of in Truely's office, the one that Mary said her mother-in-law gave her. But it wasn't Mary wearing the pin. It was Amelia Hart.

Heaven made it through the crowd and down the stairs as fast as she could but the crowd stopped her for snacks several times. She tried to stay in character as a food vamp, ready to lead folks astray with the vice of snacks, but she wanted to just dump the whole basket on the floor and let it go. By the time she made it down to the first floor, Amelia was nowhere to be seen.

Heaven grabbed the arm of a man dressed in a diaper. "Have you seen Amelia Hart, the television reporter?"

"Look out in the plant. That's where the band is," he replied and started sucking his thumb coyly. Heaven took it for flirtation and turned quickly away.

There was a steel-and-glass walkway between the house and the plant similar to those used to connect the garage and the home in "moderne" homes. In Kansas, they called them breezeways. Now Heaven heard music coming from the other end of the breezeway. Just inside the plant proper, a large space had been cleared, a stage had been constructed, and the Iguanas were playing. There must have been three hundred people at least, crowding the dance floor and lined up for drinks at bars set up in the corners of the room.

Heaven saw Mary for the first time tonight, looking like a cigarette girl in a 1940s nightclub. She spotted Heaven and waved happily. It was the first true smile Heaven had seen on her face since last Saturday. Could it just have been a week ago she was plating up Nola Pie with no inkling of what was to come?

Heaven looked frantically for Amelia Hart in the crowd. If she didn't find her and snatch that pin off her pretty little suit, Mary wouldn't be smiling too much longer. It seemed that when Truely told Will he bought Amelia something nice at the end of their affair, he had borrowed something nice that belonged to his wife instead. What nerve. And what nerve of Amelia Hart to wear a piece of jewelry that Mary Whitten would recognize as her own to a party for the memory of Truely Whitten. Midwesterners just wouldn't even try to pull this stuff off, it was way too nervy. Then Heaven realized Amelia might not have an inkling that the pin had been Mary's. Amelia could be in for a nasty surprise right along with Mary Whitten.

Heaven was stymied.

She hadn't seen Will.

Mary was swallowed up in the crowd.

No sign of Amelia.

Heaven walked slowly around the dance floor, craning her neck. She saw Leon Davis talking to Mary and they were laughing. Maybe Mary *had* decided to sell the business to Leon. That would explain why Will went out and retrieved him from the guard.

She spotted Nancy Blair but she was surrounded by people, so Heaven kept looking. Behind the stage area there were wide sliding doors, similar to the ones at the warehouse. She looked down that wall and found a people-sized door that seemed to go into another section of the plant. What the hell. She hadn't given this place a look-see. It couldn't hurt and it would be better than the frustration of trying to head off the inevitable confrontation between Mary and Amelia. Maybe she'd be lucky and they'd see each other while she was taking the tour in the back. She could survive very well without witnessing that cat fight and the enjoyment it would bring the crowd.

Heaven stepped through the door, put her basket of goodies down and followed a hallway toward noise. It wasn't the raucous noise of the party, but the business-like hum of machinery and human voices calling out instructions to others. Heaven was surprised that the plant was operating tonight. Surely Mary had invited all the employees to this blast. But maybe a small crew was keeping the roasters going.

Heaven started to walk into the room where the noise was coming from, but she found the door at that end of the hall locked. The hall dead-ended there but there was light shining from an opening down the wall. It seemed like another large room was on the other side, probably similar to the one the band was set up in. She walked down the wall and found a large opening covered with strips of heavy plastic, like the ones they used to cover walk-in refrigerator doors, in cold-storage facilities. Light and activity were in there but now Heaven was cautious. Something about that locked door had activated her adrenaline. She stood at the very edge of the opening and pushed aside one of the plastic flaps just a tiny bit.

The place was a beehive of activity. There were two women stuffing something into smaller burlap coffee bean bags, about a twenty-pound size, Heaven figured. One man was sewing the tops of the filled bags with some coarse string threaded in a big needle. He was very good at this, fingers and string flying. It took the man about a minute to close up the tops of the bags, which he tossed on the floor beside him. Two other people, a man and a woman, were packing one of the smaller bags inside a larger burlap bag, like the ones in which the coffee beans arrived at the Magazine Street warehouse. Then those two held the bags under a big funnel-like device, pulled a handle and the bag filled up with roasted coffee beans. When the larger bags were loaded, they sewed the tops shut, one holding the bag upright, the other sewing quickly. Then they stacked them on a pallet. On the outer side of the building there was a loading dock with a truck backed up to the opening. And there, heaving those hundred-pound sacks into the truck like they were Styrofoam packing peanuts, was Durant la Pointe.

Heaven was excited. This was it. Truely hadn't been smuggling something into the country. He'd been smuggling something *out* of New Orleans in bags of roasted coffee beans, with the help of that creepy Durant. She just couldn't figure out what it was.

Heaven moved away from the doorway so she wouldn't cast an accidental shadow and scooted to the other side of the opening, closer to the small bags. When she peeked in from the opposite edge of the door, it was just in time to see Will and Mary, arms around each other, enter the room through the locked door Heaven had tried earlier. It took a minute for the scene to sink in.

Two things stuck out. Although Will and Mary were normally affectionate with each other, it had seemed more like brother and sister affection. Not tonight. This didn't look like platonic friendship anymore to Heaven. Will's hand wandered all over Mary's body as he talked with la Pointe. At one point, he leaned into her and kissed her neck.

They were lovers, there was no doubt about it. Mary's face was a mass of contradictions. One moment she looked radiantly happy. The next minute she looked panic-stricken. But her eyes never left Will. Heaven didn't know if she'd just been blind to it all the time or if it was a recent development. Maybe they'd sought solace in each other after Truely died. Or maybe before.

The second thing that stuck out wasn't a puzzle like how long Mary and Will had been lovers. It was now obvious that the two of them were well aware of

Truely's scheme, whatever it was, and had taken it on as their own.

What was the scheme? Heaven stepped nearer to the opening and poked her head a little farther into the room. Will had asked the workers to come over to where he and Mary were standing, and the women packing the little bags left their work as well. Will gave each person several hundred-dollar bills and shook hands with them in turn. A little voice in Heaven's head said Will looked too comfortable, too much in charge. Maybe this scheme wasn't Truely's after all.

Heaven turned her attention back to the little bags and squinted, trying to decipher what they said. The writing on the small packages they were putting in the burlap bags said pseudoephedrine. Heaven's mind was so full of new information that she drew a blank for a minute. Then she remembered. It was an ingredient for cold medicine—and for methamphetamine. They weren't manufacturing meth, they were just providing the key ingredient. Clever. It was like that operation that Murray had told her about over the phone, the one in Los Angeles.

Heaven look over at the happy couple and realized that Mary didn't have her cigarette girl costume on anymore. She was dressed in one of her lawyer suits, very businesslike. It was the last thing she noticed before the world went black.

When Heaven woke up she was being carried over someone's shoulder like a sack of coffee beans. Her vision was swimming for a minute as she tried to focus her eyes. Pain at the back of her head indicated the spot where she must have been hit. She tried to remain relaxed so her captor wouldn't know she had regained consciousness. But when she realized her hands were bound together at the wrists she instinctively stiffened and a strong hand reached over and steadied her mid-section. "Be still now," a voice said. Even though she'd talked to him only twice, Heaven was sure it was Durant la Pointe carrying her. She grabbed at his belt with her bound hands and yelled, "Help," as loud as she could.

Durant stopped walking and swung her down to the ground roughly. It was then she realized her feet were bound as well. This was not a good situation.

"We're around the bend from the plant. With all that music, no one can hear you, Missy. You can either settle down and be carried or I'll drag you on the ground by your feet. It don't make no difference to me." Durant spoke dispassionately, looking down at Heaven.

"I'll take being carried. What girl wouldn't?" Heaven said lightly, still trying to assess the situation. He hefted her back up on his shoulder and resumed walking. "So, did Will and Mary find out about your little scheme and you had to cut them in?"

Silence from Durant. She tried again.

"Do you by any chance have a pickup truck? Did you follow me and run me off the road? Shoot at me?"

"For all the good it did," Durant muttered. "You still sticking your nose in things."

"Where are you taking me?"

"For a little dip."

Heaven couldn't believe it. Surely her friends didn't know what Durant was doing. She just couldn't believe they'd want her to be tossed in the Mississippi River.

"I hate the water," Heaven noted from her upside-down position.

"That's what Mary said," Durant said flatly.

"Where is Mary? I know if I could just talk to her we could work this out."

"They're gone."

"Gone, like left the party?"

"Gone for good," Durant said and reached over, pulled Heaven off his shoulder, and stood her up. She stumbled but regained her footing. She couldn't make a real step, but could hobble forward slightly. Durant turned her toward the river. They were on a concrete lookout perch up on a slight rise right by the river. There were no hills in New Orleans since the whole place was under sea level, but this artificial rise must have served some purpose for the Corps of Engineers, Heaven thought. The water must be fifteen feet below. Just the thought of being dropped in the dark toward the treacherous Mississippi made Heaven almost black out. She stumbled and fell down.

"Why are you doing this?" she asked, borderline hysterical.

"It's my job," Durant said as he lifted Heaven up on a metal rail. With little effort he sent her over the side. Heaven fell in the darkness, frantically trying to free her hands as she hit the water. The river was warm and she could feel a current pulling at her legs. She tried kicking as best she could and her head broke the surface. She shrieked "help" once then realized she couldn't afford the energy that took. She tried to tell herself what her childhood swimming teacher had told her. "Use your lungs as a flotation device," he used to say. "Full lungs, float. Empty lungs, kick." Heaven filled her lungs and tried to get her bearings. She wasn't far from the rocky shore, but it might as well be the length of the English Channel as far as her ability to get there was concerned.

It was true that Heaven didn't like water, and she couldn't believe Mary remembered that. She must have been very vocal about it. She'd taken swimming lessons with all the other kids, but she never felt comfortable in the water. It scared her. If she ever got out of this river, she'd have to remember to not mention her fear anymore. Who knew when an old friend would use the knowledge to try to knock her off?

Heaven expelled her breath, kicking furiously and trying to scream. It was silent above and she thought Durant had left, unconcerned about watching her drown, confident the river would have her soon. She filled her lungs with air again and tried to calm down. In the meantime she was being drawn farther from shore.

All of a sudden, a strong blast of light shone down from the riverbank. "Yell for me once more," someone commanded.

"Here. Over here," Heaven yelled with all her might.

"I'm throwing you a round preserver. Here it comes," the voice said. Heaven heard the splash but the preserver wasn't within her reach. She expelled air and quickly filled her lungs again. Full lungs, float, she said silently as a mantra. The flashlight or lantern played over the water and finally landed on the bright orange ring.

"I see it," Heaven yelled impulsively and felt herself being pulled under the water. She pulled her head up and tried frogging toward the life preserver. The light hit her again and she felt hope.

"Just go easy now, it's just a few feet," the voice said,

playing the flashlight back and forth between Heaven and the preserver.

The life preserver was almost in her grasp, if she'd been able to grasp. And then she felt its slippery, rubbery surface and threw her arms on top of it, hooking herself around it as best she could with her hands tied together. "I got it," she yelled, triumphant.

"Hold on now. I'm going to pull you in."

Heaven was amazed how close she was to the riverbank. In just a minute she banged up against the rocks that were piled there. She couldn't let go of the life preserver and she heard a high-pitched wail that she thought was coming from her.

"Easy now. You're just fine. Take my hand," the voice said.

"No. Can't let go," she stammered. A strong arm grabbed her by the elbow and jerked her half out of the water.

"Help me here. Use your legs to help get you up on the bank," the voice commanded.

Heaven wiggled her knees into the rocks, feeling the sharpness. Pain shot through her legs as her knees were cut on the rocks. It felt so good she could hardly stand it. She was now two-thirds out of the water, still clutching the preserver.

The arm pulled her another few feet. Now her whole body was on the rocks but because of her bindings, she resembled a trussed chicken, unable to scramble up the bank. The flashlight beam caught her right in the face. She smiled what must have been a ghoulish smile.

"Let's untie your hands. Then you can help crawl up here. I don't want to get too far down there and fall in myself," the voice explained. The flashlight was placed on the ground and the man bent close to Heaven to untie her hands.

When Heaven saw who had pulled her out of the drink, she reacted so violently that she almost pitched herself back in the water. Her rescuer was the big man.

She fainted.

Beignets

2 cups all-purpose flour
2 T. baking powder
1 T. sugar
1 tsp. kosher salt
1 cup plus a little milk
2 T. canola oil
1 large egg
canola oil for frying
powdered sugar

Although many beignet recipes call for yeast, this version is great for those afraid of yeast breads and the time they take, and it's still delicious. If you have a New Orleans–style brunch, you will need one person assigned to making beignets as they will disappear as fast as you make them. In a large mixing bowl, combine everything with ½ cup of milk, either with an electric mixer or by hand. When you get the lumps out of the batter, it will be stiff; add the rest of the milk to get a thick pancake batter consistency. Let stand at room temperature for an hour or make the night before and bring to room temperature.

In a heavy skillet, heat about 2 inches of oil to a medium temperature. Carefully drop a spoonful of batter at a time in the oil, turning with tongs until they are brown on all sides. Be careful not to heat the oil too hot or you'll have a raw middle in your beignet. You should do a trial run or two. They don't have to have a consistent shape. When they are browned and beautiful, drain them quickly on a paper towel and drop them in a bowl of confectioner's sugar and roll them around. The idea is to get the sugar on while they are still hot.

Twelve

Heaven was lying on an examining table in the first aid station of the plant. Someone had brought her one of the white disposable hazmat jumpsuits that factory workers sometimes wear and she'd slipped it on over wet underwear. Her costume was wadded up on the floor. Her high heels were at the bottom of the river. Policemen were milling around but so far they hadn't located Durant la Pointe. "So let me get this straight. Truely hired you to investigate his own business?"

The big man, whose name was Sam Delgado, nodded. He insisted on staying with her, only stepping out of the room for her to change clothes. "Truely knew something was up. He was missing coffee, not enough to be financially damaging, but the losses were steady and he couldn't for the life of him figure out what was happening. So he hired me to do some spying."

"And you're a PI?" Heaven was pretty sure she'd ask him all of this before but it was taking a while for it to sink in.

"Yes, ma'am. Licensed by the good state of Louisiana. Truely would not believe me when I told him what was going on, that people close to him were involved. He said he had to see for himself. Didn't know a thing about meth. It was the death of him. He should have just let me turn them in right then. He thought he could talk to them, stop the whole thing."

"Stop Durant la Pointe, you mean?"

Sam looked at her like she was dense and shook his head. "No, his wife and that so-called friend, Tompkins Tibbets. Durant just worked for them."

"So when Durant said to me they were gone for good, he didn't kill them?"

Sam chuckled. "No, tonight was their last shipment, I reckon. They planned this big shindig as their going-away party, not Truely's. They were taking off for Brazil, as it turns out. I bet we'll find out Mary, with her inter-national law background, stashed some assets in those off-shore banking countries."

"How will we find out? Isn't Brazil one of those places without extradition?"

"Well, it used to be. The laws are a little different now. But it don't make any difference 'cause the plane they chartered had to stop in Miami. A little trouble with one of the ailerons sticking. Otherwise I guess they'd be in the Cayman Islands by now, picking up some cash. My friends at NOPD alerted all the airport police in coastal towns. Mr. Tibbets and Ms. Whitten are in Dade County lockup."

"Can they be charged with Truely's murder?" All of a sudden, Heaven wanted blood. She had been so flim-flammed by those two!

Sam ducked his head. "Be hard to do that. The boy you thought was Mr. Whitten's killer is dead, of course.

Person who did him seemed like a professional, what with the two shots at the base of the brain like that. The cops have no clues on that. My idea is that Mr. Tibbetts and, uh, Miz Whitten kept the kid somewhere, told him they would get him out of town soon if he would just lay low. They probably took him to another rental property that Mr. Tibbetts owned. It was easy to send a second guy, probably from out of town, to clean up the loose ends."

Heaven felt her face turn hot. She knew she was blushing from the embarrassment of being so fooled. "So what can they be charged with?"

"Conspiracy to distribute methamphetamine, which is a pretty good federal rap. Hard to beat, under the circumstances. Even if la Pointe doesn't testify against them, the other workers didn't make enough to lay down for Tibbets and, eh, your friend."

Heaven sat up on the side of the table, her legs dangling over the side. "Some friend." She gingerly felt the back of her head and her knees, which were a mess, skinned and caked with dried blood. "I have two more questions, then I have to go home, I mean to Truely's. After Truely was killed, why did you stay on the case and what were you doing trying to break into Truely's house?"

"Well, Truely had given me a big retainer when I started working on this. He still had five K credit and in my book, he still needed my help, even if it was posthumously. I never thought anyone would be downstairs that night after Truely died. I was just going to take a look in his library. Didn't really know what I was looking for. You were there, asleep on the porch. I didn't spot you until you screamed."

All of a sudden Heaven felt dizzy. She ached all over.

"Sam, I have my car here but would you follow me home? Back to Truely's, I mean, not Kansas City."

Sam held her arm. "Why don't you let me drive you? You're not in such good shape."

"Because tomorrow I don't want to have to come back here for that rental car. I want to drive it right to the airport and go home, where I belong."

Nancy Blair and Amelia Hart were standing in the doorway. Heaven didn't know how long they'd been there.

"Heaven, honey. You go with this nice investigator," Nancy ordered. "Amelia and I will see to your car and bring it to you in the morning. But not too early. You go rest now, you hear?"

Heaven wanted to argue but she still had a few things to clear up with those two, so she smiled wanly. "Deal. See you around ten or eleven?"

"Deal," Amelia Hart said.

Heaven saw the television cameraman behind Amelia in the hall. She supposed she'd been photographed, out like a light and wet as a river rat. She didn't care at this point. "Sam, take me home," she said and walked barefoot on his arm out into a party that was still going strong, Kermit Ruffin and his band wailing in the background.

A little attempted murder and drug trafficking wasn't going to stop Truely's wake.

Heaven was almost packed. She'd slept like a rock until eight, then woke up with only one desire: to get out of that house and New Orleans as soon as possible. All kinds of scenarios went through her mind as she showered and packed. She saw Mary and Will escaping from jail and driving cross-country in a stolen SUV to get her. She worried about Durant still on the loose, although for the life of her she couldn't imagine why he'd hang around New Orleans just to torture her under the present circumstances.

It was a beautiful day and, after closing her suitcase and putting it outside by the front door, Heaven began to feel better. She'd be out of here soon. She went into the kitchen and made coffee, read the *Times-Picayune* that she found on the porch, checked her watch for the tenth time. It was almost ten. If Nancy and Amelia didn't show up soon, she'd call Amelia's cell phone.

In the meantime, she'd find her plane ticket, down at the bottom of the big purse somewhere. She rummaged around and pulled out the list of property owners that had been part of the investigation of the nuns' problems. As she started to throw it in the trash, she glanced at the names again. She really hadn't looked at it after Amelia had given her the information and she'd realized no one company or person owned all or most of the property around the convent. Now the names had some meaning to her. But why? She stared hard at them for a while. Then it clicked, just about the same time the front doorbell rang.

Amelia Hart and Nancy Blair let themselves in. Heaven had set her suitcase out on the porch and kept the door ajar for them. "Yoo-hoo," Nancy yelled.

"Come on back here. You want some coffee?" Heaven asked.

"Sure," Amelia said, "we brought beignets." Nancy nodded yes as well. Soon the three of them were laughing around the table, eating and drinking, as Heaven tried to recount her trip in the river for them. "And I'd decided that Big Man, as I called Sam Delgado, was some kind of a crook. I'd seen him at Truely's office and he'd been hanging around here. So when I saw who had rescued me, I thought I'd just gone from the frying pan into the fire. That and the river water I'd swallowed sent me right out."

"To use a cook's term," Amelia observed.

"Speaking of going from the frying pan to the fire, what in the world made you wear that pin that Truely gave you to the wake? Did you want to rub Mary's nose in it or did you not know it was her pin?" Heaven asked Amelia.

Amelia's face was blank. "Heaven, I don't know what you're talking about. Nancy and I went to the party together last night. When I got to her house, she said my costume needed that Uptown wives' touch. She went and got that pin for me to wear. It doesn't belong to me."

Heaven was floored. She turned to Nancy. "I know that pin was given to Mary by Truely's mother because I saw a Polaroid of it here just the other day and asked about it. How did it get to your jewelry drawer, Nancy?"

Nancy Blair laughed heartily, seemingly cool as usual. "Why, it was just a small token of affection, from Mary to me. I found someone who knew someone who was in a position to get Mary something she wanted. I'd always loved that pin when Truely's mother wore it. You might call it my finder's fee."

"You set her up with a supplier of pseudoephedrine is my guess," Heaven said heavily. "Aren't you worried about the news that Mary and Will were caught?"

"I don't know anyone in the pharmaceutical industry, my dear."

"Oh, I'm sure you covered your ass," Heaven said as she tossed the paper with the names of the property

holders toward Nancy. "Just like you covered your ass when you bought up all the property around the Sisters of the Holy Trinity convent. What did you want to build there, Nancy? A casino is my bet."

Amelia pulled the paper over toward her and looked puzzled again. "This is the list of owners around the convent. What makes you think Nancy owns any of this property?"

"I took a look at this list again today. When Nancy and I had lunch the other day, we talked about her husbands." Heaven pointed down at the paper. "Wayne Bernard was your fifth husband, wasn't he, Nancy? Charles McCoy was the cop, number three or four as I remember. And Jimmy Stouffert is the last one, the one that you say you can't find. Did you pay all of them to hold these properties?"

"All but Sam, who is deceased," Nancy said, her eyes narrowed.

Heaven wagged her finger at Nancy. "This conversion to religion didn't take very well on you, did it? You're the one behind all the vandalism. Trying to scare those poor little nuns into selling you their property. When were you going to set it up? Tell them you could stop the problems if they would just sell the convent to a friend of yours." Heaven looked down at the list. "Let's see, which ex-husband is left? I suppose you'd use your first husbands name, Andy Blair, since it's the same as your own."

Cool as a cucumber, Nancy Blair sipped her coffee. "You sure have a good memory for names, Heaven. You can't trace any of the poor sisters' vandalism to me, of course."

"The thing I really wonder about is how you sent all those poison-pen letters to all the various cities. Those

letters show your true colors, Nancy. Only a really bad person would have thought of that. And me, what a chump. I thought we were getting to be friends. Did you pay someone to rough me up?"

"Amelia was correct. They have mailing services for that. And as for your problems, Heaven, just the one time was from me, when you were warned up on the Moonwalk. The other times, out on Highway 90, that must have been your friend Mary. Her husband fell victim to their greed. Poor thing. I always liked Truely."

"Of course, that's what Durant was trying to tell me. I was being chased and suffocated and run off the road and shot at and dumped in the river by two distinct and different groups of criminals," Heaven said with a smile. For some sick reason, she was enjoying this. "I'm glad you told me about the finder's fee that you got from Mary. Now I want a finder's fee from you."

"And what for, Heaven? What can you do for me?"

Heaven got up and stood behind Amelia's chair. "I'll need Amelia's help for this one. But the favor I'm going to do you is see to it that Amelia doesn't do a fun little report about how the cross you gave back to the nuns was a brand-new copy and the true cross somehow just happened to get sent to New York to an auction house."

Amelia turned sharply in her chair and glared at Nancy. "Is that for real?"

Heaven circled the table. "Nancy, I think you'll want to cancel your trip to New York. I called Sotheby's and told them I thought there was a mistake because the cross they had looked just like one that had been stolen in New Orleans. And I also called the nuns and told them they might look at the back of their cross, where that tiny little scratch was, where the metal looked brand-new. But so far your name hasn't been men-

tioned. I'm sure the two parties can work out a reasonable way to return the cross to its rightful owners without naming names. Or maybe not."

The old lady looked from Heaven to Amelia nervously. She wasn't quite as cool now. "You can't prove a thing."

Amelia nodded. "No, but I could remind the whole city that you were the one that found the so-called original cross under mysterious circumstances. You're too old to relocate, Nancy. You have that nice house on Governor Nicholls."

"It would be a shame if you couldn't show your face at Antoine's anymore. They like you so much there," Heaven threw in.

Nancy Blair shrugged. She knew when she was beaten. "I guess this is where I ask what your finder's fee is, Heaven."

Heaven leaned down and took one of Nancy's hands in hers. Then she whacked it hard with her other hand, twice. Nancy winced in spite of herself. "You are so naughty. If I ever hear of anything happening to the Sisters of the Holy Trinity again, I'll consider this deal broken. If they sell their convent for a casino, I'll be on a plane down here so fast it'll make your head spin. If you ever try to scare someone by threatening them with bodily harm like you did me, I'll consider the deal broken, even if it's not about the sisters. And that filth you wrote about all of our restaurants. I will keep asking my friends and if you ever do anything like that again, I'll lie to get you put in jail if I have to. I don't want anyone else to have to go through what you put us through. Amelia, are you with me on this? I know you're not fond of the nuns."

"I think it evens up the odds for the sisters to have

you and me keeping an eye on Miss Nancy Blair," she said. "I'm in. But I may have to do a story about the fake cross. It's news."

"Fair enough. Just keep something for us to use to keep this one in line. Nancy, I'm going to start taking the *Times-Picayune* just so I can keep tabs on you. And remember, I'll lie and cheat if I have to. Now let's get out of this place. Poor Truely. He didn't deserve a two-timing wife and a two-timing best friend," Heaven said as they walked toward the front door.

"It's the South," Nancy Blair said, looking no worse for the negotiations that had just taken place.

"No, it's New Orleans," Amelia Hart pointed out as they closed the door.

Heaven stepped out of the shower. She could hear Bob Dylan playing in the bedroom. Hank was much too young to like Dylan. He must be playing it for her. She slipped into a big terry cloth robe and toweled her hair.

"Thank you for picking me up at the airport," she said as she went out into the big bedroom/study. Hank had a bottle of Veuve Cliquot in a wine bucket and two champagne flutes by the bed. "I've never been so glad to be home in my life."

"You'll be even happier in an hour. I guarantee it or your money back," Hank joked as he popped the cork on the champagne. "But before we get to that, call your daughter. She's in some town called Buzios, Brazil. She said call day or night. She's worried about you. Here's her number."

Heaven jumped on the bed and adjusted several pillows behind her. She pulled the phone in bed with her and received a glass of Veuve from Hank, who slipped in bed beside her as she dialed.

When Iris answered, Heaven's face broke into a smile. "Hi, honey. Happy Sunday. Now don't start yelling at your mother like that. I'm just fine. But wait till I tell you what happened. Someone threw me in the Mississippi River. It was my first time."

Hank raised his glass and they silently toasted each other. He started tracing the outline of her face with his finger.

"Honey, can I call you back tomorrow morning?" Heaven asked suddenly. "I'm too tired to tell the story right tonight and it's a doozie. I love you too." She hung up and put her glass on the bedside stand. She put one hand on Hank's shoulder and the other on his lips.

There were a few things in life better than Veuve Cliquot.